The Con

Kitty sat across from Lord Haverhill in the close coach, and tried to keep her pistol steady. It would not do to have him see the weapon waver. Not when she knew how ruthless he was. And not when he was so tall and powerful.

Somehow she had not expected him to be so large. Or so handsome, with his classic good looks and deep red hair.

Even more troubling, the fear she expected her pistol to inspire was curiously absent from his gaze. Smilingly he regarded her, like a tiger sizing up his prey.

Kitty began to sense how dangerous this journey might be—and what a scandalously wrong turn it might take . . .

SIGNET REGENCY ROMANCE
COMING IN APRIL 1991

Carla Kelly
Libby's London Merchant

Melinda McRae
The Duke's Daughter

Gayle Buck
Mutual Consent

Miss Gordon's Mistake

by
Anita Mills

A SIGNET BOOK

SIGNET
Published by the Penguin Group
Penguin Books USA Inc., 375 Hudson Street,
New York, New York, 10014, U.S.A.
Penguin Books Ltd, 27 Wrights Lane, London W8 5TZ, England
Penguin Books Australia Ltd, Ringwood, Victoria, Australia
Penguin Books Canada Ltd, 2801 John Street,
Markham, Ontario, Canada L3R 1B4
Penguin Books (N.Z.) Ltd, 182-190 Wairau Road,
Auckland 10, New Zealand

Penguin Books Ltd, Registered Offices:
Harmondsworth, Middlesex, England

First published by Signet, an imprint of New American Library,
a division of Penguin Books USA Inc.

First Printing, March, 1991

10 9 8 7 6 5 4 3 2 1

A special thanks to
Susie Schoenebeck,
my reader for this work.

KITTY GORDON dropped the curtain guiltily, but not before her aunt chanced to see Jess and Lord Sturbridge riding in. The older woman's mouth, which had been drawn into a smile, flattened perceptibly in disapproval. Her eyes narrowed as Kitty flushed.

"If Sturbridge would fix his interest with you, how is it that he is forever with Jessica?" she wondered aloud, the edge in her voice unmistakable.

"I had the headache, and as 'twas too pretty a day to waste, I asked them to go on without me," Kitty answered, crossing her fingers behind her at the untruthfulness.

Her aunt stared sharply for a moment, assessing her shrewdly, then she relented. "Be that as it may, Catherine, if you do not have a care, you will have whistled Sturbridge's not inconsiderable fortune down the wind," she warned, "and I should hate to see it." She lifted the curtain herself and peered out regretfully. "As it cannot be Jessica, I should be grateful 'tis you he pays court—I have hopes on that head at least." She sighed, shaking her head. "If only—well, it does not signify . . ." Her voice trailed off, and she met Kitty's eyes resolutely. "Surely after a year and more of his attentions, he means to come up to scratch soon."

"Aunt Bella—"

"I know the Trevors are dreadfully high in the instep," the older woman mused, ignoring her, "and her ladyship cannot quite like it that you are American—half-American," she amended quickly—"but with this unpleasantness now past us there, I should hope . . ."

7

Kitty smiled faintly at the thought of Charles's mother. "She calls me 'brown,' " she admitted. "And an ape-leader, I am told."

"Brown?" For a moment Bella was at a loss. "But you are not brown at all!" Her eyes traveled over her niece, reassuring herself of the girl's exquisite blondness, of the clear blue eyes, the rose-blushed fair skin. "What nonsense! 'Tis a hum, I'll be bound, Catherine! Now if she had said you are a trifle too forward or that your American manners are too free, I should have believed that—but *brown*? There's not so much as a freckle on you! No, she cannot fault you for your looks, my love—not at all," her aunt decided definitely. "Although I own 'tis fashionable to be a trifle taller, but we shall not repine too much on that. I am quite certain that Sturbridge does not think you *brown.* "

"Lady Sturbridge believes all Americans to be somehow relations to the Indians," Kitty murmured.

"What a preposterous notion, to be sure—why you are Gordon and Whitwood through and through! As though my dear brother should have consorted with Indians! Though I must own that I find your fascination for pistols most disconcerting, my love, and I cannot think of any reason—" She stopped, perceiving that she heard the young couple in the hall, then turned her attention to Kitty again. "Pinch your cheeks and put your best looks before Sturbridge. Ten to one, 'twill not matter what his mama thinks in the end, for I know a besotted man when I see one!"

"Aunt Bella, I do not think—"

"And if you are fearing that *he* thinks you an ape-leader, he does not. You cannot be faulted for a war, after all, and had there been the time or the place for a come-out, I am certain your papa would have done as he ought. Sturbridge is not so blind that he does not know you would have been taken on the instant had you been presented."

The door opened behind them, causing the older woman to start. "La, but 'tis Sturbridge, my love!" she announced a trifle too brightly. "No doubt he is come to see if you are better!"

The tall, fair-haired young man entered after the slender, flushed girl. Both stopped guiltily at her words. "You are ill?" Jessica demanded. "Why did you not say—?"

Casting a warning glance at her cousin, Kitty smiled. "Had I complained, the two of you would have sat cooped up in here with me, would you not? And then we should all have missed the beauty of a rare sunny day."

"Oh, but—"

"I say, Miss Gordon, but you ought to have apprised us," Lord Sturbridge chided. "I am sure that Jessica would have—" He stopped, aware of Mrs. Merriman's frown. "I am sure that *Miss* Merriman would have forgone the ride," he finished lamely.

"And why should you?"

"But you are never ill—I did not know—" Jessica floundered.

"Nonsense," Kitty interrupted the other girl quickly. "I am often given to these little megrims—'twill pass."

"I have never known you to have an ill day in your life," Isabella Merriman declared flatly. "You must not make poor Sturbridge here think otherwise," she added significantly. Then, reaching to pinch her daughter's elbow, she told her, "As soon as Sturbridge will excuse you, I'd have you come up to me. The latest plates are arrived from Paris, and I'd share them with you. Besides, I cannot but think that if dear Catherine would show him how the bulbs are blooming, the air would do her good." She smiled at the young man, holding out her hand. "So kind of you to take my poor Jessica up today, my lord," she murmured.

He bowed over her hand and lifted it to his lips. "Dear lady."

"Be done with you—you must not think I require you to dance attendance on me. Jessica, I will be awaiting you."

After she left, the girl turned on her cousin. "Really, but I did not know you were ill."

"I wasn't," Kitty admitted baldly. "But I had to tell her something, since she believed you were casting lures at my beau." Noting that they exchanged glances and colored, she nodded. "Just so. 'Tis a devil of a coil, is it not?" she observed wryly. "And I absolutely refuse to wed Sturbridge so that you can have him, Jess." Her blue eyes met the young man's. " 'Tis where we are headed in everyone's mind, you know."

"What! Oh, no, but—" Jessica protested.

"Miss Gordon, I assure you—"

"My aunt is expecting you to come up to scratch momentarily." Even as Kitty said it, tears welled in her cousin's eyes. And Lord Sturbridge's hand reached reassuringly to clasp the young girl's hand. "You cannot keep on courting Jess, my lord, under the guise of seeing me," Kitty continued gently. "It makes all of us into less than admirable sneaks. And I am done with it."

"Kitty!" Jessica wailed.

"I repeat—I absolutely refuse to wed him for you, Jess." She turned to face her cousin. "I don't suppose 'tis called wearing the horns when one is a female, but whatever it is, I won't do it."

"Miss Gordon!" Sturbridge choked.

"Which brings us to the unthinkable," Kitty went on resolutely. "Either you will have to cease this—or a way must be discovered for you to be together."

"You know there is no way! 'Tis cruel, what you suggest!" Jessica cried.

Ignoring her cousin, Kitty appealed to the young man. "My lord, think what you do. I collect that Jess has told you of Haverhill, hasn't she? While 'tis not common knowledge, 'tis still an impediment, you must own."

"Don't listen to her, Charles! Kitty, how *could* you?"

But Charles met Kitty's eyes and nodded. Exhaling slowly,

he conceded, "You are quite right, of course. To continue this way is to invite disaster on her head, but—"

The color draining from her face, the younger girl stared at her beloved in disbelief. "Charles, you cannot mean—that is—I should perish without you!" she wailed dramatically.

"Jessica, I have not the right to ask you—I'd not make you an *on-dit* for the gossips!" He ran his fingers through his pale hair in distraction, and his handsome face betrayed his helplessness. " 'Tis foolish to mire ourselves deeper when we cannot act, but—"

"Charles!" Then, perceiving that he was serious, Jessica burst into tears, covered her face, and fled.

He would have gone after her, but Kitty stepped into his path. "Since you appear to have the sense, I believe we ought to speak plainly, my lord." He reached out his hand toward the doorway, then dropped it helplessly. Kitty walked to the door and carefully closed it. Then, with her hands clasped together, she faced him. "There is no future for Jess like this," she said simply.

He nodded dumbly.

"Do you love her?"

"More than my life."

"More than your mother?" she persisted.

"I fail to see what that is to anything, but—" He stopped, quelled by the look in her eyes. "Yes," he answered finally.

"Enough to take a divorced woman?" she continued brutally.

For a moment, his eyes betrayed hope, then he shook his head. "He will not divorce her," he decided heavily.

"He might. It has been years, and there's not been so much as a word exchanged between them since the wedding."

"He has abandoned an angel. How any man could look on her and—"

She cut him short. "Marriage was not on his mind, or so I surmise," she snapped with a trace of asperity. "Angel or no, he had no wish to tie himself to her. Indeed, but if Jess can be believed, he was too disguised to compromise her," she added in disgust. "I doubt he even recalls what she looks like. After all, she was but sixteen and still a schoolroom chit."

"No man could forget her," Sturbridge maintained loyally.

"Well, apparently Lord Haverhill has. It has been six years, and he's done naught but send her an allowance through some man of affairs. If he'd had the least interest, he'd have done something beyond that, I'd think," she observed practically. "No doubt he is content to keep his mistresses and his barques of frailty instead."

"Miss Gordon, 'tis improper to say such," he pointed out feebly. "Gently nurtured females do not speak of such things here."

But she'd walked away suddenly, moving to stand at the window, and she stared out, chewing pensively on her thumbnail. "No, 'twill not be an easy task," she mused aloud. "An annulment would be best, of course, so we will attempt that first." She swung back around. "Well—if she were free, would you marry Jess?"

"But she's not, and—" Her blue eyes held his, making him wonder how it was that people said she was a delicate female. "Yes," he answered. "But—"

"No 'buts,'" she declared firmly. "And if your mama objects?"

"My mother does not have the ordering of my life," he retorted. "But I fail to see—I mean,'tis all very well to speculate, but just how do you think I am to persuade Lord Haverhill to give Jessica a divorce?"

"An annulment would be better," she repeated.

"All the same, I fail to see how that I—well, I cannot but think that her family would not wish me to know of the matter. Indeed, but I was utterly shocked myself when first Jessica told me." He stopped. "You do not think that *I* should approach him, do you?"

"No, no, of course not, my lord. And if you were directly involved, the scandal would be too great. No, it will have to be one of her family, I think. But if you will not cavil at taking her despite the scandal, I am hopeful she can be freed of him.'' She looked up at him again, searching his face. ''You might have to take her away for a while, you know.''

''I have an estate in Ireland,'' he answered, warming to the thought. ''Miss Gordon, if it meant that I could have Jessica, I should be happy to go into exile.''

''And you would wed her?''

''Yes—how could you think anything else? Surely you do not think that I would wish it otherwise,'' he protested.

''I think Haverhill might be persuaded,'' she decided. She smiled up at him. '' 'Tis the best answer, don't you think? Otherwise, I am expected to wed you, and I am certain we should not suit.''

''Be honored to have you, but—'' he began gallantly.

''Fustian. You require someone who both likes and admires you, my lord.'' Her blue eyes sparkled mischievously for a moment. ''You are too comfortable for me, you know.''

''Miss Gordon, if you can persuade Rollo to approach Haverhill, I will be forever grateful,'' he promised, grinning.

''Rollo?'' She started to give her opinion of her young cousin, then thought better of it. ''Oh, yes, I daresay he might do it.''

Much later, after he had gone, she sat for a time considering what she'd suggested, and the more she thought on it, the more she believed it could be done. Surely Lord Haverhill could not wish to keep a wife who clearly meant nothing to him.

She closed her eyes, and the homesickness washed over her. Why could no one see that she did not belong here? That she longed to be useful again? She could almost smell the cotton and tobacco that came into her father's Carolina warehouses, and she could almost hear him say, ''Cat, you've got a good head on your shoulders.'' Much good it did now, for there seemed to be none to value a good head here.

But her papa was dead, carried off by a tidewater fever contracted in Virginia, and there'd been no other relations there. Even now she could remember her shock when his will had been read and she discovered she was to live with his sister in England. His business had gone to his partners and her money had gone into trust. A stranger in London sent her a quarterly income, and in that at least, she was no better off than Jess. Despite her financial competence, she was still constrained to be what the *ton* accepted as a lady.

Resolutely, she drew her thoughts away from her own problems. 'Twould take some doing, some subterfuge, but she meant to get to London to see this odious Lord Haverhill. Maybe she'd come back in such disgrace that everyone would cease throwing eligible *partis* at her head. Maybe they'd even consider sending her to her real home. As it was, her American sense of independence had little patience with the matrimonial games expected of her. No, she would help Jess, and maybe her Aunt Bella would come to realize that it was too late to make Kitty Gordon into an English lady.

With that happy thought, she rose to fetch her papa's pistols. Today, when Jem showed her again how to use them, she meant to see if she could hit the cider jar rather than the tree several paces to the left of it. In the weeks she'd been practicing, she'd gained a greater respect for the soldiers who could not only actually hit moving targets, but who could also load, wad, prime, and fire often enough to be effective. The way she saw it, she'd have been dead before the powder ignited.

"I HEARD HAVERHILL cut up pretty warm," the young man observed, dropping into one of the wing chairs. Turning his head despite the high points of his collar, he gazed admiringly about the paneled bookroom. "Not at all what you are used to, is it?"

"No."

"Couldn't believe m'eyes when I read it—Red Jack Rayne, a baron—now there's justice, if there ever was any. You going to live here?"

"I haven't thought about it yet. 'Twas a trifle unexpected," Jack admitted. "He was not much above fifty, you know, and I rather thought he'd produce an heir before he died."

"Thought he was a bachelor."

"He was, but there was always the possibility he'd marry." For a long moment, Jack stared unseeing across the room, then he straightened. "In my business, a man lives for today rather than on expectation."

"You ain't thinking of selling out?"

"I suppose. The war's done, anyway, and it doesn't look like Boney'll rise again," he conceded.

"An army without Red Jack Rayne?" The younger man lifted a disbelieving eyebrow. "Coming it too strong! We got to have our heroes, Jack—we got to."

The warmth faded from the hazel eyes. "I'm not a hero, Tony."

"What the deuce—how the devil can you say that?" his friend choked. "Everybody's heard of Red Jack! Why, you was there at Talavera, Cuidad Rodrigo, Badajoz, Salamanca, Victoria, and—'' He ticked off the victories on his fingers. ''Well, you was in the dispatches, Jack!''

''I was a survivor. The heroes are all dead, Tony.''

''Dash it, but how can you talk like that? Why, we read about how 'twas you as led the charge at—''

''I am not one who enjoys reliving horror,'' Jack cut in abruptly, stopping him.

''You was decorated for it—aye, 'twas in all the papers how the Prince Regent himself received you, how Parliament voted—''

''I said I did not wish to speak of it.'' Jack's voice, though quiet, had a definite edge to it. ''The war's over for me. If you would lionize those who survived, look at the poor devils who beg on the streets now.'' He rose and walked with a decided limp to the window. ''Look out there—they are everywhere—the ones who came back not heroes to this, Tony. Then look at me. Baron Haverhill—'tis a jest, is it not?''

Not knowing how to answer him, Anthony Marston fell silent for a time. Finally, he cleared his throat. ''All right— you ain't a hero then. Divine Providence made a mistake and you was left alive.''

''Something like that.''

''So what do you do now? I mean, you got a title, property, and a little fortune, don't you? Seems to me as you ought to get on with it.''

''I will—if fools don't keep reminding me.''

''Leg hurt?''

Jack smiled ruefully and nodded. ''Only when it rains, which is too damned often.'' He came back to sit again. ''I am thinking of politics,'' he admitted suddenly.

''With your rep—'' Tony caught himself and stopped. ''Well, it might not be a bad thing—bound to be those as would favor you. But 'twill have to be Lords now—I mean—''

''Aye.''

"You a Whig or a Tory?"

"Actually, I hadn't given it much thought until lately. But I suppose a Whig, for they are the most inclined to act. I mean to try to help those who have come back to nothing, Tony."

"Now, you ain't going to be one of those deuced reformers surely? I mean, I don't think I could stand it."

"Maybe."

"What you need," Tony pronounced definitely, "is a night at White's—good games, good company, good supper, and plenty of drink. Make you forget the war—make you forget Haverhill even," he coaxed.

Jack shook his head. "Got too much to tend to—Cousin Henry left his affairs pretty tangled, by the looks of it. Maybe by next week."

"If that don't beat the Dutch!" Tony snorted in disgust. "Red Jack Rayne don't have time to play anymore! Time was, Jack, when you was the first to the tables and the last to leave—and don't you think I don't remember it! The demned war has taken all your pleasures, ain't it?"

"Something like that."

"Listen—it don't have to be the games—I had it from Biggleston that there's a new gel a-singing at Haymarket. Prettier than Vestris, if Ponsonby can be believed."

The new baron leaned toward the cluttered desk and lifted a sheaf of papers for Tony to see. "Not tonight. I've got my uncle's man of affairs coming in the morning, and I'd have a notion where I stand. Thus far, I don't know what's paid and what isn't."

"If it's tradesmen, they can wait."

"It's thinking like that that sends a fellow into exile," Jack warned his friend. Then, seeing Tony's face fall, he relented. "Tell you what—come to dinner at half-past eight Tuesday, will you? I'll send around to Ponsonby and Crisswell and Wrexham, and we'll make an evening of it," he promised.

Marston studied Jack for a moment, seeing the fatigue lines that deepened at the corners of otherwise fine hazel eyes.

And even as he stared, Rayne passed a weary hand over his forehead, brushing back the thick mahogany-colored locks that fell forward. There was no question about it, the famed—or infamous, depending on whom one asked—Red Jack was exceedingly tired. It crossed Tony's mind that he looked more than his thirty years. The war and the wound had taken their toll on what had once been a hell-or-nothing handsome countenance. Fighting his disappointment, he rose.

"Tuesday night, it is." Impulsively, he leaned to grip Jack's hard shoulder. "You get some rest—ain't right for Red Jack Rayne to go around looking like death's head on a mop stick, you hear?"

"I am all right—been up since six, that's all."

"Six?" Tony recoiled visibly. "Well, no wonder! Don't think I was abed much before then." Seeing his friend start to rise, he hastened to reassure him. "No, no—no need at all, old fellow. Time ain't come yet as when Tony Marston cannot find his way out."

After he left, Jack moved to the desk and poured himself a drink from the decanter. Resting his head on an elbow, he read down the column of figures he'd been writing. Only one item puzzled him—an annuity to a Jessica Merriman. Had it been less, he'd have assumed it was a pension, but one hundred pounds per year was exorbitant. He opened the ledger book again to check the figure, and there in a neat hand it was. And thumbing backward, he found it had been listed for as many years as the book had been kept. Intrigued, he wondered if perhaps the Merriman woman represented an old liaison of sorts. And somehow it gave him a chuckle to think that Old Henry had been caught enough to pay, for he'd never seen a colder fish in his life.

Making a checkmark beside the figure, he moved on down the page, noting the rest of the list. A careful totaling revealed what he'd suspected—Henry had left him a tidy fortune even after all was paid. He leaned back, sipping his drink slowly, savoring it, and looked about him. It was in truth a fine house also, he admitted it. The devil of it was that he really hadn't needed one.

Ten years in the army, seven of them with Old Douro himself, had taught him that a man's needs were actually quite few. He'd gotten on more than tolerably well with naught but a batman to take care of him. And here he was, Baron Haverhill of Haverhill, surrounded by servants, possessed of a considerable fortune. It was funny.

A cynical, derisive chuckle escaped him as he thought of how he'd once been—a young fool filled with notions of honor and glory. He lifted his glass in a mocking toast to the young John Rayne, the boy he'd buried somewhere in Spain, the boy who'd been killed as surely as if a French ball had taken him. His hand rubbed along the top of his thigh as though to reassure himself it was still there. The pain it gave him was little enough payment for keeping the leg. "To a bloody fool," he said softly.

He supposed he ought to be grateful to Henry for rescuing him from the army, for he'd lost his taste for it somewhere in the Peninsula. Too many dead friends, too much destruction. It finally got to where it scarred a man's soul. He drained his glass and poured another, then sprawled back to commence another night of holding the demons at bay. Maybe if he had enough, he would forget how it had been— maybe he'd forget the sounds and the stench of war.

Kitty eased the door open, peering inside to make certain he was alone. Thus far, gaining entrance to his house had been almost too easy, for the butler, taking in her plain cloak and gown, had accepted her explanation that she sought one of the housemaids, and he'd sent her around to the back. It had helped that Jem had been able to discover a name from a footman to make her story more plausible.

Drawing the faded cloak over her arm to cover her hand, she stepped gingerly into the bookroom. It took a moment to adjust her eyes to the dimness, for there was but one brace of candles lit, and the fire had all but died.

She stood there, afraid her courage meant to desert her, then slowly crept across the room to where the chair had been pulled between the fire and the desk. She could see the outline of the man, and her heart pounded as she approached him, afraid that he'd swing around and see her ere she was ready. But he did not move.

He was sitting—sprawled actually—in the chair, with his long legs extended, his boots resting on the polished marble hearth. His head was leaned back, his eyes closed. For a moment, she thought he slept, then she saw the half-filled glass in his hand. Her fingers tightened on the pistol as she moved closer, stepping to his side.

This then was the notorious Baron Haverhill, the odious villain who stood between Jess and her happiness. For a long moment, Kitty stared at him curiously. Perhaps it was that his face was unguarded from the drink, but he did not look so very terrible. In fact, he was rather handsome, if one did not mind the unruly auburn hair that fell over his forehead. He had a strong, almost classical face, she decided dispassionately, and he certainly did not look as old as Jess had painted him to her. But Jess had been but sixteen and inexperienced before the world then, and certainly with none but Rollo for measure, she could be forgiven the error of a few years. Her eyes traveled the length of him, and she realized he was far bigger than she'd imagined. She felt almost intimidated looking at him.

Resolutely, she let the cloak fall back. "Baron Haverhill —my lord—"

The most arresting hazel eyes she'd ever seen flew open, and he sat up, startled. "What the deuce—?" He blinked, trying to gain his bearings as he found himself facing the merest slip of a girl in the plain dress of a housemaid. "Must've dozed," he mumbled apologetically.

His first impression was that she could not be above sixteen or seventeen, for she was quite small and delicately made.

His eyes traveled appreciatively from her narrow waist to her face, and there was no disappointment there either. Had she been taller, she must surely have been considered a beauty, but even as she was, she was extremely pretty in a rosy, soft blond way. There was even a hint of humor in her lovely blue eyes. It was the first time he'd ever seriously considered dallying with one of the maids.

"Are you Baron Haverhill?" she repeated, this time more definitely.

"I am." Despite his fatigue, he managed to flash what he hoped was his most engaging smile. "And you are—?"

"Smith," she lied.

"I see. Miss Smith?"

"Yes."

"Well, usually we address those who are employed here by their given names."

"But I am not employed here," she murmured, raising her hand.

His gaze dropped to the pistol, and his smile broadened into a grin. "If 'tis a jest, you'd best put that down, Miss—er—Smith, is it? Coming it too strong, even for Tony." He started to lurch to his feet.

"Stay where you are," she ordered coldly. As she spoke, she carefully cocked the gun with her other hand. "I can hit a cider jar at twenty paces, my lord—and you are considerably bigger than a cider jar." She took a step backward, making certain she stayed out of his reach. "Now—you will rise that we may leave."

"I beg your pardon?"

She moved the pistol, gesturing toward the door. Perceiving that she was somehow serious, he measured the distance between them. A faint smile curved her mouth, and she shook her head. "I should not think to try it," she advised.

"As I am considerably stronger and faster, I could argue the matter," he murmured.

"You could, but I will not hesitate to shoot. And do not

be thinking 'tis not loaded for firing, my lord, for I have measured the powder, placed the ball and wadding, and checked the flint myself.''

"I see." His eyes flicked over her, betraying a glint of amusement. "I cannot think a female as pretty as yourself would have to resort to such drastic measures, my dear."

"I am not your dear," she retorted.

"And I suspect you are not Miss Smith either," he retaliated.

"Who I am is nothing to the point." She took another step backward, being careful to avoid the table behind her. "You will, of course, go first, my lord."

"Er—do not think 'twill be remarked when I leave without so much as my coat in this weather?"

"Get it then. And do not be thinking to sound a warning, Baron Haverhill, for I shall be directly behind you." Her eyes met his steadily. "I should hate having to shoot you." When he made no move to follow her direction, she leveled the pistol until it was in line with his heart. "Have you seen the damage a ball can do, sir?" she demanded.

"Have you?" he countered.

He knew he could rush her, yet he was not so sure but what the foolish chit just might hit him. Besides, 'twas an utterly ludicrous situation—the six-foot-tall Red Jack Rayne held at bay by the merest dab of a girl. How would it look if she did put a ball into him? And after he'd faced Boney's best? No, 'twas better to wait, to catch her off her guard, for if there was anything he'd learned in his thirty years, 'twas that a pistol made equals out of nearly everyone.

"We have not all night, my lord."

"I collect you mean to abduct me," he murmured sardonically as he rose from the chair. "Did none ever tell you 'tis usually the other way 'round—'tis the fellow who does the abducting?" Her finger appeared to be tightening, prompting him to add gallantely, "But I shan't repine, Miss Smith. Lead on."

"You will walk out the front door, my lord, and turn

directly left. We are awaited just beyond the corner.'' Warily, she watched him pass her. ''If any asks—''

''If any asks, I shall merely say I am going walking with one of the housemaids,'' he decided. ''Though 'twill cause comment, I am sure.'' One corner of his mouth quirked upward despite his attempt not to smile. ''Usually, I suspect that sort of thing is done indoors, you know.''

She had the grace to flush. ''And I suspect you know a great deal more on that head than I, sir,'' she responded tartly. ''In fact, I am sure of it.''

''Am I to collect you do not mean to compromise me?'' he asked wickedly.

''Not in the least. But we waste time, sir. I shall be but a few paces behind you.''

''Ah—you favor the Indian style, I see.''

''I beg your pardon?''

''It does not signify.'' He opened the door and noted a trifle regretfully that there was no one in the hall. And again, he considered swinging around in an attempt to disarm her. But there was still the chance that the pistol would discharge accidentally. He picked up his beaver hat from the table just inside the door. ''To the left, you say?''

''Yes.''

Any other time, he was sure he could have depended on his late cousin's staff to be everywhere, but not this night. He walked across the deserted foyer and let himself outside. The chill, damp air hit him, clearing the wine from his mind. For a moment, he stood there, seeing the row of gas lights glowing like yellow dots in the fog.

''Go on.''

He shrugged, then hunched his shoulders against the cold and walked down the steps. A carriage rolled past in the street, its wheels spraying the gutters before it disappeared somewhere into the swirling mists. As usual, he reflected wryly, it had been raining. His abominable luck.

He walked with a limp, favoring his right leg. Behind him, she kept her eyes trained on his back, ever wary lest he bolt and run for help. But he did not. The thought crossed her mind as she followed him that he was very tall—and certainly more than able to overpower her—especially once they were inside the cramped confines of the carriage. She would have to exercise great vigilance if she were to get him all the way home.

"I don't suppose you mean to tell me where we are going?" he wondered aloud, as though he could hear her thoughts.

"No."

" 'Tis a blind adventure, is it?"

"Yes."

A coachman stepped out of the fog and led the way to a decidedly old-fashioned carriage. "Gor—is that 'im, miss?" he asked, looking up at Red Jack.

"Get in," she ordered. And as Jack complied, she nodded to the fellow. " 'Twas an easy task, Jem—the baron was in his cups."

Taking great care to keep the pistol on her prisoner, she climbed into the coach and took the seat opposite him. He sat, his head leaned back, his face in deep shadows, his hands crossed over his waistcoat, and his legs stretched out to take up much of the space between them. She pulled her cloak closer about her shoulders, then settled against the cracked leather squabs. Jem closed the door behind her and swung up into the box.

"I hope," Red Jack drawled lazily as the coach lurched forward, "you do not mean to doze, Miss Smith. I should not advise it."

"No."

The carriage picked up speed, rolling through the wet streets. Jack sat there in the darkness watching her, ever alert for some sign that she meant to relax her vigilance. Finally, he exhaled deeply and rubbed his aching leg.

"Where are you taking me? Surely there can be no harm in telling me now?"

"Home."

"I cannot say as I recognize the accent," he murmured, "so perhaps you would enlighten me as to where you are from?"

"America. Charleston, to be precise."

To his credit, he did not even blink. " 'Tis a trifle far," he commented mildly.

" 'Tis not to that home I mean to take you, my lord," she explained coldly. "We are going to see Jessica Merriman."

That piqued his interest. "Ah, yes—Jessica Merriman. I own I had wondered about her."

The bland way he said it infuriated her. "You fiend," she muttered under her breath. "You bloody fiend."

"Acquit me," he retorted. "I cannot say I know the woman."

"Of course you do not! Why would you? It has been six years, after all! What sort of man are you, anyway, that you can just go away and forget what you did?" she demanded angrily.

"I don't think I did anything. In fact—"

"Oh, I know she told me you were three sheets into the wind, but 'tis not sufficient excuse, my lord! How is it that men can debauch, then plead innocence by reason of drink?"

"I assure you that I can remember every female I have debauched, Miss Smith, and I do not recall—"

"You think that money buys everything, do you not? Well, it cannot! There are feelings to be considered, sir!"

It came home to him then that her grudge was against his late cousin, and for a moment he considered telling her just that. But she intrigued him. Jessica Merriman would surely apprise her of her mistake soon enough, and when she did, he was going to enjoy seeing Miss Smith, whoever she really was, squirm.

He leaned his head back and tilted his hat over his brow

at a decidedly rakish angle. "I shall most certainly look forward to renewing the acquaintance. If she is truly persuasive, mayhap she can keep you out of Newgate, my dear."

DESPITE THE TOSSING of the less-than-well-sprung carriage, and despite the pain in his leg, but perhaps because of the wine he'd drunk, the new Baron Haverhill managed to doze. Kitty Gordon watched him with an increasing sense of ill-usage, for she herself did not dare fall asleep. Instead, she sat still, her body at attention, her mind as alert as she could keep it, while her hand stayed on the pistol in her lap.

As a sort of mental exercise, she repeated her earlier inventory of Lord Haverhill, noting again his almost reckless good looks. It was most unfair, she decided, for how was an innocent like Jess supposed to be proof to one who looked like that? Indeed, but had she herself not known what he was, she'd have been inclined to like him also.

And it was certainly not a matter of his address, she had to own truthfully, for he seemed sadly lacking in that department. His manners, what she had seen of them, were less than polished, after all. Why he'd spoken openly of debauching females even, as though 'twas naught to him. No, if anything, his free manners had mocked her, and rather than being frightened by his predicament, he seemed inclined to be amused.

Even now, she was not entirely certain that he slept, that 'twas not a ruse on his part to lull her. Very quietly, she leaned across the seat to peer into his face, ready on the instant to snap back if he should move. He did not.

Jess had called him old, and no doubt he was, for debauchery sometimes set well on the worst of men. Still, it made her wonder just what Jess thought old to be. Baron Haverhill, Kitty judged, was possibly thirty-five to thirty-eight, or so it seemed when he was awake. Asleep, he looked at least ten years younger.

In the dimness of the carriage, the darkness lightened but slightly by the slice of moon that appeared from time to time between the clouds, his red hair seemed black, and his strong, well-defined features were muted by deep shadows. And his even breathing was oddly soft, nothing at all like the snoring of either her father or her late Uncle Edwin. It was, she realized suddenly, the closest she'd ever been to any man who was not a relation. And that alone, excepting the circumstances even, gave an exhilarating sense of danger.

It was as though he felt her scrutiny, for one eye opened, followed by the other, and he sat up. "I trust," he drawled softly, "that you have uncocked your weapon. Otherwise, you are in danger of shooting yourself in the leg."

She jumped, caught in the act of studying him. "I know how to use it, sir," she retorted stiffly.

"If you do, you must surely be the first of your sex to admit it. Ladies usually do not own up to anything beyond a talent for watercolors and often indifferent singing voices," he chided. "Ah, but then I forgot—you are American. No doubt a proclivity for pistols is more useful against the Indians."

"Are you never civil, sir?" she demanded acidly.

He favored her with a wry, twisted smile. "Am I supposed to be? You perhaps expected a more urbane debaucher of females? Alas, but I am seldom at my best when faced with a gun of any kind—and certainly not when 'tis held by a female of dubious nerve." He shifted his weight, easing his stiff leg.

She raised the pistol menacingly. "Do not move, my lord—every time I think of Jess, the temptation to make her a widow is great."

For a moment, he was not sure he'd heard her aright. "A widow? My dear Miss Smith—"

His words were cut short by a warning shot fired outside.

The carriage braked so suddenly that she was thrown across the seat, but she managed to right herself and keep the gun in her hand. "Whatever—?"

" 'Twould seem we are about to be robbed," he observed dryly.

"Robbed?" She peered out the window at the two shadowy figures on horseback. As she watched curiously, one dismounted and approached the carriage, calling out, "Your money or your lives!"

And before Jack could stop her, Kitty Gordon pushed open the hinged pane, leveled the barrel of her gun, and cocked it. "Stay where you are!" she shouted back. "Otherwise, I shall fire!"

"Don't be a fool—there are two of them," Jack warned her, reaching for her arm.

"The swells is armin' the females!" Laughing derisively, the highwayman swaggered toward her. "Lookit, Billy—"

She jerked free of Jack and squeezed the trigger. The hammer clicked, followed by a deafening report. The recoil sent her back against the seat, and a thick, black billow of smoke blew back into the coach.

"Owwwwwww! Th' bloody witch 'as 'it me, Bill!"

Choking, with tears in her eyes from the acrid black powder smoke, Kitty felt rather than saw Haverhill wrest the gun from her hand. "I hope you have powder and balls at hand, Miss Smith," he told her grimly. "Otherwise, we are in the basket."

"No—yes—"

She bent over to retrieve her reticule from the floor. As she fumbled for the ammunition, the fallen man's companion rode up to the carriage and shot inside. Fire belched from the barrel, sending a new cloud of thick smoke into the passenger compartment. She groped for the pull handle on the door.

"Damn it, stay down!" Jack shouted above her, pushing her.

She hit the floor and lay there coughing, aware only that

his body covered hers. The two men outside yelled at each other, then there was the sound of horses beating a hasty retreat. It was several seconds before she could breathe.

Jem wrenched open the door as she attempted to disentangle her legs from Haverhill's. "Gor! Miss Kitty, ye got one of th' bloody bastards!" Lifting the lantern from the top of the coach higher, he peered inside. "Lud!" he exclaimed in shock. "What's ter do now?"

Kitty pulled herself into her seat shakily and looked down. The baron still sat on the floor, his back against the rise of the seat, his hand holding his left shoulder. For a moment, she thought he was but winded, but then she saw the blood that seeped between his fingers. His vest, where his coat fell away, was already wet as the stain spread. She stared in dawning horror.

"Oh—my. Are—are you all right, my lord?" she asked foolishly.

The question brought a decided lift to one of his brows. "Aside from the fact that I am bleeding like a stuck pig, Miss Smith, what do you think?"

"Oh, dear." She forced herself to lean closer, despite the sudden knot that formed in the pit of her stomach. "We'll have to get to a doctor," she decided. Then, daring to meet his eyes again, she asked anxiously, "Is it serious, do you think?"

With an effort, he coughed, then winced from the pain. "If there is blood in my mouth, 'tis serious," he murmured. "If not, I shall probably survive." He swallowed, then shook his head. "The ball missed my lung at least."

"If you will agree to a divorce, I'll take you back," she offered.

"No." Pushing himself up with an elbow against the seat, he managed to heave his tall frame onto the leather-covered bench. He closed his eyes briefly, then opened them again. "I hold you accountable for this, you know."

"I didn't shoot you," she protested. " 'Twas the one called Billy. And we must get you back to London, I think."

"No. I've no wish to look the laughingstock. No—you have piqued my interest in Jessica Merriman, Miss Smith."

"But I cannot take you with a ball—that is, dash it, sir, but you are wounded!"

"Deuced perceptive of you." He forced a smile despite the burning in his shoulder. "I'm afraid I am in your hands, aren't I?" This time, his hazel eyes betrayed his pain. "Got to stop the blood."

"Oh—yes, of course. Jem—"

"I ain't no hand, Miss Kitty—I—" The coachman held the lantern closer and shuddered. "Bleedin' bad, ain't he? Best thinkin' I ought to go for help, miss. Bad business if he was t'die, don't ye know?"

"He will not die," she promised grimly.

"Jes th' same—"

She cast about wildly for the means to stop his bleeding, then reached beneath her cloak. Bending low, she caught the hem of her petticoat. "Papa always said to tie up anything that bled," she muttered. "Do you have a knife at least?"

"No."

"Jem?"

"Allus carries one, miss." To demonstrate, he drew out a small blade. "Ain't much fer looks, but 'tis a good sticker." He handed it over, then threw back. "Still think as I oughter get help fer ye."

Unable to work within the close confines, Kitty stepped down from the carriage and disappeared behind it. There, under cover of darkness, she lifted her gown to untie her petticoat, letting the undergarment fall to her ankles. Stepping out of it, she picked it up and returned to the lantern light, where she tried to cut it. Pulling mightily, she managed to tear several strips of the fine lawn.

"Can you get out of your coat, do you think?" she asked Jack as she climbed up again.

"With aid. But I'd not advise it. I'd roll that and put it beneath the vest," he suggested. "And then I'd button it as tight as I could."

"Yes, of course." She rolled two strips together, making a pad of sorts, and then loosened his vest and his shirt. His skin was warm beneath her fingertips. Resolutely, she thrust the pad against the wet flesh. "Is this where you would have it?"

"Yes." His hand came up to press the cloth, holding it. "See if you can get anything buttoned over it."

"Doesn't the ball have to come out?" she asked, kneeling on the seat beside him to do as he directed.

"Yes, but if you think I mean to let you probe with a dirty knife, Miss Smith, you are very wide of the mark." He winced as she pulled his vest tightly over the wadded cloth. "I'd as soon do it myself."

"As if you could." She finished with his buttons and settled back on her haunches to survey her handiwork. "Do you think 'twill stop bleeding?"

"I certainly have hopes of it." He closed his eyes again, but kept his hand tight against his shoulder. "If not, you will have a devil of a time explaining this to the constable, I should think." Sucking in his breath, then letting it out slowly, he spoke again. "Do you think your coachman has any rum?"

"I shouldn't—"

"Aye, miss." Jem shifted nervously under the sharp look she gave him. "Keep it fer the cold," he explained defensively. "Get him some," he mumbled, drawing away. When he came back, he held out a nearly full flask.

Kitty took it and attempted to pour a little into the cap, but the baron shook his head. "Just give it to me," he muttered through clenched teeth.

"But—"

"Miss Smith, I intend to drink all of it."

"You'll be disguised!"

"How very perceptive of you again." Releasing his shoulder momentarily, he took a big swig of the liquor and swallowed. "I hope we are near to where we are going."

" 'Tis not above another fifty miles, but—"

"I think 'twill take more than you and er—Jem, is it?—to

get me out by then.'' He drank deeply again. "I trust there are servants?''

"Yes.''

"Good.''

The carriage swung into motion again, and it was then that the enormity of what she'd done came home to her. She'd merely meant to make Baron Haverhill face Jess, to see what he'd done to her. And she'd hoped to persuade him that Jess's affection for Sturbridge was genuine, thinking that surely he would set her free. It was not as though he himself had wanted her, after all. But she'd bungled the matter badly, and now she would have to explain not only how he came to be there, but also how he came to be wounded. Her eyes rested on the sticky red stain that spread across his chest. She devoutly hoped he survived.

He replaced the lid and wiped his mouth with the back of his hand. Setting the flask between his legs, he again reached to hold his throbbing shoulder. Across from him, the girl was watching him with enormous blue eyes set in a very pale face.

"Buck up—it takes more than this to plant R—to put me in the ground,'' he amended.

"You act as though you are used to taking balls,'' she observed in a low voice.

"One is never used to it, Miss Smith—though I admit to having acquired my share.'' When she did not respond to that, he cocked his head for a better look at her. "Before we get wherever 'tis we are going, don't you think you owe me your name? Miss Smith sounds a trifle unlikely, you know.''

She sighed and nodded. "I am Catherine Gordon, my lord—Kitty to my family.''

"A relation to Byron's? I always thought he was a havey-cavey fellow myself.''

"No.''

They fell silent for a while, each lost in thought, and when she looked across at him again, she thought he slept. The flask was still between his legs, but his face was turned into the corner of his seat. She sat there, her hands twisting the thin fabric of her skirt, trying not to dwell on what her aunt would say.

"How old are you?" he asked suddenly.

"What?" Startled by his voice, she sat up. "I don't—"

"You do not look above eighteen."

"Well, I am four and twenty, my lord, but—"

"Good," he murmured obscurely.

For a moment, she wondered if she'd imagined he spoke, for he still appeared to be asleep. Then she noted the tightness around his mouth, and she realized he was conserving his strength. It was obvious that the shoulder pained him.

She reached out to touch his arm gingerly. "My lord—perhaps 'twould be best if I took you back. I—I can quite see now that 'twas a foolish venture on my part, and perhaps 'twould be better if Rollo spoke with you on Jess's behalf."

"No."

"But you cannot wish—that is, I did not expect—"

His eyes opened again. "Miss Gordon, I have finished every adventure I have ever begun, and I should expect to finish this one," he told her patiently. "I look forward to seeing Miss Merriman, I assure you. It *ought* to be an enlightening experience for the both of us."

"But—but on reflection, my lord, I cannot think she will wish to see you!" she blurted out. "And I cannot think Aunt Bella will be pleased under the circumstances, either," she added candidly.

"Then let us hope you are as resourceful as you are impetuous, Miss Gordon. I own I am fascinated by the thought of what you mean to tell them."

Her chin came up, and her blue eyes met his soberly. "I shall tell the truth, of course."

"I DUNNO. It don't look ter me like he'll go much further, Miss Kitty," Jem muttered, removing his hat to scratch his head. "Lost too much blood, he has."

Kitty surveyed the baron worriedly. His condition had seemed to worsen greatly over the last few miles, and now he was difficult to rouse. " 'Tis the rum," she ventured hopefully.

"No, it ain't. Feel 'im," he urged her. "The man has got to 'ave a doctor."

She lifted Haverhill's hat to touch his forehead with her fingertips. Despite the fact that it was chilly inside the coach, his head was clammy, as though he sweated. She peered closely while Jem held the lantern above his face.

"My lord—Haverhill!"

He did not open his eyes. "Too tired—" he mumbled thickly. "Got to sleep."

"Lost too much blood," Jem muttered.

Kitty looked down to the bulge between the baron's vest, and the stain was still wet, proving that he still bled. "My lord," she uttered urgently, "can you hear me?"

"Yes."

It was little more than a croak and certainly nothing to reassure her. "You are bleeding—we've got to get aid for you," she said more loudly.

"Aye."

It was the first time since her father had been so very ill that Kitty felt panic rise in her breast. But she could not succumb to hysterics, not now. She had to remain calm.

"Jem," she said, measuring her voice carefully, "we shall go to the nearest inn."

"Aye, miss—but what's ter tell 'em when they asks?"

"We have been accosted by robbers, and we are in need of a physician immediately." She straightened up resolutely. "They cannot turn us away surely."

"I dunno—female and gennulman alone . . ." His voice trailed off doubtfully.

"We shall deal with that when it arises."

Yet when Jem had returned to the box and she was again alone with the baron, she was by no means as assured. She stared across the darkened compartment to where he slumped against the seat, and a sense of hopelessness enveloped her. That there would be no way she could ever explain was secondary to the thought that Haverhill might die there. And as much as she might dislike him for what he'd done to Jess, she could not wish that. Besides, he did not seem so terribly odious, after all. Perhaps there was a reason—perhaps he'd been too angered with himself even—perhaps he could not face Jess after what had happened.

"So tired. Thirsty."

His voice was somewhere between a croak and a whisper. She slid across the seat to brace him. "Would you have more of the rum, sir?" she asked helplessly.

"No."

He was heavy, far heavier than she'd expected, and he seemed to be dead weight against her. The thought crossed her mind that perhaps she ought to keep him talking, but then she wondered if it would not use his strength to do so. His head slid from the back of the seat to her shoulder. She half-turned to catch him, and found she held him against her breast. Where his body touched hers, it was wet and sticky, and it seemed as though the whole compartment was filled with the smell of blood. Maneuvering her hand between them, she discovered that the soaked pad had slipped.

How could anything bleed so much? she wondered. Then,

as she felt the panic increasing, she determined to do what she could. Still bracing him, she leaned across to retrieve the rest of her petticoat, then wadding it into a ball, she thrust it against the wetness. Pressure—it required pressure—and she was a small woman. Throwing modesty to the wind, she pressed him down against the seat and lay over him, turning her shoulder against the wound so that it bore much of the weight of her.

He flailed weakly, struggling as though he would rise, then his back arm fell over hers, holding her in a macabre embrace. She pinned him down, her head turned into the hollow between his chin and his neck, her body against his. His breath was shallow, but reassuring above her head.

Dear God, but how far could it be? It seemed that they careened through the darkness toward eternity. The rain, which had held back for much of the journey, struck with full force, hitting the side panes furiously. And the wind howled, swirling about the carriage as though they traveled through a black maelstrom. She held onto Haverhill tightly and prayed, saying every rote prayer she ever knew, until the rhythm of the repetitions calmed her.

The storm was such that the carriage had braked to a stop before she realized they'd reached something. Even then, when she straightened up to peer outside, she could see almost nothing through the wall of rain. A sheet of water poured through the door when Jem wrenched it open to shout above the din, "Hawk and Pig, Miss!" The lantern he carried chose that moment to die, leaving everything in a furious darkness.

"See if there is help to get him inside!" she yelled above the storm.

The door banged as he shut it, leaving her again alone with the wounded baron. She tried to smooth her bloodstained gown, all the while wondering what she could say to an inn-keeper that would not get them turned away. Picking up Haverhill's hat from the seat, she placed it on his head to keep him from getting wet when they took him out in the rain. It was a foolish, futile gesture given all else that had happened to him, and she knew it.

"We are arrived at an inn," she said loudly, lowering her head close to his ear.

"Good," he answered weakly.

"Can you sit up, do you think?"

"Aye." He made a feeble move to rise, then fell back. "No."

Once again, she slid across the seat and tried to pull him up. It was, she reflected dispiritedly, much like trying to lift a log. But as she tugged, bracing her feet against the bench seat opposite, he pushed also, and somehow between them, he managed to sit.

"Liked it better the other way," he mumbled.

Given the noise from the storm and the lowness of his voice, she couldn't be sure she'd heard him correctly. "Help is forthcoming!" she shouted again into his ear.

"I am wounded—not deaf," he protested in croaks.

"Oh. Yes, of course." Then, seeing a glimmer of light that must be the inn door, she said quickly, "Whatever I tell them, do not dispute me, I pray you."

"Won't." His hand crept to his bloodied vest, then fell. "Funny."

Again, the carriage door was pulled open, and again they were soaked. Two men came with Jem, ready to carry Haverhill inside. With a great deal of difficulty, they managed to pull him out, and as two took his shoulders and one his feet, they lifted him. Kitty slogged through the muddy yard after them.

"Lud a-mercy!" a fat woman exclaimed as they made it inside. "Put him abed atop the stairs," she ordered, turning her attention to Kitty. "What happened ter ye?"

Kitty looked down, grateful for her cloak, for what she could see of her wet dress was quite revealing without her petticoat. And even as she looked, the red stain that covered much of the front, ran downward, dripping a puddle of pink on to the spotless floor. Pushing back her soaked hair, she gulped for air before answering.

"Robbers! We were beset by robbers, and—"

"And yer husband's been shot," the woman finished for her, nodding. "Aye, bad business 'tis when decent folks cannot keep the roads t'night." There was sympathy in her eyes. "Well, me and Mr. Turner runs a respectable inn, missus, so ye've come ter the right place."

"Thank you. But my husband—"

"Well, Tom's been sent to fetch old Burke fer ye, and we can hope he's sober enow to come. Here now—ye got to get outer the wet things."

Kitty shook her head. "I've got nothing else, and I'd stay with him."

"Aye—spose you would. Well, up wi' ye then, Mrs.—" She hesitated, waiting for Kitty to supply a name.

"Smith—Kitty Smith."

"And yer husband?"

Not having any notion of Haverhill's Christian name, Kitty rechristened him on the instant. "John."

"John Smith? Sounds like a Puritan, he does."

"Yes, but I call him Johnny," she added hastily. "He much prefers it."

"Shouldn't wonder at that," Mrs. Turner murmured. "Well, Mrs. Smith, ye'd best go up and get 'im ready fer Burke, if he comes. And don't worrit none—I'll find something dry to cover ye."

"*If* he comes? He's *got* to!"

"Humph! Seems ter me yer better off wi'out 'im," the woman muttered. Then, realizing Kitty's anxiety, she added grudgingly, "Ain't half bad when 'is rum's gone, I guess. Ye go on—me and Turner'll come up if ye need us."

When Kitty reached the room at the top of the stairs, she discovered that they'd laid him on a sheet of oiled cloth spread across the bed. Jem hovered over him, his face worried, but the others had left. Kitty approached the bed with some trepidation.

"Is he better, do you think?" she asked, knowing he could not be.

"Nay."

She looked down, seeing the baron sprawled on his back, his closed eyes looking like bruises on his pallid face. Bending over, she tried to keep her voice low enough that she would not be heard outside.

"My lord, we are at an inn, and the doctor has been sent for. I—I had to tell them we were wed, lest we should be turned away." One hazel eye struggled open at that, prompting her to add defensively, "Well, I had to say it! And if any asks, you are Smith." Looking from him to Jem, she warned, "And no gossiping over your cups. We were robbed on the road, and our money is gone—do you understand?"

He nodded. "And who'm I ter be?"

"That does not matter," she reminded him severely.

"Beggin' yer pardon, Miss Kitty, but if he don't make it, I don't want ter have ter answer fer it. I'd as lief not have it knowed I was here, ye know."

"He will survive. He has to." She looked down again. "Mrs. Turner says we are to make him ready for the doctor."

"I spect she means 'is clothin'."

"Yes, of course." For a moment, Kitty was non-plussed. "Yes—well, I will remove his boots whilst you get the rest."

The coachman looked at her, tilting hs head askance. "Seems ter me," he said, "as 'twould be more useful t'other way.. Ye ain't a-getting 'is boots off, I'll be bound. And I got ye here, but I ain't stayin' t' explain as how his lordship got shot, I ain't," he maintained stoutly. "I ain't swingin' on the Nubbing Cheat fer it. I was a bloomin' noddy fer comin', anyways."

"Jem—"

"I'll get 'is boots, then I'm going."

"In this rain? Jem, you would not leave me surely." Her eyes met his reproachfully.

He looked away. "Miss Kitty, I ain't nobody—they'll hang me if he was ter die."

"Jem, I cannot manage alone. If you take the carriage, I am discovered." She could almost see the struggle between his conscience and his rational mind, and she pressed her advantage. "Please, Jem. I'll not ask you to do more than take his boots. You can play least in sight after even, until we are ready to leave." Laying a hand on the coachey's shoulder, she cajoled, "I'll see you are paid for this, I swear."

"I got ter look ter the horses," he muttered.

"But you will come back?"

It was as though the resistance melted beneath her hand. A sigh of capitulation escaped him. "Aye, but—"

"I'll tend him," she promised quickly. "And if aught happens, I will swear you had nothing to do with what has happened."

He looked doubtfully to where Haverhill lay on the bed. "I dunno—it ain't seemly fer ye to do it, but—"

"If this gets out, my reputation is in shreds, anyway," she countered. "Just get his boots and tend the horses."

"Ye can manage the rest?"

The thought of undressing a man was unthinkable, and Kitty was not at all sure she could do it. In fact, she expected she would die of embarrassment. Nonetheless, she nodded. "I think so," she mumbled, coloring.

It was not until Haverhill's boots stood neatly at the bottom of the bed and Jem had left that Kitty realized the enormity of the task. The baron must surely be a full foot taller than she, and certainly she knew he was heavy. But the physician would have to see the wound, she reminded herself practically. It was clearly no time to be missish.

Moving to the head of the bed, she leaned over, assessing the task. He'd have to come out of the coat, the waistcoat, and the shirt. More than that seemed little to the purpose.

"If you can aid me at all, 'twill be to the good, my lord," she told him, not knowing if he could even lift his arm himself. When he did not respond, she sighed heavily, and sat down to pull on one sleeve. The gentleman's fashion of well-fitted coats was a nuisance, she reflected with resignation. "This is going to hurt," she muttered.

By the time she'd pulled and stretched and forced until she got the coat off his shoulders, she knew she had to have help. She was about to roll off the bed and call downstairs when she realized that Haverhill was conscious.

"You are awake," she accused him.

"I could scarce be anything else." His voice sounded stronger, and his hazel eyes were fixed on hers.

"Can you not help at all?"

He looked to where she knelt on the side of the bed, her wet dress pulled up almost to her knees. And as tired and as weak as he was, he nodded. "Help me to sit."

She pulled on his good arm until he sat up, but the room swam around him. For a moment, he weaved uncertainly, unable to get his bearings. "Lost too much blood," he muttered thickly. Then, forcing himself to the matter at hand, he held out his arm.

She tugged the sleeve off and peeled the jacket around his back, then carefully edged it down the other arm, turning the other sleeve inside out as it came off. Her fingers fumbled at the buttons on his waistcoat, releasing them. It came off far more easily than the coat. He swayed beneath her hands.

"We are nearly done," she encouraged him. "There is but the shirt."

He nodded.

The creamy lawn was stained darkly where it clung to his chest. "At least the ball did not pass through," she observed with some satisfaction.

"'Twould have been better if it had," he muttered, wincing as she stripped the stiffened shirt from his shoulder. He tried to look down, but the angle was wrong. "Still bleeding?"

She lifted the soaked pad gingerly, then peered at the welling hole. There appeared to be the rudiments of a clot forming. "Not so much as 'twas, I think," she murmured, dabbing at the edges to check it.

"Thought you might lie on it again." This time, when he swayed, he leaned over, then lay down. "Pardon—too tired." The oiled cloth that protected the bed crackled beneath him.

Mercifully, the doctor arrived, bleary-eyed but sober. Surveying his patient, he asked only how long ago Mr. Smith had been shot, then shook his head. "Ball's got to come out."

"But the bleeding has just stopped!" she protested.

"Lead—at least two hundred grains of it—festers if 'tis left inside." He looked up at her. "Don't want him carried off with a fever, do you?"

"No, of course not."

"Didn't think so." Even as he spoke, he rolled up his sleeves, then dug in his bag for an evil-looking probe. "Fetch the washbasin, will you?" He eyed her curiously, noting the expression on her face. "If you ain't got the stomach, send up Mrs. Turner."

"I have the stomach," she answered, swallowing the gorge that rose in her throat.

"Good. Like to see a woman as stands with a man. These days, there ain't too many of them." Then, almost as an afterthought, he added, "Best get a cup for the laudanum, 'cause he's going to need it."

"No." It was the first time the baron had spoken since the physician had arrived. "No," he repeated succinctly. "Too much rum."

The doctor shrugged. "He'll swoon then."

Later, Kitty would be hard-pressed to describe anything about the procedure. She washed away the clot, then held the basin while Dr. Burke probed for the ball. Finally, he inserted an evil-looking pair of thin tongs and pulled it out triumphantly. Haverhill had gone rigid for a moment, then fainted. It was a mercy, for Kitty discovered that the wound had yet to be cauterized to stop the bleeding. It was not until his shoulder had been neatly bandaged that she had the stomach to look again.

In the end, Burke stood up. "Lost too much blood, but the body's a wonderous machine, Mrs. Smith. If he keeps quiet and drinks enough, the blood will replace in a matter of days. He ought to feel better by day after tomorrow—unless there is an infection," he hedged, qualifying his rosy prognosis. "Ought to get him out of his wet clothes, though, and keep him warm. Let him drink broths and avoid wine." He looked from Haverhill to her, seeing the utter fatigue in her eyes. "Want me to help you undress him? Don't suppose a little thing like you can manage, can you?"

"Thank you," she murmured gratefully.

"Don't know why big men like him always pick little females," he went on, reaching to unbutton the baron's tight-fitting breeches. "Makes 'em feel strong, I suppose." As Kitty turned away, he peeled the pants down. "How'd he get wounded?" he asked conversationally.

"I told you—robbers—"

"No. No, I meant this."

Despite her resolve, she looked to where Burke pointed at an angry scar that dented deeply into Haverhill's thigh, thinking it explained why the baron favored the leg. The muscle puckered around it.

"Suppose it was the war," he decided. "Nearly lost the leg by the looks of it—broke the bone."

"Yes."

"Peninsula?"

"Er—yes, I believe so."

"Haven't been wed long, have you?"

"No."

He stood again. "Can always tell the newly married ones."

"Oh," she asked cautiously. "How is that?"

"They still blush."

Long after the doctor left, Kitty sat on a chair pushed against the wall. She'd never been quite so tired in her life, and she was beginning to wish she'd said she was Haverhill's sister. Then she could have requested a separate chamber. As it was, she was doomed to sit up with naught but her unhappy thoughts for company.

She thought of the lines by the Scottish poet, Robert Burns, that went "The best laid schemes o' mice and men gang aft agley; an' lea'e us nought but grief and pain, for promis'd joy." How very true, she reflected dispiritedly. Instead of going home to America in disgrace, she would more likely go to prison. And Jess would never get Sturbridge, because her husband would be too intent on revenging himself against Kitty.

The candle guttered in the dish, spluttered valiantly one last time, then died, leaving her in darkness. Outside, the storm still raged, pelting the many-paned windows like a host of pebbles.

"I'd have—a drink."

At first, she thought her ears tricked her, that 'twas the wind, but then she realized he spoke to her. Rising, she made her way unsteadily across the room on cramped legs. "Yes?"

"I'd have a—drink," he repeated, his voice little more than a whisper, his words separated by effort.

She sparked a candle wick with the flint, then turned to find the water pitcher and was in the process of pouring some into a cup when he spoke again. "Have you thought—what you'll—tell the magistrate?" he asked low.

"What?"

"The magistrate. You reported a—robbery."

A deep, cold chill crept down her spine, making her fingers shake. "I did not think of that, my lord—I was but wishful of getting you to the doctor."

"Then say—you—saw nothing."

"You do not mean to give me away?" she asked, turning back to face him.

"No." Despite the pain he felt, his mouth turned down wryly. "Tale would do—nothing—for my credit." His hazel eyes seemed dark in the faint light. "Tell me—what name did you—give me?"

"John Smith."

"Inventive," he mumbled as she sat beside him to hold the cup to his lips.

"Well, I did not know your name beyond Haverhill, sir—and I could scarce use that," she explained practically.

"Name is John."

"I said you were called Johnny."

He drank thirstily of the water, draining the cup, then fell back. She moved back to the chair, and sat again, stretching her legs to ease them.

"Won't molest," he said finally. "Cannot. You can lie down also."

"No. I suppose you can be forgiven for thinking me that sort of female, my lord," she admitted tiredly, "but I am not. This whole day is but a mad scheme gone awry, I assure you, and I am heartily sorry for it."

When he did not respond, she thought he meant to ignore the apology, and she could not blame him if he did. She leaned back against the wall and closed her eyes, hoping that somehow she could waken on the morrow and discover she had but dreamed an utterly awful dream.

"Never been Johnny in my life," she heard him say. " 'Twas always—Jack.''

"WHERE CAN SHE HAVE GONE?" Mrs. Merriman demanded, facing her eldest daughter. "And never say that you do not know, Jessica, for 'twill not wash!"

"I thought she was visiting Squire Marsh's daughter," Jess protested. "Indeed, but I know she said 'twas Amelia, and—"

"She is not there!" her mother announced dramatically. "Moreover, neither Jem nor the carriage has returned!"

"But how—?"

"One of the March grooms rode over but a few minutes ago with a message for her. And when I said I thought it quite odd that Amelia should write to her here if she is there, he said they had not seen her, missy." Isabella paced the floor of the small back parlor, her agitation evident even to the young man who lounged with his feet up on her favorite settee. "You do not think 'tis an elopement? Surely Sturbridge would not be so lost to propriety that—"

"In our carriage, Mama?" Roland asked incredulously. "A man don't take a female to Gretna in her equippage—takes his own cattle. Where *is* Sturbridge, by the by?"

"Charles will be here directly," Jessica volunteered.

"And I cannot like that, missy! It seems to me that he spends as much time with you as with Kitty, and how's he to fix his interest there, I ask you, if you are forever in the way?"

Roland choked. "Charles and Kitty? Coming it too strong, Mama! She don't like him much better'n she likes me, if

47

you want the truth of it. And if there's any as says otherwise, 'tis a faradiddle they've told you.''

"Rollo, you stay out of that which you do not know,"
his sister warned him. "I am sure she thinks a great deal
of him."

"Humph! Don't show it if she does."

"If you would pay attention to the world rather than dwell
in the clouds, fancying yourself a soldier, you might see
something," Jessica retorted. "But every time you are down
from Oxford, you spend your days with naught but those
musty war books for company, and you know 'tis the truth!"

"Please!" Mrs. Merriman put her hands to her temples
as though to block out yet another brangle between her two
eldest. "Of course there is a *tendre* there. Why else would
he be forever here? But that is nothing to the point now,"
she recalled. "Where *is* Kitty?"

"Don't know," Roland muttered. "Ten to one, she went
to a turn-up or something—be like her to go off to a mill,
if she wanted. Gel don't go on as she ought, you know."

"In the Carolinas, I daresay females are more free in their
manner," Jessica observed loyally, coming to her absent
cousin's defense. "And she is not exactly a green girl, after
all. I mean, she is even older than I. Moreover, she did take
Jem."

"It *ought* to have been an abigail," Mrs. Merriman
muttered.

"But she don't—well, she ain't used to the ways of the
ton," he pointed out. "Dash it, Jess, but she don't try to
fit in!"

"All the more reason I had such hopes of Sturbridge,"
his mother admitted. "He did not appear to note her—" She
groped for a word. "—well, her *candor*—or her lack of
refinement, I suppose I should say. Indeed, but I had
thought—"

"You mean her eccentricities, and if he did not, you can
be sure his mama did," Roland cut in dryly. "If ever there

was a Tartar, 'tis she. No, you'd best not count on Charley Trevor coming up to scratch for Kitty, I can tell you.''

"Of all the unfeeling—"

"Ain't unfeeling—just don't see it, that's all. Dash it, but he'd be more likely to offer for you than Kit!" He rounded on his sister. "At least you got a notion how to go on!"

"How would you know? You do not pay attention when you are at home," Jessica shot back.

"My hopes in that quarter are quite cut up," Mrs. Merriman sniffed. "Had it not been for Haverhill, naturally I should have wished—" Her voice trailed off wistfully. "But there *is* Haverhill, of course, and there's naught to be done about that. Your dear papa did what he thought he ought, after all. And we cannot say that the money the baron sends Jessica has not been a blessing. Indeed, but since Mr. Merriman passed on, I know not how we should have survived without it."

"Fiddle. Uncle Thomas left Kitty enough for all of us," Roland reminded her.

For a moment, his mother looked as though she would cry. "No, no he did not." Then, when both of her children turned disbelieving eyes on her, she shook her head. "I'd not meant to tell any—that is, I'd hoped that Sturbridge would have offered first—"

"Doing it too brown, Mama!"

"Oh, Rollo, you know how Kitty is! If she should discover the reverses the Funds have taken, she will not accept his suit! And she must!"

"Are you telling me that Kitty has no fortune?" Jessica demanded incredulously.

"Well, there is a little, but nothing like there was, my love. I had it of that wretched man your papa appointed to oversee our affairs. No, 'twould seem the end of the war has thrown the economy into disarray—or some such thing." She twisted the handkerchief she carried. "But if Sturbridge is besotted with her, I am sure 'twill not matter. If naught else can be said of the Trevors, they have more than enough money to be generous, my love." Isabella met her daughter's eyes and nodded. "Suffice it to say that she *must* take him, for there does not seem to be anyone else on the turnpike, does there?" she asked rhetorically.

"No!" Then, perceiving that they both turned to her, Jessica colored guiltily. "That is, if she does not want him—"

" 'Tis nothing to the point. They will deal well together, I am sure," her mother declared flatly. "I promised Thomas I should see her settled, and if it takes my last breath, I shall."

"Gel's at her last prayers, Mama."

"She is four and twenty," Isabella acknowledged, "but she does not show it, after all. Indeed, but with her looks and her natural liveliness, I am sure she could have found a husband anywhere." She eyed her son speculatively. "Indeed, I have often thought that if you were older—but then I suppose the situation with the Funds would have changed that, in any event."

"Egad, no!"

They were interrupted by a footman, who peered inside to announce, " 'Tis Viscount Sturbridge, madam—shall I direct him in?"

"Yes—no—oh, dear!" Looking to her offspring, she wavered. "Whatever shall we say? We cannot tell him she has disappeared, after all, but—" Squaring her shoulders, she collected herself. "You will, of course, direct him to the front saloon."

"Tell him she's visiting," Roland suggested.

"Where?"

"It don't make no difference where! Dash it, but he ain't going to pry, Mama! You have but to say she is out."

"But where *is* she?"

"Ten to one, she's gone shopping somewheres and forgot to tell you. Do things differently in America, after all," Roland uttered bracingly. "Be home ere nightfall, no doubt."

"Overnight? Kitty would never—oh, dear—do you

suppose there has been an accident?'' Jessica wondered nervously.

"I am sure I do not know, but I would not think so, else we should have heard.'' The older woman sighed. "There is no help for it, is there? Jessica, you will have to make an excuse for Kitty to Sturbridge, for I do not think I could face him without betraying my worry.''

"Well, if she don't want him, it ain't impossible that she's fleeing 'cause of him,'' Roland hazarded.

"Do not be absurd, Rollo,'' his sister retorted. "Charles is a catch.'' Her chin came up and her eyes defied him to dispute it. "Very well, Mama, I will see him.''

"What the devil ails her? Did I say he wasn't? You know, Mama, if she wasn't wed to Haverhill, I'd think she was head over heels for Sturbridge herself!''

"Well, if she is, she'd best rid herself of any foolish notions—there is Haverhill, after all.''

Jessica closed the door on them and crossed the hallway to the front saloon. As she stepped inside, the fair-haired young man jumped up, smiling expectantly. She stared at him as though she would remember him always with just that expression on his face.

"Jess?''

"Oh, Charles!'' she wailed, her face crumpling. "You are going to have to marry Kitty after all!''

"I beg your pardon? Jessica, whatever—?''

" 'Twas impossible to think otherwise!'' she blurted out. "One of us has to wed you—and you know I cannot!''

"Oh, my love . . .'' He crossed the room, reaching his hands to her.

"No, I pray you will not.'' She backed away. "Charles, we must give up this foolish dream of ours. And Kitty will make you an unexceptional wife, I am sure. She is pretty and lively and—''

"Jess—''

"And while your mama cannot like her breeding, I daresay

she will come to admire her for her mind. Kitty is quite clever, you know, and—"

"Jess—" He moved closer.

"No! What I am telling you, Charles, is that Kitty has to marry you!"

"Jess, I know not what goes here, but Kitty would be the first to tell you we should not suit. She'd have me in Bedlam within a fortnight, love."

"Please—you do not understand!"

" 'Tis nonsense—Kitty Gordon has no interest in me, and well you know it," he murmured soothingly.

She turned away. "She will discover one, no doubt."

"She wishes to return to America."

"With what?" Spinning around, she raised tear-filled eyes to his. "Charles, she has no money—'tis gone."

"Gone? But how could that be? 'Tis common knowledge that Gordon left her well fixed." He stopped, seeing that his beloved was indeed quite serious. "Egad—*all* of it?"

She nodded. "Enough, I am afraid. So you see, if you love me, you will take her. I should rather think of her having you than someone else. At least I should still see you."

"Jessica, what you suggest goes against every feeling! I am not such a man as—"

"No, of course not," she cut in quickly. "I did not mean that, Charles." The tears spilled onto her cheeks and trickled downward. "It was always a hopeless passion, you know."

"But Kitty—she would not—"

"She will. As Mama said, there is no one else."

MORNING CREPT UP SLOWLY, bringing with it not the rosy hues of dawn, but rather the faint light of a rainy day. Jack roused, aware at first of an almost overwhelming thirst, then of the ache in his shoulder. His eyes opened, and for a moment, he thought he was again in Portugal—or Spain perhaps—and he half-listened for the cries of others, more sorely wounded soldiers. But there was not the stench of death about him, only silence. His eyes traveled over the dingy room warily.

Then he saw the girl. Her small body was folded like a concertina, compressed to fit the plain wooden chair. A tangled riot of pale gold hair fell over her arm where it cradled her face against the wood. Her gown twisted about her legs, giving him a view of stockinged ankle above her ruined slippers. What he could see of the dress bore mute testimony to what had befallen them—the front was stiff and brown, stained with his blood.

He struggled to sit, then leaned back, too dizzy to rise from the bed. He must have bled more than he ought—that accounted for the thirst. His head pounded like the devil's hammer inside, and he remembered the coachman's rum. Not only had he been shot, but he'd been bit by the proverbial barn weasel also. His mouth tasted as though Boney's army had been through it. Must've been cheap stuff.

Just as he was about to try his legs again, someone pounded on the door. The girl roused, coming awake guiltily. She sat up and pulled her dress down.

"Who—who is it?" she asked cautiously.

53

"Jem!"

She stood unsteadily on cramped legs, then hobbled to let the coachman in. He doffed his cap respectfully, mumbling a greeting. "Morning, Miss Kitty." His eyes strayed to where Jack sat on the edge of the mattress, holding his head, and his relief was evident. "He's better, eh?"

"What—? Oh." She turned around slowly, afraid of what she'd find. Where the covers fell away from his body, he was bare. "Oh, dear."

Jack lifted a weak arm, then let it fall. "Weasel-bit," he croaked. "Need a drink." Then, seeing that she looked away, he pulled the blanket up over his chest. "Pardon."

"Outer rum—drank it all," Jem told him plaintively.

"The last thing he needs is spirits. Indeed, but the doctor said he must drink broths. I—"

"Don't want broth. Water." As she reached for the pitcher, he nodded and wished he had not. He had to hold his pounding temples to keep his bearings. He groaned. "Lost too much blood—must've hit a good-sized vein."

"By God's grace 'twas not yer lung," Jem muttered. His face clouded momentarily. "They's goin' ter send fer the magistrate, Miss Kitty. Told 'em he couldn't talk to 'im, but guess they ain't listenin' ter me."

Jack took the cup she offered and gulped greedily. Even the noise of the liquid going down reverberated through his head. "Tell him you say nothing—'twas too dark," he advised between swallows. The blanket slipped to his waist.

"Will I have to swear to it?"

"Why?"

"I should dislike lying."

Both men stared at her. " 'Twould seem, Miss Gordon, that your scruples are discovered a trifle late," the baron observed dryly.

She had the grace to color. "Yes, well, I suppose it must seem so to you, but I could justify what I did to you, sir— 'tis quite another thing to lie to a magistrate." Aware of the lift of his brow, she added defensively, "Well, I had to make you understand about Jess."

"Ah, yes—the Merriman female."

"Your—"

"Mrs. Smith, Colonel Barswell is come to see you!" Mrs. Turner called through the closed door.

Kitty cracked the door cautiously. "Colonel Barswell? But I don't know any—"

"The magistrate, mum."

"Oh, but I—my husband—well, we are not prepared!"

"Says if they are to catch the miscreant, they got to get the report, missus."

"Lud."

"He'll come up ter see yer husband arter."

"Damn!" Jack muttered.

"But he is not able!"

There was a pause, then the woman spoke again. "Says he won't tire 'im, missus."

"Go on—got to buy time," Jack urged. "Don't tell him anything—say you swooned."

"I have never fainted in my life, my lord."

"Nonsense. You are a female."

"And what will you tell him?"

"I don't mean to tell him anything. Go on—else he'll come up here and I've no wish to see him. I'd not be recognized, if you'd have the truth of it."

"But—"

"Miss Gordon, it is in your best interest to divert him," Jack reminded her. "Take your time—pretend you are trying to recall. Cry if you think 'twill help."

"I seldom cry either," she muttered with asperity. "Jem—"

"I need Jem with me—cannot stand unaided, I fear."

Despite her resolve not to look again, her eyes strayed to his bare chest, and the thought occurred to her that he probably wished to be dressed. "Oh, yes, of course. I daresay Jem can assist you, sir."

With great trepidation, her heart pounding, her stomach churning, she made her way down the narrow wooden stairs. It was not until she'd reached the bottom that she became aware of the curious stares. She looked down, seeing the thin, blood-stained gown, and wondered if any could see through it.

"Mrs. Smith?"

A tall, courtly gentleman well into middle age stood in the doorway of a side parlor. "Colonel Barswell," she managed through lips almost too dry for speech.

"Yes. Oh, not a colonel anymore—but people hereabouts are slow to forget. Was in the dragoons, actually, until last year." He smiled. "But 'tis not of me I would speak, madam." His gaze took in the gown, and he shook his head regretfully. "Bad business, I know, and I shall contrive to make this as brief as possible, you know. But if a man is robbed in my district, I'd pursue the matter forthwith."

"Yes, of course." She walked past him into the private parlor.

"Ordered breakfast for you. Woman said you had not eaten, and stands to reason after what has befallen you, food would be the last of your thoughts." He gestured to a table set for two. "You will join me, will you not?"

She had little choice. "My thanks, sir."

"Nothing of it," he assured her, waiting for her to sit.

Even though it still rained and the light that came through the window was gray, she tried not to let it shine through her gown. Moving quickly to the chair, she dropped down.

"London female," he guessed, his eyes on the dress.

"Actually, I am American." It was, she decided almost as soon as she'd said it, the wrong thing to admit. His smile faded immediately. Thinking to retrieve the situation, she hastened to invent a reason for her existence there. "Alas, but I was orphaned, and my only relations are here, you see, and then I met John . . ." Her voice trailed off as though that explained everything.

"Don't look old enough to be married," he decided, tucking his napkin over his yellow waistcoat. "Thought there must be a mistake when I saw you."

She was used to that at least. "I am four and twenty, sir. 'Tis my height, or lack of it, I suppose, that makes one think otherwise. My mother was short also," she confided, reaching for a slice of bread. Hopefully, if her mouth were full, he would forebear asking too much.

He poured himself a cup of coffee, then chiseled a chunk of sugar from the loaf. Stirring it into the steaming liquid, he leaned back to watch her. "I'd have you tell me what happened on the road—all of it."

The bread seemed like a lump of dough too large to swallow. She chewed valiantly, shaking her head, then gulped, forcing it down. Reaching for the teapot, she poured herself some and drank it plain. The hot liquid scalded, choking her, and she began to cough until tears came to her eyes.

"Ought to take a little sugar and cream in that," Barswell told her, waiting.

She nodded and reached for the loaf, buying time by chipping off a piece of it. Stirring that into her cup, she picked up the cream pitcher. "Well, I did not actually see anything," she said, her voice still strangled. "It was dark and raining."

"Approximately where did the attack occur?"

She considered telling him, then realized that he'd surely wonder why she'd traveled hours more with a wounded man. "Well, I am not certain—a few miles back, I should guess," she answered vaguely. "In truth, I was so upset that I cannot recall anything but the fact that my husband was shot, sir."

"I suppose I will have to get that from your coachman," he conceded. "Now, how did the actual shooting occur?"

"Someone fired a pistol."

He favored her with a pained expression that told her he considered her little better than half-witted. "I surmised that much, Mrs. Smith. What I meant to ask was if the door were opened, if the highwayman actually approached the carriage for your money? Did your husband struggle for possession of the pistol?''

She started to say no, then recalled she'd had Jem tell the innkeeper that they'd been robbed. "Yes."

"He struggled with your husband, and yet you did not see him?''

"There were two," she volunteered. "Two of them. And neither of them actually entered the carriage. They ordered us to throw our valuables out. No, my husband did not struggle with them," she added.

"Do you have any notion as to why they shot him? Or perhaps you were so fearful that you did not look? Perhaps being female you hid your face."

She buttered her bread and took another leisurely bite. His attitude was annoying in the extreme. "Actually, I suppose 'twas because I fired at them. John advised against it, but I did not wish to lose our money."

"You fired a pistol, madame?" he asked incredulously.

"Well, 'twas my husband's. He keeps one under the seat," she explained, warming to the tale. "But it was on my side, so 'twas I who retrieved it and fired." Her blue eyes met his over the rim of her teacup. "I should have listened to John—there was only one shot, you see, and two of them. When the first fellow—the one who was picking up the money we'd cast out—well, when he bolted, the other one fired. The ball struck my husband."

"I thought you did not see anything," he murmured, bemused.

"Well, I did not, but I fired in the general direction of his voice. And it happened so very quickly, sir."

"And what was your coachman doing during the robbery?" he wondered.

"I suspect he was attempting not to be noticed. They did not seem particularly interested in him, anyway," she recalled. "But after I shouted that John was shot, he applied the whip, fleeing while they were still in disarray. No doubt they were more interested in the money than in us, anyway, don't you think?''

"Undoubtedly." He took a bite of his sausage and leaned back to watch her as he chewed. "You are a remarkable woman, Mrs. Smith."

She wondered if he meant her story or herself, but she chose to brazen it through. "John likes to think so. But then, I never was a dieaway miss." She met his gaze wide-eyed. "I am afraid 'tis all there is to the tale, sir. I do not think I could identify anyone."

"Yes, well—we can hope that your coachman or your husband can give a better description."

"John does not recall much—the wound, you know."

"Burke tells me 'twas a near thing—a trifle lower and— well, shouldn't speak of that, I suppose. Suffice it to say that he is fortunate 'twas only blood he lost." Perceiving that perhaps he touched upon her fears, he forced an encouraging smile. "A few days and he'll be up and about, I daresay," he added heartily. "Well, finish your food, ma'am. Soon as mine's done, I shall go up to see Smith."

She happened to glance out the paned window behind him, and what she saw almost made her heart stop. "Uh—" She pushed away from the table and started to rise. "I really think I ought to tend to him, sir—to make certain he is presentable."

"Nonsense! Told you I was a soldier, didn't I? He won't be the first fellow I've seen in this condition, I assure you! Best eat—need your strength for the task of caring for the fellow."

"Yes—well, I cannot say that I have the appetite this morning, sir. If you will pardon me . . ."

It was then that he noted her pallor, and reluctantly he rose also. "Forget what 'tis like for the females, don't I? Ought to ask your pardon for bringing up such things, but business, you know," he murmured apologetically.

"It *has* been oversetting," she agreed. "Even I must own that. I thought I'd lost John, you see."

"Blood can be replaced—just takes time to make more of it. Daresay he'll be up and about in a matter of days, ma'am."

Behind him, her carriage moved slowly toward the corner of the innyard. "Yes, well—I really must look in on John," she murmured. Extending her hand, she added hastily, "So good of you to come, sir—I hope you will discover the culprits."

He held her hand a trifle overlong, bowing over it gallantly while she wished him at Jericho. "Smith's a fortunate fellow, my dear," he told her.

"You are too kind." She retrieved her fingers, trying not to betray her panic. "Do finish your breakfast, sir—I am sure Smith is going nowhere in his condition, after all."

"Course he ain't—be abed a few days. You tell him I shall be up directly, will you?"

She made good her escape, slipping not up the stairs but rather out the front door of the establishment. And once outside, she broke into a most unladylike run, lifting the hem of her ruined gown as though a few mud spatters would matter. Around her, the men in the yard turned to watch and grin, but she was beyond caring about that.

Breathless, she found her carriage standing just beyond the main roadway. Wrenching open the door furiously, she discovered the baron inside. Without waiting for Jem, she threw her body into the coach, ripping the seam of her narrow skirt.

"Of all the awful things to do!" she rounded on Haverhill. "I should have looked the veriest fool—and worse! What was I supposed to say when my wounded husband disappeared?"

"Wasn't disappearing." He leaned back, his face pale beneath the auburn hair that fell over his forehead. "Sent Jem to tell you." He shifted slightly, wincing. "Didn't want to face Old 'Swell—be all over the country in a sennight I'd been shot." He caught his breath and grimaced again.

"We cannot just leave! My lord—think of it, I pray you! How's it to look if we run?" she demanded.

"Do you—want to sign an affidavit?" he countered. "Only crime I can attest to—abduction by you." Beads of either perspiration or rain shone on his brow. "Too much to explain."

"But the bill—someone must pay the shot," she protested.

"Told 'em we were robbed," he reminded her. "Send it to 'em later. Promise."

"Can't find 'er, my lord," Jem announced, opening the door. "Ain't with th' magistrate, and ain't—" He stopped, seeing Kitty. "Oh—yer found." He wiped the rain from his face. "Near thing—was afeard he meant ter ask me, but he was feedin' 'is face. Said he'll speak ter Smith first. Well, none's the harm t'day. Where d'ye mean t' take 'im, Miss Kitty?"

The baron's hazel eyes were on hers. "Yes—where now, Miss Gordon?"

He was rumpled, his bloody shirt open over the bandages, his face in desperate need of a shave. The thought came to mind that he looked more like a ruffian than like Baron Haverhill. Then she looked down again at her soiled, torn gown. And no explanation she could think of would suffice, she was sure of it. Indeed, by light of day, the whole affair seemed too preposterous for repeating.

"Well," she sighed, exhaling fully, "I shall have to take you home, I suppose."

"To London?" One of his eyebrows rose.

"No—to my aunt's house, though what she will say, I cannot imagine. I hope, when she comes to understand why I have done it, she will not cut the connection entirely."

Jem looked from her to the baron, shaking his head. "Take yer there, I will, but I ain't stayin'. Yer can tell 'er I give m' notice ere she turns me off." He backed out of the doorway and closed it. "Ain't stayin' here neither," he acknowledged, climbing onto the box.

She clasped her hands in her lap and stared downward. "I can only hope you will be persuaded to do the right thing were Jess is concerned, my lord. Then 'twill not have been entirely for naught."

"Miss Gordon, I do not—" His words came to an abrupt end as the carriage lurched violently forward, throwing him back against the leather-covered seat. He went white, biting his lip against the pain.

"Are you all right, sir?" she asked anxiously.

"No. Be damned fortunate if I don't bleed some more," he gasped. "Got a devil of a head and a hole in my shoulder—of course I am not all right!"

"No, of course not."

She looked even younger and smaller as she sat, her head down, and he felt goaded. "No Cheltenham tragedies, please—'tis I who am injured," he muttered. "Only thing worse that ever happened to me was the ball in my leg."

"Dr. Burke said you must have nearly lost it."

"He was right." He closed his eyes and swallowed. "Damned thirsty."

"You drank all the rum last night."

"I know."

There seemed to be nothing else to say to him, nothing to the point, anyway. Sighing again, she turned to look out the window into the dreary day. If she had it to do all over again, she would have asked Rollo to write him. It would not have been impossible, she supposed. She could have flattered her young cousin by reminding him that he was the head of the house, after all.

"No," he said suddenly. "The leg was not the worst of it. 'Twas the suffering and dying of the others."

"I beg your pardon?" She looked up, seeing a very different pain in his eyes, a pain that made them seem almost green. They were, she realized, quite the most beautiful eyes she'd ever seen. " 'Twas as Burke thought—you have been in the war?"

"I have been to hell, Miss Gordon." His mouth compressed into an almost bitter line. "The fire, the brimstone, the smell—all of it. There are no terrors left for me."

And in that moment, her heart went out to him. "How awful for you," she whispered, swallowing the ache that rose in her throat.

"It makes what passes for fashionable life utterly frivolous."

"Yes." She sighed heavily. "I would that Rollo knew it, but he is only sorry the war ended ere he was old enough to go."

"Rollo?"

"Roland, actually—my cousin, Roland Merriman."

"The young fool."

"Does it pain you very much—the leg, I mean?" she asked him.

"Only when it rains—I have said it until it does not bear repeating, you know, but 'tis the truth." He looked at the drizzle that streaked the carriage windows. " 'Twould be a jest if the infernal rain ever stopped."

"I am sorry for it."

He leaned forward, and his eyes seemed to warm. "I like it much better, Miss Gordon, when you show your spirits. I've had a surfeit of sympathy—'tis company I need."

"I am not an entertaining sort of female, I fear. My conversation always seems to be of the wrong sort for fashion over here."

"But you are, Miss Gordon—you are," he said quite definitely.

She'd been wrong—his eyes were gold. "Spanish coin, sir, but at this point in my existence, I shall take it."

IT WAS HIS WEAKNESS, she supposed, but the baron slept much of the remainder of the trip, leaving Kitty to worry about her reception at home. If they disowned her, it would make leaving easier, she told herself. She could return to America unencumbered. No, 'twas not the truth—for despite her homesickness, she had to own that her aunt and cousins had been more than kind to her. She looked across to where Haverhill's head rested in the corner between the seat back and the side panel of the coach. If only a way could be found to keep the matter hushed—then they could forgive her ere she left.

A wheel hit a deep, water-covered rut, and for a moment, she thought they would turn over. Above, she could hear Jem swear at the horses. The carriage teetered, then righted itself to continue on the road.

Haverhill's head snapped back as the wheel found the pavement again, and he came reluctantly awake. Passing a hand over the stubble of his face, he sat up. His other hand touched the bandage as though to make certain it was still in place.

"The road is in sad need of repair," she observed.

"If you believe that, you ought to try the Spanish ones."

"Does your head still pain you?"

"Only when I think, so probably not overmuch. 'Tis the thirst that plagues me."

"You ought to have brought some water."

"As I recall the matter, there did not appear to be any time.

I could not know that while my stomach grumbled, Old 'Swell was feeding you.''

"I collect you know him then?"

"A passing acquaintance at best, but I think he would have remembered me," he answered in modest understatement. "Where are we, by the by?"

She looked out the window. "Not above another two or three miles from Rose Farm, I should think."

"Rose Farm?"

She nodded. "An ancestor of Aunt Isabella's husband named the place for his wife—'twas in the seventeenth century, I think. He bought it from a Catholic who went to Maryland, or so the story is told."

It occurred to him then that he knew next to nothing about the girl across from him. Nothing except that she had been born in America. "Your family over here is of the gentry?"

"Yes."

"Have you been here long?"

"No." Realizing how uncivil she must sound, she unbent to explain, "I came but last year, delayed by the troubled situation between England and the United States. My papa had died the year before, you see, and although it was his express wish that I come to live with my relatives, 'twas not practical until the hostilities ended."

"And they have not discovered a husband for you yet? My dear, over here a twenty-year-old female is quite on the shelf."

"So I have found," she noted dryly. "But I cannot say they have not put themselves to the task. Had I not been so long in the tooth, I should have been dragged to London for the Season."

He shook his head sympathetically. "I have never understood it myself. I find it unfathomable that a man of the world, after sampling most of life's pleasures, should think it desirable to wed an empty-headed widgeon whose experience is limited almost entirely to the schoolroom."

His gaze traveled lazily over her. "I have always liked a lady old enough to share interesting thoughts."

"No doubt," she muttered, recalling how he'd abandoned Jess.

"Didn't mean to put you up in the boughs, Miss Gordon, I assure you. So—they have been throwing you at the gentlemen's heads, have they?"

"Only one. Actually, there are not many eligible partis in our neighborhood, for which I suppose I must be thankful. Lord Sturbridge is quite enough."

"Your swain?"

"If Aunt Bella has her way, he is." She considered confessing about Jess and Charles, then thought better of it. Too much depended on what he did with Jess, and she'd not betray her cousin. "I expect that the whole of Sussex, with the exception of Sturbridge's mama, expects the announcement momentarily."

"His mother objects?"

"Oh, no. She is quite careful of what she says of me. Clever of her, really. No, I am brown, and my manners she pronounces unconventional but not unpleasing."

"Brown?" He lifted his eyebrow. "I should rather call you fair myself."

"It is her way of reminding him that I am not English, my lord. We Americans are thought to have consorted overmuch with the Indians, I suppose."

"And so she deals in half the truth, eh?" He tried to straighten his tired body, and was instantly sorry for it. The pain that shot through his shoulder was like fire. "Damn!" he muttered.

"If nothing else goes wrong, how long will it take for you to heal?" she asked curiously.

"What difference does it make?" he asked through teeth clenched against the pain.

"I should like to know you have survived ere I go back to my home—to the United States."

"Good of you." He clasped his shoulder and held it tightly.

"Especially since I should not be in this case were it not for you."

"I said I was sorry for it—and you said you disliked sympathy," she reminded him.

"There is sympathy—and there is sympathy, Miss Gordon."

"And there are riddles, sir."

"Needle-witted also, I see." Then, noting that she still waited for an answer, he relented. "With food and rest, I ought to mend enough to ride within a couple of weeks, I should suppose. Naught's broken, after all. Now, if I take a fever . . ." He let his voice drift.

"But you will not," she was positive. "I mean, we had the doctor."

"Optimistic, too," he murmured. "You've got more faith in the surgeons than I." He shifted his weight, moving his leg, and he blenched anew. "Would've taken m'leg, if I'd let 'em. Had to hold 'em off with my pistol."

At that moment, the wheel dropped into another rut, throwing them against the sides. There was the crack of shattering wood, then nothing—the coach just seemed to settle at an angle. Kitty righted herself to open the door.

"Damme if the wheel ain't broke, Miss Kitty," Jem explained. "Throwed me off'n the box." To show her, he lifted a muddy sleeve.

"It cannot be!"

"If it ain't, then my name ain't Jeremy Miller!" he retorted. He looked past her to the baron, who leaned back, one hand on his shoulder, the other on his thigh. Haverhill was deathly pale. "We done it now, miss—what's ter do?"

She looked around her, gaining her bearings. In the distance, she recognized the monolithic Blackstone Hall of the Trevors. Her gaze dropped to the torn, bloodstained dress that now clung indecently to her.

"I do not suppose you would seek out Lord Sturbridge, would you?" she asked hopefully.

The coachman's eyes followed hers. "And tell 'im what?"

he fairly howled. "How we's abducted a swell, and ain't nuthin' been right since? I was leavin' ye ere we got ter the gate ter Rose Farm, ye know. They ain't clappin' me up, I'll be bound!"

"If you would but get word to Lord Sturbridge—'twould be all I'd ask," she promised.

He wavered. "Un-uh. Miss Kitty, we—" The appeal in her blue eyes was unmistakable. "Ye goin' ter visit me in jail?" When she said nothing, he exhaled and nodded. "If he ain't ter home, I ain't comin' back." Shrugging his shoulders helplessly, he started off.

Yet another wave of guilt washed over her. "Jem—" She waited for him to turn back to her. "Jem, I don't mean for this to touch you, you know. I intend to tell everyone the fault was mine—that you attempted to dissuade me even— and I am sure they will believe me." When he said nothing, she added, "They will think it all of a piece, don't you see? I have not gone on as I ought since I arrived here."

"But I oughter have knowned better," he answered glumly. "And so's the mistress ter say."

As he walked down the narrow country lane, she felt sorry for him. Life as a stableman was not easy, and whilst she had been inside the carriage, he'd been soaked above. And now she had more than likely cost him his position at Rose Hill. She turned back to where the coach sat atilt, and her already low spirits plummeted. That it was not her aunt's only conveyance was little consolation, for Isabella could not wish to go everywhere in the cabriolet, particularly not since there would not be room for the family in it. The carriage would be but one more item on a list growing ever longer, more fuel for the peal her aunt would ring over her.

Dispirited, she climbed back into the coach to tend to the baron. "Are you all right?" she asked anxiously.

"No."

"Your shoulder—'tis not bleeding again, is it?"

"No." There was a whiteness about his mouth, and his hand gripped his thigh as though he would strangle the pain there, but his eyes still betrayed the barest hint of humor. "Tell me, Miss Gordon—would you lie upon it again if it were?"

"I beg your pardon—" She felt an involuntary rush of embarrassment as her face went hot. "Oh—but you are not supposed to recall that, sir."

"I could scarce forget." Despite the condition of her gown, despite the bedraggled appearance of damp hair that flattened against her face, she was still more fetching than most, and he relented. "I possibly owe you my life for it," he added quietly. "I have seen men bleed to death from wounds that weren't supposed to take them."

"I did nothing that anyone I know would not have done, my lord," she protested feebly, disconcerted by the sudden warmth in his eyes. Once again, they seemed to be gold.

"You must have a remarkable set of acquaintances then, my dear."

She stared out the window toward the misty shadow in the distance, wondering what Sturbridge would say when Jem apprised him of what they had done. "Let us hope so," she said, her voice low. "I suppose," she mused, more to herself than to him, "that I must be thankful for my competence at least. 'Twill repair this and pay my passage to America."

He could see her swallow, and he had a fair notion that she was far more upset than she would admit. "What will you do there?" he asked quietly.

She turned sober eyes on him. "I have hopes that my father's partners will welcome me back. We had a shipping business, you see, and I am accounted a fair hand with the figures. While Papa lived, I assisted with the books."

"And yet you came here, where a female cannot pretend to such skill."

" 'Twas Papa's wish," she said simply.

"Why?"

'I don't know—my English heritage, I suppose. Despite the war, despite the need to keep his politics to himself, I think Papa never forgot he was born here. And—" She looked again to the window. "And he wanted me to marry well—better than the sort of gentlemen in his business. He was a younger son, you see, but I was his only issue. He said he made his fortune that I would not have to."

"And you dislike this Sturbridge fellow?"

"Oh—no. No, 'tis not that precisely."

He waited for her to enlighten her as to why she did not just take his lordship, but she said nothing. "His title must weigh with you surely."

"As he has not actually offered, I should not discuss it," she answered, evading the question. " 'Twould be improper to deny what has not been asked."

The rub must be her suitor's mother, he decided. And yet the thought crossed his mind that perhaps she cared more for Lord Sturbridge than she wished to admit. And surely, mother or no, his lordship could not be blind to Kitty Gordon's loveliness. Despite his resolve to drop the matter, he could not quite resist wanting to know.

"Why do you dismiss this Sturbridge? Is it the Old Tartar?"

Her eyes widened at his directness, and then she blinked. "Let us just say there are two important impediments to the match." A slow, rueful smile curved her mouth. "Really, my lord, I should expect such impertinence from myself, but from an English gentleman?"

"I suppose I ought to know a set-down when I get one, eh?" he conceded, grinning. "Very well, Miss Gordon, I shall pry no more. Where are we now, by the by? This Rose Farm must surely be closer than when last I asked."

"We are awaiting Lord Sturbridge, I hope."

Somehow he thought perhaps that explained her agitation and her forlorn countenance more than any consideration for the coach. "I see," he said softly.

"No, you don't," she retorted peevishly. "What he is to think of this, I don't know. But just now, I shall have to consider him my only ally."

They had not long to wait. Within the space of a quarter

hour, the viscount appeared, alone, driving a tilbury with its leather top pulled up against the mist. Jack followed Kitty's apprehensive gaze, hoping to see a slender fop, a frippery fellow like so many of the *ton*. But as the equippage barreled into view, he was dismayed to discover that not only did Sturbridge drive to an inch, but he was also quite an amiable-looking gentleman. In fact, although Jack was not overgiven to appraising the looks of his fellow man, he could recognize this one as being rather handsome.

"Miss Gordon, I came as soon as your coachman explained!" Lord Sturbridge called out, jumping down.

Kitty took a deep breath, mumbled a quick prayer, then twisted the door handle, hoping to be able to speak before he saw the baron. But the viscount pulled the door from her hand and peered inside. The first thing he saw was her wet, bloody dress, its skirt torn past her knees.

"Egad! Miss Gordon—Kitty! Whatever—?"

Owing to the tilt of the carriage, when she leaned forward, Kitty quite literally fell into his arms. He staggered slightly, then righted both of them, steadying her. His arm went around her protectively, a gesture not lost on Jack, who watched with interest.

"I say—are you all right, Kitty?" His eyes went from her to the man still in the coach. "What the devil—did he do this to you?" he demanded.

She gulped air, then before her courage deserted her, blurted out baldly, "It's Haverhill, Charles—and he has been shot. I abducted him in London."

At first, her words went past him. "If he has—Haverhill!" Then, as her meaning sank in, he groaned. "You shot Haverhill, Kitty?"

"Of course not! I shot one highwayman, and the other shot him. There is but one ball in a pistol at a time, you see," she added, as though that must explain everything. "Oh, Charles—we have had the worst time of it!"

"There . . . there . . . of course you have," he murmured soothingly, holding her. "But—"

"First we were beset by robbers, then he was shot—and he bled so much—" She looked down to where her stained gown clung in indecent invitation against her breasts. Crossing her arms to cover herself, she went on. "And we— Jem and I—thought he would die of it. We took him to an inn, that a doctor could be summoned, and it was terrible. I assisted while the ball was removed. Then this morning, there was the magistrate we fled, and now the wheel is broken—Charles, I am at the end of my wits!"

"Of course you are, but—"

"He's wounded badly. The ball's out, but it will take him weeks to recover, and—" She had to catch her breath momentarily. "Can he stay here until he can be moved?" she finished quickly.

"Here? Kitty, I don't . . . Mama . . ." Then, perceiving the appeal in her eyes, he protested, "Dash it, but what am I to say to her? If she don't get the story of me, she'll pry it out of him!" With one arm still holding her, he reached with his free hand to brush back his hair distractedly. "Kitty, abduction's a crime!"

Jack lurched into the doorway. "A very affecting reunion, I am sure," he muttered thickly, weaving. "But I need water and . . ."

"Egad!"

Both of them lunged to catch him before he lost his balance and fell. Sturbridge shoved a shoulder beneath his arm, trying to brace his greater weight. Kitty slid both arms around his waist and held on. Jack caught her, returning her embrace with his good arm, then leaned like dead weight.

"Got to get him inside—lay him down—" the viscount decided. "Cannot take him to Mama—she'll have you in Newgate over this, Kitty." He adjusted his weight beneath Jack's. "Here—I've got him—too heavy for you by half." Twisting his head sideways, he asked him, "Can you walk between us, do you think? Put you in m'rig."

"Yes."

They walked him, Kitty supporting more than her share

due to a propensity on his part for leaning to her side. "Ain't got but two seats," Sturbridge recalled. "Have to ride on the groom's shelf, Kitty. Tell you what—take him to the crofter's cottage—the Kerrs is moved out and it ain't let yet."

"There are times, Charles Trevor, when I could kiss you!" Kitty breathed, relieved.

"Servant," he murmured, reaching for the side of the tilbury. "Can you step up?" he asked Haverhill. "I can push."

"Yes." Jack caught the side bar with his hand and, taking a deep breath, swung shakily up. Sturbridge threw his weight beneath him, effectively pushing him into one of the two seats. "Gad, but I'm tired," Jack said, closing his eyes.

"Can you ride back there, Kitty?"

"Of course."

She hung onto the wet iron as the two-seater took the rutted road. The mud splashed from the wheels, spattering the hem of her gown and her stockings. It was all of a piece, she decided wearily, for nothing could harm her dress further anyway.

The cottage was dry enough, but musty. After they got Haverhill to the bed, Sturbridge moved about the place opening the windows just enough to admit a little air despite the spring chill, then busied himself starting a small blaze in the dusty fireplace. Kitty managed to find a battered cup, which she carried outside to the well. Returning with it filled, she handed it to Jack.

" 'Tis the best I have just now, my lord."

He sat, head in hands, on the side of the bed. When he looked up to take the cup, he stared into the swell of breasts outlined beneath the damp fabric. And suddenly the dryness in his mouth had little to do with thirst.

"We'll leave him here until a reasonable explanation can be contrived," he heard Sturbridge say in a tone that indicated he expected hell would freeze first. "And I will, of course, take you home."

"But who will tend him?" she asked anxiously. "He is in no case to care for himself."

"No, of course not. Cannot just send anyone though."

"Jem."

"That coachey of yours?" The viscount laughed. "He begged twenty pounds of me, saying only that you told him to ask. By now, my dear Kitty, I suspect he is halfway to Scotland, running as though hell pursued him."

"Oh—no! And I had hopes of persuading Aunt Bella that I'd duped him into this. Oh, dear."

"He'll come about," Sturbridge promised her. "Ten to one, he'll have a position ere he reaches Gretna. The problem is Haverhill."

Jack drained the cup, then rolled onto the bed, where he lay exhausted. He was about to tell them to leave him be, that all he needed was rest, when he heard her tell Sturbridge that if none could be found, she'd come back herself.

"Dash it, Kitty, but you cannot!" The viscount cast an aggrieved look Jack's direction. "You are forgetting what he did to Jessica!"

"But if he cannot tend himself—"

Jack forced himself to groan loudly.

"I suppose I can look in on him," the viscount conceded, "but I am no hand with the sick." He moved closer, staring down on the baron's pallid face. "He don't look good, does he?"

Jack rolled onto his back, holding his shoulder as he moved, and beads of perspiration damped his forehead. "Deuced good of you to note it," he muttered dryly.

"I shall have to come back," she decided. "I cannot abandon him, no matter what he is."

"And tell Mrs. Merriman what?" Sturbridge demanded incredulously.

"I'll have to tell her something, anyway." Kitty looked down on her ruined dress and sighed. " 'Tisn't as though she will not ask."

"Tell you what—if you can mollify the old girl, we'll come

back together. She ain't going to cavil if you are in my company, after all. Say we're going driving.''

"In the rain?"

"It don't signify, Kitty. Lovers don't pay much heed to weather—and neither do matchmakers. Look in on him every day, if you want. Then, when he is better, we'll think what to do.''

She moved back to the side of the bed. "I am going to have to go home, my lord, but as soon as may be, I shall come back. Is there anything you'd have me bring you?"

"Damned near everything." His hazel eyes traveled upward the length of her soiled gown to her face. "But mostly yourself.''

Despite the flush that heated her cheeks, she felt an odd thrill course through her. "I'll bring a basket of food.''

"If you were able, I'd be tempted to call you out, sir,'' Sturbridge told him coldly.

"If I were able, you would not wish to," Jack retorted.

As they left, the baron turned his face toward the wall, denying the stab of jealousy he felt. The viscount's voice floated back. "Did you mention the divorce?''

"An annulment would be better," she replied. "And there was not the time.''

He began to think differently of Henry—the old stick had had a secret life, after all. And by the looks of it, the chickens were coming home to roost on his heir.

IT WAS LATE AFTERNOON when Kitty and Lord Sturbridge arrived at Rose Farm. As they climbed the steps of the house, he offered her his arm, but she shook her head. The butler opened the door, stared, and stepped back. The expression on his face spoke more than words, saying that he thought she had exceeded all bounds of decency. The housekeeper, a buxom woman named Crane, came into the foyer and stopped.

" 'Pon my word!''

"Summon Mrs. Merriman, if you please,'' the viscount ordered a stunned footman.

"I say, but what's the commotion?'' Roland demanded, emerging from the front saloon, a book of military history still in his hand. "Egad—Kit!'' His eyes took in her wet, bloodstained gown. "Who did this to you?'' he demanded. "I'll see him pay for it!''

"Oh, Rollo, 'twas—''

Her words stopped as her aunt came from the back of the house, shadowed by the footman who'd fetched her. Isabella looked Kitty up and down. Charles Trevor's hand reached to support one of Kitty's elbows.

"I trust, Catherine, that you have an explanation?'' was all Isabella could think to say.

All of the excuses, all the plausible stories she'd concocted in Sturbridge's tilbury, deserted her in favor of the truth. Kitty sucked in her breath, then nodded. Exhaling slowly, she looked to the saloon. "If we may all be private . . .''

Her aunt turned on her heel and walked into the room,

with the others filing after. Sturbridge was about to shut the door in the faces of the curious servants when Kitty stopped him. "You'd best get Jess also."

She waited, painfully aware of the scrutiny of her family, while Jessica came down. Then, shutting the door herself before a disappointed Crane, she turned to face her aunt. " 'Tis a long tale at best, Aunt Bella. Suffice it to say that I have brought Haverhill here—well, to Sturbridge's actually," she amended truthfully.

"You *what*?"

"I abducted Baron Haverhill."

"Kitty!" Jessica wailed. "How *could* you?"

Roland looked again to her dress. "Fellow must've put up a devil of a fight—pardon my saying so, coz, but looks like you slaughtered him. Not that he did not deserve it," he added hastily.

Isabella Merriman sank into a chair nervelessly, and sat fanning herself with a newspaper. "I should ask for the vinaigrette, but I have never fainted in my life, and I shall not do so now," she assured herself. "I have never succumbed to the vapors." Her eyes, when she raised them to Kitty again, were full of reproach. "The whole story, if you please—and do not think to spare me, I pray you."

"You brought Haverhill here?" Jessica demanded almost hysterically. "*Why*? Has he not done enough? Could you not let me forget the humiliation?"

"Sit down, Jessica," her mother ordered. "Let her speak."

"But I *hate* him!"

"Ain't fit to live," Roland agreed.

"I did it for you, Jess."

The room went silent. Kitty looked from the sympathy in Sturbridge's eyes to the tears in Jessica's, then to the incredulity of her aunt's. "Six years is a long time for a young girl to pay for that which was not her fault, do you not think?" she asked softly. "And now that—"

"No! I pray you will not say it! Not now—not yet!" Jessica implored her.

"All right. Suffice it to say that you are tied to a man you cannot love, one who does not hold you in the least regard, Jess." She turned her attention again to Isabella. " 'Tis no life for a vivacious girl to be cooped up here, the object of pity among the neighbors." She watched her aunt stiffen. "The object of pity," she repeated. "For as long as there is Haverhill, she cannot wed, and if he does not acknowledge her, 'tis assumed she is naught but an ape-leader rather than the truth."

"I do not think that Lord Sturbridge ought to have to hear our family scandals, Catherine," Isabella interrupted her uneasily. "Perhaps he would prefer to come again later."

"If he is to become a member of this family, he has a right to know."

"It ain't for you to tell 'im," Roland protested. "As head of this house, I—"

"Do *you* wish to tell him?" Kitty asked, turning to him.

"No—of course not. And you ought not neither," he muttered defensively.

"All of this brangling is nothing to the purpose," Isabella conceded wearily. "Apparently, he has a fair notion already, I suppose. Go on, Catherine."

"I have hopes that Haverhill will give Jess a divorce, Aunt Bella—or perhaps an annulment. I have not broached the specific subject with him yet, but—"

"A divorce!" Roland choked. "Brand her for life! Might as well call her a—a—well, you know—" he finished, his face reddening. "Kitty, what was you thinking of?"

"I was thinking of Jess."

"You have explained nothing, missy!" Isabella snapped, losing the battle for control of her nerves. "I'd hear how it is that you have been gone for two days and one night, how you have come home in the company of Lord Sturbridge—" She rose to face her niece, her voice rising as she catalogued the perceived sins. "—how it is that you look as though you have been slaughtering in a pigsty—and without your petticoat, missy!'' Her eyes took in the offending dress as though it was in itself proof of her perfidy. '' 'Tis positively indecent! I have seen more clothing on a— a—''

''Now, Mama, you ain't seen any of 'em, I'll be bound,'' Roland hastened to assure her.

''—a lightskirt!'' she finished triumphantly. Her temper vented, she sat back down. ''Well, Catherine, I am waiting for the rest of this tale.''

''I went to London, Aunt Bella, with the express intent on abducting Haverhill, and—''

''Ohhhhhhhh,'' her aunt groaned. ''Kitty, how could you?''

''Little thing like you?'' Roland scoffed. ''Couldn't have made a flea jump.''

''I used a pistol, Rollo. Anyway, I got him into the carriage to bring him here, but unfortunately we were beset by highwaymen, and he was shot.''

''Shot!'' Isabella fanned faster, making the paper almost snap. ''With what?''

''Daresay it must've been a gun, Mama,'' Roland told her.

''If you say anything more, Rollo, I shall not continue,'' Kitty threatened him. ''And after he was shot, he bled rather a lot, so much that we feared he would die from it. I had to stop to get help for him.''

''Where?''

''I don't know—the Hawk and Pig, or some such—yes, that was the name of it. I shouldn't recommend the place, in any event. But the doctor came and removed the ball, and the blood was finally staunched. Hopefully, in a few weeks he will have recovered.''

''I don't want him to recover!'' Then, seeing that everyone turned to her, Jessica colored. ''He is a hateful, odious man—I shall never forget the wedding. I wish Papa had not insisted, for if none was to discover I'd been compromised, there was no need for it!''

"Perhaps he's changed, Jess. Perhaps he regrets it as much as you," Kitty ventured.

Her cousin stared as though she'd lost her senses. "Changed? He could not! And what if he should decide not to divorce me? What if he should wish to live with me? I could not bear it!"

"He ain't divorcing you—not if I got breath," Roland promised grimly. "Don't want m'sister in a scandal broth."

"And he is at Sturbridge's?" Isabella asked suddenly. "Lud, but what is your dear mama to think, Charles?"

"Well, actually he is in one of the cottages," he admitted, not wanting to meet her eyes. "I did not think Mama could be brought to understand, and under the circumstances, it did not seem the politic thing to do, ma'am. But Kitty and I mean to tend to him until he can be on his way again."

The woman blinked. "Do you now? And have you thought what that will do to my niece's reputation?"

"If she's been to the Hog and Whatever with Haverhill, rep's in shreds, anyway," Roland pointed out. "Don't see—"

"You stay out of it, young man!" Isabella told him furiously. "Haverhill cannot wed her—he is Jessica's husband!"

"What's that to anything? Don't nobody know that—all they'll hear is how Kitty was at some inn with him! Ruined all the same," he finished defiantly. "Ruined. Ought to be clapped up in Bedlam!"

"Stop it!" Kitty put her hands to her head as though she would block out the arguing. "There is no need to send me to Bedlam, for I think I am already there!" Unused to hearing any outbursts from her, everyone was suddenly silent again. "Thank you. Now—'tis my fault he is hurt, and 'tis my fault he is here, after all, and I shall take full responsibility for it. I will tend him, and perhaps none will know of it. But if they do, blame it on the country of my birth." Her face flushed, she pushed a straggling lock of hair from her eyes. "It seems to me that there are enough people here ready to condemn me for that, anyway. And when he is well, I shall ask him to give Jess an annulment.'' The lock fell forward again, exasperating her. This time, she brushed at in angrily. ''Failing that, perhaps Sturbridge can be persuaded to introduce a Bill of Divorcement into Parliament. After all, Haverhill has not lived with her these six years past,'' she pointed out reasonably.

''No! Dash it, but it ain't done!'' Roland shouted. ''You don't know! Daresay things is different in America, but this is England!''

Ignoring him, she continued, ''And when 'tis settled, I shall return where I belong. No doubt I can ask Papa's partners to allow me to assist with their books.''

They exchanged glances of consternation, then Jessica stepped forward. ''I thank you for trying, Kitty, truly I do, but 'twill not fadge. Haverhill punishes me for his own folly, and he is not like to cease simply because we ask it.'' Her eyes beseeched Sturbridge. ''Please, Charles. After all, she is in the basket because of me.''

''Ah-hem.'' It suddenly seemed as though the frog in his throat was more like a rock. Manfully, he squared his shoulders to face Isabella. ''Mrs. Merriman, there is no need to worry over Miss Gordon, I assure you.'' For a moment, he looked again at Jessica, then he exhaled, resigned. ''It is my intent to make her my wife.''

''*What*?'' Kitty choked. ''Oh, no, but I—well, I cannot!''

It was as though night had changed to day. Isabella's face broke into a smile on the instant. ''I *told* you, my love!'' she crowed to Kitty. ''Our little Catherine a viscountess! Lud, but this calls for a celebration!''

''I say—'tis the answer!'' Roland agreed readily. ''Don't have to worry about the business at the Hog—if he don't care, ain't none to complain.''

''The Pig—'twas the Pig,'' Kitty managed to correct him. ''Charles, we should not suit! Your mama . . .'' She cast about wildly for an excuse that would not cause Jessica more difficulty. ''Well, your mama dislikes me, after all!''

"She don't dislike you, Kitty—thinks you are a trifle brown, that's all. Though where she gets that, I am sure I do not know. Eyesight must be failing."

"Well, I don't know whether I am on my head or my heels, I am sure," Isabella announced happily. "A summer wedding."

"No!"

"At four and twenty, you cannot think to get a better offer, Kit," Roland reminded her.

" 'Tis sudden. No, I—"

"Nonsense, my love. Sturbridge has been most assiduous in his attentions for a full year." Isabella turned to her daughter. "Would you not agree, dearest?"

"Yes—yes, of course. I wish you happy, Kitty."

"Well, I won't do it," Kitty maintained stoutly.

"Don't listen to her, Charles," Roland advised. "Being missish, that's all. Well, 'tis settled then. Now, what's to do about Haverhill?"

" 'Tis not settled, Rollo!"

"Jessica will take care of him, of course. We shall have to send the carriage to Blackstone to fetch him here. And if anything is said, there's none to cavil with that."

"Mama—no! I won't do it! If he should so much as lift one finger to touch me, I should be sick!"

"In truth, he did not appear so terrible to me," Kitty admitted. "And there is no question but what you will have to face him—how else are we to persuade him that he ought to free you?"

The younger girl shuddered visibly. "He is a veritable toad, Kitty!"

" 'Tis your overwrought imagination, love," Kitty soothed her. "I did not find him toadish at all. In fact, there are probably some to account him quite handsome."

"Handsome? Haverhill?" Jessica choked.

"No need to be in a pelter, Miss Merriman," Sturbridge spoke up. "Not a reason in the world why Miss Gordon—

why Kitty and I cannot tend to him. Engaged, after all.''

"But we are not!"

"Kitty, might I speak with you for a moment? Please, Mama, but I think I can make her understand how it is.''

"There is no need to make me understand anything, Jess— I do not believe Sturbridge and I should suit. And you must surely know the reason why!''

"Very well, Jessica, you have my leave to talk sense to her.'' Isabella rose and gestured imperiously to her son. "Rollo, you and Sturbridge will take brandy in the bookroom while I see to the ordering of the carriage.''

"Aunt Bella, the carriage—''

"Regardless of who cares for Haverhill, 'twill be done here. Cottage indeed!''

"Then you will have to ask Sturbridge for the loan of his conveyance. The coach must needs be repaired,'' Kitty said low.

"*What*?''

"The wheel is broken,'' she added more loudly. "We struck a rock or a rut, I know not which.''

To her credit, Isabella Merriman did not lose her temper. "I see,'' she said through tightly compressed lips. "Then I suppose he will have to stay there tonight at least.''

"Yes.''

"And I suppose Jem is dead also?'' Rollo asked sarcastically.

"Er—I believe he bolted,'' Sturbridge answered for her. "He was of the opinion he would be turned off.''

"And so he would,'' Isabella sniffed. "Come on, Rollo.''

"You go also,'' Jessica told the viscount. "Please.''

He wavered briefly, then capitulated. "All right.''

No sooner had they filed out than the younger girl shut the door carefully behind them. "You've got to take Charles, Kitty—you've *got* to.''

"Thank you, but I've no wish for a husband who cares more for another,'' Kitty retorted acidly. "What am I supposed to do, look the other way? And what if I should discover an affection for another myself? I realize that 'tis fashionable to dally after the heir is assured, Jess, but I've no desire to have one for Charles Trevor—and I should think 'twould be a trifle difficult to explain if you do.''

"I suppose I deserved that," Jessica admitted. "But 'tis more than that." She turned away, twisting her hands, then blurted out, "You cannot go home, Kit."

"I can and I will."

"There's no money." She looked up, aware that she had her cousin's attention now, and plunged ahead in explanation. " 'Tis the Funds—there have been reverses—I suppose 'tis the aftermath of the war. In any event, our man of affairs has advised Mama that the losses have been dreadful, and there's almost nothing left."

"But—but Papa left—"

"I know. So you see, you cannot go back, Kitty. One of us must take Charles, for he is very rich, and 'tis foolish to hope that it can be I."

For a brief time, the room seemed to spin around Kitty as the meaning of Jessica's words sank in. There was no money, she was saying. There was no return to America, unless she went as a beggar to her father's partners. Kitty exhaled heavily.

"I would beg in the street before I should stoop so low as to take Charles Trevor for his money, Jess."

"But can you not pretend? I mean, can you not agree to wed him? Later, if something happens, you may cry off. Besides, 'twill make Mama forget the loss of her carriage," she coaxed.

"If what happens?"

"I don't know!" Jessica's eyes filled with tears and her chin quivered. "I j-just know I shall not survive, Kit! Maybe you can persuade Haverhill—maybe something will come of that! But if you do not accept Charles now, Mama will make me see my husband—and I cannot! And then I shall never see Charles again!"

"Peagoose! You'll have to see Haverhill! Tell him you've found another, Jess," Kitty responded. "He does not seem to be such a terrible fellow to me."

"Well, he is! Kitty, if you can but delay—if you can but let Mama think—otherwise she will not allow Charles to run tame here anymore!"

"Can I not just take the offer under advisement?"

"No, but you can cry off later," Jess persisted, sensing that Kitty wavered. "And I can tell you with a certainty that Charles Trevor will not treat you as Haverhill treated me. Even if you were wed to him, he would not."

"Just what did Haverhill do?" Kitty asked curiously.

"He got me alone, and he—he slobbered on me! Then he—well, he was so disguised that he fainted, but Papa would not listen to me. He said that since Haverhill—since he had— torn my dress—that I—oh, 'tis too awful to tell!" And, as though to give credence to the horror, Jessica dissolved again into tears.

"All right—all right." Clenching her teeth to stifle her exasperation, Kitty gritted out, "I will agree to pretend to affection for Sturbridge, Jess, but you will have to agree to see Haverhill. We shall take Sturbridge with us, and I can assure you that amatory pursuits are beyond your evil baron's abilities at the moment."

"I could not."

"Then I cannot allow Aunt Bella to believe an arrangement exists between Charles Trevor and myself. 'Twill be bad enough when word reaches Lady Sturbridge, I assure you. You can believe that she will discover me to be spotted," Kitty muttered dryly. "And then she will allow as how spots are quite fetching—so very savage, you know. For every criticism, she is careful to couch it as though the fault is not mine, as though she balances it with tolerance, which she does not."

"You will stay in the room with me?"

"With a pistol at full load, if you wish it."

"And you will have Charles there also?"

"Yes."

"All right."

Kitty forced a tired smile. "Now that we are decided, I think I shall change my gown. I should very much rather not wear Haverhill's blood any longer, thank you." She reached for the door. "Wear something sensible yourself, for we shall have to share one seat between us. Charles has brought his tilbury."

"But what if Haverhill decides he wishes to live with me?" Jess asked in a small voice behind her.

"Then I suggest you make yourself as plain as possible. Though quite frankly, he is in no case to offer violence to anyone just now."

"But Charles—"

"Charles is *my* betrothed now," Kitty reminded her grimly. "And so long as he is, I refuse to let either of you make me into an object of sympathy, do you hear?"

"Yes."

"And the first time that I discover that I am pitied, I shall throw him over. Do you understand me?"

Jessica swallowed and nodded.

WAITING FOR KITTY GORDON'S return seemed like an eternity to Jack. He lay upon the bare bed, shivering, and he knew not whether it was from the cold or his wound. But for whatever reason, he knew he felt about as bad as he'd ever felt, with the exception of the time they'd wanted to take his leg. Finally, to pass the time and take his mind from the ache in his shoulder, he relived what he could remember of Miss Gordon.

The girl had pluck, he'd give her that. Spirit and beauty—it was rare to find both in the same compact package. And compact she was, barely reaching to his shoulder. Fine-boned, delicate, tiny almost. With nerve. He closed his eyes and tried to bring her face into focus. There was a pertness to it that made her more pretty than beautiful, he decided, a certain rosiness that warmed it, keeping her from being another cool, insipid blond. He tried to decide whether her hair reminded him of gold or wheat as he recalled the spun softness of it beneath his chin. It was gold, he guessed. And those eyes. Three-quarters of the Englishmen he knew had blue eyes, but none so lively as hers.

It was the liveliness about her that drew him. The daring. And the unselfishness. Why had she done it, dared to abduct him? For someone else, for the one she called Jess. Jessica Merriman, a girl his cousin must have wronged terribly. For a moment, he was puzzled, then he shifted his aching body against the lumpy mattress and told himself that it would no doubt be revealed, that he would see this Merriman female and judge for himself.

He forced his mind again to Kitty Gordon, remembering
how she'd tried to stop the bleeding with her small body,
remembering how, despite his pain, she'd given him thoughts
that ought to damn him. Even now, as he recalled the smell
of his blood, he could also smell the scent she'd used on her
hair.

Four and twenty and unwed—it seemed in truth an impos-
sibility. But she would not long remain so, he was certain
of that. Despite the protestations, despite her impatience with
her family's matchmaking plans, there was no question that
there existed between her and Sturbridge an ease of manners.
And once again, he felt a twinge of jealousy. Sturbridge
would not know what to do with a female like Kitty Gordon,
he feared, and more likely than not the viscount would spend
a lifetime trying to make her into an English lady. And that
would be a shame.

He heard the wheels of a vehicle roll up, breaking into
his reverie. And then he heard her voice, complaining, "I
know not why Jess will not face him, and I think it positively
poor-spirited of her, if you would have my opinion of it.
To have changed her mind after I agreed to this passes all
bounds," she added peevishly.

"The remembering would be too terrible," Sturbridge
answered.

"Fiddle. When I was quite a small child, my papa told
me that the best way to drive terrors from the mind was to
face them. I had nightmares then, after Mama died, you
know," she confided artlessly. "But he was right. Instead
of cowering on my bed, I forced myself to get up and look
under it. And every time the dreams frightened me, I lit my
candle and showed myself that there was nothing to fear.
Eventually, they ceased."

"Alas, but not every female is possessed of your common
sense, my dear."

"No, I suppose not." She sighed. "But I do wish that Jess
could be brought to at least face Haverhill, you know. She
might discover he is but an ogre in her mind."

"She has sensibility."

"A surfeit of it," Kitty agreed dryly. "One could wish she were not such a watering pot sometimes."

Jack could hear them enter the outer room, and then she appeared in the doorway. Her arms were laden with what appeared to be folded linen.

"Well, you are still alive, at least," she observed, moving closer. "How do you feel?"

"Like the very devil, but 'twill pass."

"Well, I have brought sheets and a blanket, my lord, that we may make you more comfortable. And Charles will go up to the house to find a nightshirt for you. Unfortunately, I did not think to bring one of Rollo's."

"I should rather have clothes, I think."

"As you are not able to be about, the nightshirt will suit you better."

"I dislike managing females, Miss Gordon," he managed through teeth gritted against the pain.

"Do you now? Then you will have to get well so that you can manage yourself, won't you? Charles will aid you to rise while I make up your bed, and then we shall see you are fed. I have brought bread and cheese and cold beef."

"I am more thirsty than hungry."

"And there is a jug of cider," she added, "though I am not at all certain 'tis quite the thing for you. But at least 'tis not spirits."

"I need a shave."

"Now that will have to wait. Believe me, but you cannot wish me to do that, my lord, for I should most probably cut your throat. Accidentally, of course."

"Of course."

"And Sturbridge would probably like nothing more than to put a razor to your neck. *That* would not be an accident." She stood over him, surveying him. "You look positively awful, you know. A shaving is probably the last thing you actually need."

"Plain-spoken female, I'll give you that. I'd thought you'd abandoned me," he muttered.

"Well, there was a brangle, you see, else I'd have been back sooner," she admitted, sitting on the edge of the bed. "Has the bleeding ceased, do you think?"

She gingerly lifted the blood-stiffened shirt to peer at the bandage beneath. "It does not seep, and for that we must be thankful."

"What did you tell them—your family, I mean?" he asked curiously.

"The truth. And by the time I had to explain the carriage, it appeared to be the least of my mistakes. You were saved from Aunt Bella by the broken wheel, by the by. But Jess was in hysterics at the thought of facing you again, so I suppose 'tis as well we did not go there. 'Twill take her a day or so to gain her courage, I expect."

"Miss Gordon—"

"Kitty, you ought to let me do that," Sturbridge said, coming into the room. " 'Tis not seemly."

"I was but making certain the bleeding had stopped." She looked up at the viscount. "Do you think you ought to get him the nightshirt first? I could see he is fed while you are gone. And then we can put the sheets on the bed."

"If you think I mean to leave you alone again with a man of his stamp, Kitty, you are mistaken. I have not forgotten Jessica," he added meaningfully.

"Does he look as though he is able to pounce on me? If he should even consider such a thing, I have but to strike him a blow on his shoulder, and I should imagine the pain would drive lechery from his mind, don't you think?"

"Still—"

"Can you not see he is freezing? How will it look if Baron Haverhill succumbs to a raging fever while he is here? Your mama would have a fit of vapors such as we have never before seen," she reminded him severely.

"Well, 'tis not that far to the house, I suppose."

"No, 'tis not." She rose and put another log on the waning

fire, poking it to settle it into the bed of live coals, then walked to where Sturbridge had placed the hamper on the floor. "I'll get his food, and when you return, we can do the rest."

He wavered. Turning to Jack, he warned him, "If you so much as think to offer her violence, I shall run you through."

"Thus far, all the violence has been hers," Jack retorted.

"Very well, Kitty, but I shall be back forthwith. And before we return to Rose Farm, I should like to apprise Mama of our betrothal. 'Twill give her more time to get used to the notion."

"Surely you will not need me for that—I mean—"

"Nonsense. Mama will wish to see you, I am sure."

After he left, Kitty dragged the heavy hamper closer to the bed. Retrieving a large napkin from within, she spread it out beside Jack, then proceeded to lay half a loaf of bread, a chunk of cheese, and some sliced beef upon it. "Do you take your cider with your meal or after it?" she asked, pouring him a cup.

"With." Lying on his side, he reached for the bread, then shook his head. "Would you be so kind as to tear that for me? Deuced awkward one-handed, you know. And perhaps you could roll the meat inside that I could hold it better? Sorry. Helpless as a babe, I guess."

"I don't mind." She did as he asked and handed it to him.

He bit off a piece and chewed it. Swallowing, he reached for the cup. "Betrothed, eh?"

"Yes. 'Tis the price of yesterday's mistake."

"Dashed decent fellow—Sturbridge, I mean."

"Yes—yes, he is."

He drank deeply, then handed her back the cup. "Strange he should choose you. Surprises me."

"I do not believe I wish to pursue that notion to its logical conclusion, sir," she retorted stiffly.

"Don't fly up into the boughs, Miss Gordon—meant you don't seem the sort of female as he'd want."

"I beg your pardon?"

"Seems to be a protective fellow, ever ready to defend your honor, you know, and—"

"If you say I have none, I shall run you through myself, you wretch."

"Not at all—mistake my meaning." He tried to sit up, but could not, and it was as though the world spun around him. Instead, he pushed the food away and lay back weakly. "Can defend yourself."

"Is that all you mean to eat?"

"Too tired."

"You cannot mend if you do not eat." She leaned over and broke off a small piece of the cheese. "Here."

He let her put it into his mouth and chewed dutifully. Swallowing, he shook his head. "No more." For a moment, his eyes closed, then reopened. "Weak as a babe, too."

"At least drink the cider."

"Must be that you are small."

"What?"

"Makes him think you ought to be protected."

"My lord, if you do not eat and drink at least a little, I shall wash my hands of you," she told him severely. Tearing off a piece of bread, she thrust it in his mouth. "You must get well, you know, for otherwise I shall not know what to do with you."

"A trifle late to worry now, isn't it?" Nonetheless, he took the bite.

As he chewed, she continued to tear more bits of bread. "If I have to, I'll feed you myself."

He swallowed and gestured for the cup. She balanced it in one hand and tried to support his head with the other. But he weighed too much, and the result was that his head slid into her lap. Considering all else that had occurred between them, Kitty forbore fighting him. Telling herself that he was in fact unable to sit alone, she proceeded to feed him bits of bread and cheese, stopping occasionally to give him a sip of cider.

His rumpled, unruly hair seemed an even darker red against the blue muslin skirt of her day gown. Looking down, she had to resist the urge to smooth it, and she found herself wondering how Jess could have maintained such a distaste for him. He was, Kitty thought, possessed of arresting good looks. Resolutely, she continued to feed him, telling herself she'd do the same for anyone.

It was thus that Sturbridge found them. "Kitty! Whatever—?"

She colored guiltily. "He's too weak to eat unaided, Charles. Every time I manage to sit him up, he slides down, so 'tis simply easier this way," he answered, trying to sound reasonable. "But now that you are here, you can feed him, if you prefer."

"He's had enough," he retorted curtly.

"Do you think so?" She eased the baron's head off her knee and rose to straighten the skirt of the fashionable day gown. "I daresay you are right, for I have gotten most of the cheese and the bread down him."

Jack sighed. "And I was beginning to feel like a rajah in the arms of his handmaiden." He caught her wrathful eye. "Or was that a Viking in the arms of his Valkyrie?"

"If you do not mind your tongue, 'twill be a sinner in the hands of an angry God," she countered.

"I brought the nightshirt, and if you will leave the room, I shall get him into it."

"In a pig's eye," Jack muttered, struggling up again. "Dress myself."

"Thought you said he couldn't sit."

The room moved crazily around the baron, and he felt like a child's top at the point of the string's release. He weaved unsteadily, passing a hand over his face as though he could clear the cobwebs before his eyes, then he sank down again. "Cannot."

"Does he feel warm to the touch to you?" Kitty wondered anxiously.

"Don't care if he does. Dash it, but you forget what he did to Jessica!"

"Like to see her," Jack mumbled, groaning. "Mistake."

"Mistake? Mistake!" The viscount's voice rose incredulously. "You have ruined a young female's life, and you count it naught but a mistake? I'll be damned if I'll dress you, sir!"

"If you do not, I shall have to, Charles, and I should very much rather not," Kitty protested.

"Acquit me—never molested a female in my life—none that was unwilling, anyway."

"Are you saying Jessica succumbed readily to your advances, sir?" Sturbridge demanded wrathfully. "I'll not believe it!"

"No—I'm saying 'twasn't I. Miss Gordon's mistake—"

"What sort of mistake?" Kitty demanded. "Are you Haverhill or not?"

"Yes, but—"

"Don't listen to him, Kitty! Ten to one, he's trying to turn you up sweet, just as he tried with Jessica!"

"I am not sixteen, Charles."

"And you have not been before the world, my dear. Sad to say, but you are more than a trifle green when it comes to experience with gentlemen. And Haverhill is certainly less than a gentleman even."

"Then I suggest you produce Jessica Merriman," Jack cut in wearily. "Let her tell you."

"She's too afraid of you to come." Kitty folded the napkin, taking care to keep the crumbs out of the bed. "But as she has need of your goodwill, I daresay she will have to get over it." Walking to deposit the cloth in the hamper, she looked up at the viscount. "If I must face your mama also today, I'd not have you tarry. Speak up when he is decent." Half turning back to Haverhill, she added, "You ought to feel better to get out of those clothes, after all, and certainly clean sheets will improve the situation. Then we shall decide how we are to manage caring for you, though I expect Charles will have to come back for the night.''

"She'll lead the dance for you," Jack observed as the door closed after her.

"Sit up," Sturbridge ordered.

"Call the tune also, no doubt.''

"Unbutton your shirt.''

"Alas, but I cannot—stupid complaint, I know, but whenever I move my arm, I—''

"Save the faradiddles for a female, Haverhill!'' Nonetheless, the viscount began undoing the front of the shirt, muttering, ''Ain't a valet, after all. Kitty ought to have left you at the Hog and Hawk.''

"Hawk and Pig," Jack corrected him. ''And I expect she was afraid of what I might tell the magistrate.''

"Cork-brained thing to do, anyway.'' He ripped the shirt off Jack's back, jerking it savagely over his bandaged shoulder. ''Egad.''

''A couple of inches inward, and I'd have been planted,'' the baron acknowledged. ''Inconvenient as hell to go that way—embarrassing also. Bled like a bloody pig.''

"Is everything a jest to you?'' Sturbridge demanded.

"If it were not, I should have succumbed long ago,'' Jack retorted. ''The biggest jest of all is that I am alive.''

The viscount ringed his head with a snowy nightshirt, then lifted Haverhill's arm, taking more care than he wanted, and eased it into the sleeve. When he looked down, the baron was nearly as white as the gown. But the worst was over. As he worked the nightshirt down, he removed the breeches, commenting, ''London tailor?''

"Spanish.'' Jack bit his lip against the pain, drawing Sturbridge's attention to the leg.

'' 'Pon my word!''

"It heals. At least 'tis still there—better than a lot—of poor devils,'' he gasped.

"I'll get Kitty. Keep yourself as decent as you can.''

The viscount had one hand on the door before Jack spoke
again. "Sturbridge?"

"What?"

"I hope you are never reincarnated as a nanny."

His rival jerked the knob and did not answer.

THE THIN, COLORLESS woman peered out the window of the elegant saloon. "Well, 'twould seem the rain has finally abated, my lady. Now if 'twill but dry, perhaps we shall be able to take a turn about the garden tomorrow. 'Tis so tiresome sitting inside." She sighed.

"With naught but the crocuses out? Really, my dear Pennyman, if you are restive, you have but to say so. I am sure that Charles may be persuaded to take us up in the carriage later today." Louise Trevor looked up from the book she had been reading, and favored her companion with a thin smile. "He was used to be a dutiful son, after all."

"I am not at all certain he is at home," Mrs. Pennyman ventured timidly.

"Nonsense. Where would he be on a day like this?"

"Well, Mrs. Hatcher had it of Mr. Clement that he has left twice today—once earlier, then he returned to ask Mr. Clement for a clean nightshirt and was gone again."

"A shirt, you mean."

"Oh, no, my dear Louise, 'twas a nightshirt. Poor Mr. Clement was quite positive on that head. And he took it with him."

"He took a nightshirt? How very odd."

"Mr. Clement allowed as he would pack for him if his lordship meant to leave, but Lord Sturbridge assured him that it was no such thing." The old woman looked out again. "I am sure that I do not mind the crocuses at all."

"Well, I do. There is no use to a garden, Pennyman, when there are no flowers to speak of." Lady Sturbridge snapped the book shut and laid it aside, then rose to join her companion at the window. "Lud."

The way she uttered it, Mrs. Pennyman knew she was displeased. "Whatever—? Oh."

"Just so."

They both watched Lord Sturbridge drive up, his matched pair stepping smartly despite the muddy, rutted drive. "He has Miss Gordon with him," Pennyman observed. "I did not know she was to pay us a call."

"Neither did I."

"An unexceptional girl, I am sure," the old woman suggested, then quailed at the look her employer gave her. "A trifle odd though," she added hastily.

"A trifle? Pennyman, she is not at all what one could wish for Charles," Lady Sturbridge pronounced definitely. "The girl is forward, brash, and totally lacking in feminine refinement. What he sees in her in beyond understanding."

"She is quite lovely," her companion observed.

"She lacks breeding, Pennyman," the dowager retorted. "And she is American. I cannot like that—I cannot." She looked again, seeing her son lift the object of her distaste from the tilbury, and she shuddered visibly. "If he were a second son—but he is not. One wishes better for one's only son, Pennyman."

"Yes, of course."

"Well, I shall have to redouble my efforts in that direction, I suppose." Louise moved away from the window. "Perhaps if I encourage him to go to London early this year . . ." Her voice trailed off.

Mrs. Pennyman knew better than to point out that there was not a female on the Marriage Mart Louise would approve for Charles. It was a deep game the dowager played, one where she encouraged, then discouraged whenever it appeared the viscount might fix his interest somewhere. But thus far she'd not been able to throw a spoke in the wheel where Miss Gordon was concerned. He still ran tame at Rose Farm, no matter what his mother did to deter him.

"Hallo, Mama—Pennyman." He came into the saloon with his beaver hat in one hand, Kitty Gordon's hand in the other.

"What an awful day to have this lovely child out," his mother chided, acknowledging Kitty's presence. "Lud, but you will catch your death—won't she, dear Clara?"

"Oh—yes, yes, I should think so. Cold out," the old woman agreed.

"But as she is here, you must ring for tea—or would you prefer ratafia, Kitty dear?" Then, before the girl could answer, she decided, "It ought to be tea—small females are more susceptible to illness, don't you think? What Charles can be thinking of, I am sure I do not know." Smiling brightly, she ordered, "Come give me a kiss, child, and tell me how dear Isabella fares. 'Tis an age since last I saw her, after all, and just this morning I was tell Pennyman that we ought to call on her, you know."

There was no help for it. Kitty moved closer and stood on tiptoe to brush a quick kiss against Lady Sturbridge's cheek. As she drew away, the woman caught her hand and held it. "La, but what cold hands you have, my dear! I fear you are chilled to the bone. Charles, you must be careful of her health."

"I am fine, Lady Sturbridge. Indeed, but I am never ill."

"Nonsense. Small females are noted for their delicate constitutions." She surveyed Kitty's face, then frowned. "Your skin chafes easily, does it not? You must remind me to send some lotion home with you for that."

"Mama." Charles cleared his throat and waited to gain her attention. "Mama, wish me happy—Kitty and I are betrothed."

Kitty could feel his mother's fingers stiffen in hers, and she wished she were at a greater distance. The woman seemed to have gone rigid for a moment, then she let out her breath slowly as though she counted for control.

"Betrothed? 'Tis a trifle sudden—I mean, well, 'tis not summer even, and—" She looked down at Kitty and forced a smile that did not begin to reach her cold gray eyes. "You naughty girl—I'd not even suspected. Well, this calls for more than tea, I should think. Pennyman, have Bittle bring Charles's best wine."

"Uh—"

"Lud, a daughter. I shall not know how to go on with a daughter, Charles."

"I told you she would be more pleased than you thought," Sturbridge reminded Kitty.

"You thought I would be displeased? Wherever had you that notion?" Louise asked. "What an ogress you must think me, child. I have always known that Charles would one day wed—the title, you know."

"Well, the wedding is not to be soon," Kitty hastened to tell her.

The dowager seized upon that glimmer of hope, and her smile broadened. "Of course it isn't! So much to be done, after all, I am sure. You will wish a London modiste, for they are so much better at concealing flaws, my love. I daresay with a great deal of contrivance, they will be able to make you appear taller. You must tell dear Isabella that I have the name of a shoemaker who excels in building up heels, will you? He works rather slowly, but as there is no hurry . . . Well, you must allow me to accompany you when you travel to town. Between us, we shall make you presentable." She cast a reproachful look at her son. " 'Tis the busy time now, though, what with everyone coming to town for the Season. If you would have waited a few months, I am sure—"

"Mama, I like the way Kitty looks."

"Of course you do! But then you are besotted, after all," Louise murmured. "If she is to be Viscountess Sturbridge, she must be more elegant." She studied Kitty for a moment, shaking her head. " 'Tis always difficult to make short females appear other than dumpy, but we shall manage, my love. You have good bones, so all is not lost."

"La, a wedding! I have ever loved weddings," Mrs. Pennyman admitted, then recalled herself. "That is to say—well, when is it to be?"

"I had thought perhaps August," Charles murmured.

"August! I should think not, not at all. Too soon by half, dear boy." The dowager favored her son with a look that told him such haste was unseemly. "Why, there is far too much to do, is there not, Kitty, my love? It ought to be a year, but Christmas at the very earliest, I should say. After all, if 'tis too soon, there will be those who suspect things are not as they ought to be."

"Uh—"

"She cannot possibly be ready by August," Louise continued definitely, disposing of the possibility. "I shall simply have to confer with Isabella on the matter."

"Mama—" Sturbridge was interrupted by the arrival of a footman bearing the wine and glasses. Not wanting to dispute anything before the fellow, he forbore saying anything more. Lady Sturbridge handed Kitty a filled glass before taking one for herself.

"I do not drink much wine," Kitty admitted, eyeing it doubtfully.

"Nonsense, my dear. Dr. Kimball assures me 'tis most beneficial for delicate constitutions—so soothing, you know. And we must take care of you now that you are to be our own."

"Mama, there is nothing wrong with Kitty's constitution—she is healthy as a horse," her son protested.

"Well, I should not put it quite that way, Charles! Poor Kitty cannot like the comparison, can you, dear? So tiny, so delicate—no, I should not call her a horse at all."

"But I am never ill," Kitty repeated. "Never."

"You look a trifle peaked now," the dowager insisted. "Don't you think so, Pennyman? A little air—not too much, mind you—and you shall revive directly. Pennyman, you will take Miss Gordon to the garden to show her the crocuses."

She turned again to Kitty. "They are so lovely this year that I cannot credit it. You run along with Mrs. Pennyman, and I shall send Sturbridge after you directly."

"Mama, it has been raining all morning! She'll soil the hem of her gown. Besides, you yourself said 'twas too cold."

"I meant she should not be out at length, Charles. A little air is invigorating, too much is dangerous. Go on, dear— Pennyman, watch for her gown, will you? And if 'tis too cold, do not let her stay out overlong."

"Really, dear ma'am, but—"

"Nonsense."

It was obvious to Kitty that his mother wished to read a peal over him, and there would be no end to her pointed solicitude until she did. Charles nodded, and Kitty capitulated gracefully.

"I have never seen a flower that I did not like," she declared, following Lady Sturbridge's elderly companion to the door.

"I'd hoped you would approve of her, Mama," Charles admitted.

"How can you think I do not?" Louise countered. "La, but the choice is yours, after all. And Kitty is a dear girl, I am sure—a trifle long-toothed, but still young enough to have your heir."

"Mama, she is but four and twenty," he reminded her. "You would have it sound as though she is at her last prayers."

"I never said any such thing, Charles Trevor, and well you know it. No, no, you mistake me. I shall love her dearly, though I own I could wish her a trifle taller, which I am sure you will understand. I mean, what if the boys should take her height? 'Tis so very difficult for a man to be short, you know—it makes them so very sensitive."

"As I am nearly six foot myself, I should not worry," he answered dryly.

"La, foolish me! How good of you to remind me, dearest boy—I daresay you are quite right." She looked up at him wistfully. "Lud, but I shall not know how to go on when you are married, you know."

"Mama—"

"But I suppose 'tis a good thing you have chosen a neighbor girl—'twill be more like a family that way. Though I admit I had hopes of Miss Merriman, you know."

"You did?" he asked in surprise.

"Well, I must admit a certain partiality there, for I have known her all her life. Miss Gordon, being from America, is nigh a stranger to us, after all. No, I'd been less surprised had it been sweet Jessica—such a delightful girl, Charles. In truth, I am surprised you did not note her."

"Yes, she is wonderful," he owned.

Louise pressed her advantage. "And so lovely! Not a delicate girl like Kitty—taller, too. And such pretty manners! I have never heard it said that she did not know how to go on, for she has been bred here. But—" She sighed deeply. "But you know what you are about, of course."

"I did not know you liked Miss Merriman."

"*Like* her? Charles, I have positively doted on her for an age! Indeed, but I have often considered taking her to London myself, for it seems such a shame that the Merrimans never presented her. Such unexceptional manners! Such a lovely complexion! Unlike Kitty, she will not turn brown."

"I keep hearing you say it, but there's naught brown about Kitty. She's fairer than Miss Merriman even."

"Ah, yes, but 'tis precisely what I mean—once she gets into the sun, she is more like to throw spots."

"There ain't a freckle on her," he declared.

"Yes, well, you must admit there has been no sun to speak of, so you cannot know but what there will be. Americans are not at all as we are, after all."

"Kitty Gordon is as English as you are—her papa was born in Sussex, and her mother was a Whitwood from Kent."

"But she is a Gordon, and I cannot quite like the connection. Byron—"

"Is no relation to her, and well you know it."

"There must be some connection, I am certain of it, dearest, for all Gordons come from Scotland, do they not?"

"The distance would have to be too great to note," he muttered. "Besides, you like Miss Merriman, and she is related to the Gordons also."

"Well, I am sure you are right—foolish me to worry," she admitted doubtfully. "Still, one can but wonder at the influence of a wild place like America on a young character."

"Mama, I have offered for Kitty," he reminded her grimly. "The announcement will appear forthwith, and I should hope that you will be agreeable to her."

"Charles, how could you think otherwise?" She favored him with a wounded look. "I would not for the world be anything but kind to your betrothed." Then, seeing Kitty returning with Mrs. Pennyman, she sighed. "I shall simply have to make her more presentable, that is all. The Merriman woman never goes to town and cannot know what befits your viscountess, I'll be bound. You deliver Kitty into my hands, Charles, and I will see she is a credit to you." As Kitty came through the door, she held out her hands. "Ah, dear—we were just saying how wonderful 'twill be to have you in the family. I shall delight in dressing you, I promise you."

"I thank you, but Aunt Bella—"

"Bella Merriman is a wonderful woman, Kitty dearest, but she is a trifle behind in the world. No, no—you must turn to me for direction, my love." She walked closer, surveying Kitty much as a buyer for a horse. "Yes 'tis not hopeless at all—a challenge merely. With the right clothes, we shall contrive to make you appear taller. Hmmm—have you considered drying your hair with lemon juice on it? 'Twill make it less brass and more gold, you know."

Perceiving that Kitty's jaw was taking on a decidedly mulish set, Lord Sturbridge hastily intervened. "Mama, it grows late, and I'd best take her home."

"Well, I'd hope she would stay to dine," Louise insisted. "We can send 'round a note to Rose Farm, after all."

"Really, but I should prefer—that is, I am certain I am expected at home."

"Well, if you insist. Pennyman, run get the pot of face cream off my dressing table—the one in the black jar. I'd have her wear a little to bed every night—'twill soothe roughened skin. And if you will wear it in the daytime, I have hopes 'twill stop the freckles," she added to Kitty.

"Really, ma'am, but I am not given to them," Kitty demurred.

"Well, we cannot take the chance, for Sturbridge abhors brown females, my love."

It was not until she was again safely in his tilbury that Kitty dissolved into whoops. "Lud, Charles, but what she will do to your wife, I should hate to think."

He clicked the reins over his matched pair. "She will come around, I promise you. Mama is nothing if not practical, after all." He half turned to look down on her. "And I am a man of honor, Kitty Gordon. Having offered for you, I shall keep the bargain."

PLEADING THE HEADACHE, Kitty retired early to avoid her aunt's enthusiastic plans for a summer wedding. But once inside her bedchamber, she could not sleep, and after several hours of attempting to read Caro Lamb's *Glenarvon*, a singularly self-serving work if Kitty had ever read one, she abandoned both the book and her room. Creeping downstairs, she was surprised to find Roland in the bookroom.

"I'd thought you to still be out," she murmured when he looked up in surprise.

"Just in—country pubs is deuced boring, you know," he admitted, the slight slur in his voice betraying that he was more than a little bosky. He lifted up a book. "Been trying to read, but can't seem to keep the words straight. Tired."

She moved closer to see the title. "*Alexander's Granicus Campaigns*? I shouldn't wonder."

"Got to like it," he admitted, "else it puts you to sleep. Me, I don't get tired of it." For a moment, his young face clouded. "Hate being an only son, Kitty—hate it. If Jess had been a boy, I'd been a soldier."

It was something she'd heard him say so many times she'd lost count. "I know," she sympathized.

"Wished I'd been at Waterloo—wished I'd fought Boney, you know."

She forbore pointing out that he was but twenty now, and it was unlikely he'd have been allowed to go in his teens. Instead, she said nothing, waiting for him to vent his frustrations yet again.

"But I got to be head of the family," he muttered thickly.

106

"Got Jess and Georgiana and Little Fanny to think on, don't I?" His blue eyes were almost fever-bright as they met hers. "Thing is, the younger girls is away to school, and Jess don't need me—you are more to the purpose here than me, Kit. Least you wasn't afraid to take Haverhill. Me, I never thought to do it."

"It was not one of my better ideas, Rollo," she said quietly. "Indeed, but I wish I had not. But one cannot escape one's mistakes," she added, sighing.

"Think we can scotch the scandal?"

"I think 'twill depend on whether he can be brought to pity Jess."

He nodded solemnly. "Cannot be a divorce, you know. Throw a spoke in your wheel. Sturbridge's mama wouldn't let 'im wed into the family." Reaching for the brandy decanter that he had on the desk behind him, he offered, "Want to join me, Kit?"

"Rollo, your mama would not approve at all."

"What she don't know don't make no difference," he maintained stoutly. "Come on—a man don't like to tipple alone. Besides, you ain't one of them as butter won't melt in your mouth. And 'tis real French cream I got here— genuine article." To demonstrate, he poured out two glasses. "Smooth stuff, Kit."

" 'Tis all of a piece, anyway, I suppose," she conceded, taking the one he offered her. "Maybe 'twill aid me to sleep."

"Good as laudanum."

It warmed her throat going down, so much so that it almost chocked her. He watched her make a face. "Ain't supposed to *drink* it down, you know—got to sip it. Be disguised in a trice if you was to take it like that," he warned.

"Kitty!"

They both looked up guiltily as Jessica slipped into the room, then Roland relaxed. "Oh—'tis you."

"I—I could not sleep."

"Got the ticket for you," he promised. "Get another glass from Papa's cabinet."

"Oh, but I could not. Mama—"

"Been asleep an age. If you wasn't a married lady, you'd be an ape-leader," he pronounced definitely.

"Thank you," Kitty muttered dryly. "As I am two years the elder, I suppose I am one."

"Not you—not now, anyways. Sturbridge came up to scratch." He lifted the decanter and poured a goodly amount into the glass that Jessica produced. "That's more like it." He giggled. "Tipplin' with the females—wonder what Lady Sturbridge would say to that?"

"A great deal, I should suppose."

"Was she truly rude to you?" Jessica wondered as she took a dainty sip. Before Kitty could answer, she choked. "Ugh!" she gasped.

"Got to get used to it." To demonstrate, he took a sip and held it in his mouth before swallowing. "Ahhhh—smooth as a baby's skin."

"Lady Sturbridge allowed as how I am too short, too dowdy, and too delicate," Kitty admitted, "but she will contrive to make me presentable."

"She never said that, surely!" Jessica protested. "Kitty, not even Louise Trevor would say that to your face."

"Well, she did—not in precisely those words, but I had no difficulty in catching her meaning. And neither did Charles, for he apologized much of the way home." Despite her irritation with the dowager, Kitty could not help smiling. "She sent me home with face cream—to keep me from spotting."

"But you ain't got spots!" Rollo fairly howled.

"That is not to say I will not get them," she responded, mimicking Lady Sturbridge's tone. "And the cream serves more than one purpose, after all. While I am waiting to freckle, I can use it for the chapping."

"Doing it too brown! You got good skin, Kit!"

"Thank you, Rollo. Oh—and she means to take me to London herself, for she has the acquaintance of a modiste who can conceal the flaws of my form—not to mention the bootmaker who excels in shoes to make me appear taller."

"Kitty, I'm sorry."

"Fiddle, Jess. I was vastly diverted, I assure you," Kitty managed, giggling. Abruptly, she sobered. "I would that I knew how Haverhill fared just now."

"I would that he died," Jessica declared flatly. Then, to cut off Kitty's disapproval, she sipped some more of the brandy, murmuring, "Quite right, Rollo, it does improve."

"He ain't any better? You'd best hope that he lives, Jess, 'cause if he don't, we got a devilish time explaining it. Kitty's liable to be clapped up."

"He's too weak to eat unaided."

"Egad."

"Yes, and I cannot think Charles means to care for him as he ought."

"Charles is tending him?" Jessica demanded incredulously. "After what he did to me?"

"Stuff it, Jess!" her brother retorted. "The way I heard the tale, he didn't do anything but rough you up a bit. I mean, deuced bad business, but it ain't like he ravished you."

"He meant to!" Tears welled in her lovely eyes. "Rollo, how could you say such a thing to me?"

"Of course he did! And Papa ought to have called him out for it, but he didn't—made him wed you instead, in fact. Thing is, you ain't blameless in the matter yourself. Besides, he didn't get the deed done, so you wasn't hurt none."

"Rollo!"

"Well, demned stupid thing to do, going off with him like that, Jess. And don't be watering the plants for me, 'cause it won't fadge—I ain't Mama," he told her stoutly. "You was a peagoose, and you know it."

"He said he wished to see the old miller's rock, Rollo—how was I to know otherwise?"

"Dash it, but a bosky fellow don't want to look at rocks, Jess! Fellow was three sheets into it!"

"You do not know how it was!"

"I ain't a slowtop," he retorted. "Got a notion. I mean, if a pretty girl was to go off alone with me, I'd think—well, I'd think she was inviting me to kiss her."

"And would you tear her clothes?" Jessica demanded hotly. "Would you throw her onto the ground, and—"

"Of course not! I ain't a loose screw, but you can't know that. Thing is, you don't do it, anyways, 'cause you don't know what the fellow'll do." He turned his gaze to Kitty. "Don't know why he didn't try to ravish you also. Little thing like you ain't a match for a man like Haverhill, Kit."

"I had a pistol," she reminded him.

"I suppose I could look in on him," he conceded, changing the subject abruptly. "Daresay Charles ain't much of a nurse. Me, I at least know about gunshot wounds."

"How?" his sister asked sarcastically, still stung by his words to her. "A man is not the same as game, Rollo."

"Read about it."

"Would you take me with you, Rollo?" Kitty asked suddenly. "I cannot sleep knowing he is in such case."

He looked up at the clock on the mantel, squinting his eyes to focus on the dial. "Dash it, Kit—'tis nigh to two o'clock. I said I'd go, didn't I?"

"Please, Rollo. If he should die, I don't know what I—"

"Ain't going to die! Ball's out, ain't it? If he survived that, he'll make it—unless he gets a putrid infection in the hole," he amended thoughtfully. "Just weak, that's all. But I suppose if you ain't going to rest until—well, guess we could."

"You cannot go off in the middle of the night," Jessica protested, scandalized. "What if Mama were to discover it?"

"Well, as I am betrothed to Sturbridge, you wretch, she cannot make me wed Rollo, after all."

"It ought to be you instead of Kitty, Jess. Ain't anybody

as could cavil at it if you were to take care of your husband, you know.''

Kitty finished her brandy and, emboldened by the intoxicating warmth that spread through her body, she teased her cousin. ''Yes, if you were kind to him, perhaps he might be persuaded to let you go.''

''Ought to try,'' Roland coaxed. ''If Sturbridge is there, and me and Kitty also, he ain't going to lay a hand on you.''

''He could not if he wished,'' Kitty added. ''I could put him into the floor myself. I'm telling you that he's very ill, Jess.''

''*Now?* Mama—''

''Mama ain't going to know. Be four of us there, Jess,'' he persisted. ''Don't be a coward—cowards never win any battles. Be home ere the sun comes up.''

The younger girl looked from her brother to her cousin and perceived they were indeed serious. She wavered, then drank the rest of her brandy in one gulp. Coughing, she managed to nod. ''If he offers me any violence, I shall expect you to kill him, Rollo,'' she finally got out, drawing courage from the spirits.

''Done.'' He rose unsteadily. ''Ticket out of boredom, I'll be bound. Could use a good lark.''

"I DID NOT EXPECT it to be so dark," Jessica complained as the two-seater bounced over the rutted lane.

"Don't know why not—night, ain't it?" her brother retorted. "And you got it better than Kitty. You riding all right back there, Kit?"

"Yes."

She sat with her knees drawn up onto the groom's step to avoid ruining her dress, and held on with both hands. The ruts jarred her bones unmercifully, but she consoled herself with the fact that Jess was finally going to face Haverhill.

It was not until they were almost to the crofter's cottage that she began to worry. It had been six years since the baron had seen his unwanted young wife, and much could have changed in the intervening time. What if Jess were right—what if he saw her and changed his mind? What if he should decide he wanted her after all? Somehow that thought did not bear thinking.

Rollo reined in too sharply, nearly throwing her from her precious perch. "You sure Charlie's here? Don't see his nag."

"He must be. He promised he would sit with Haverhill." She slid from the groom's step and straightened her gown. For once at least it did not rain, and for that she was thankful. As she walked toward the dark cottage, she patted her hair back into place. "There is Charles' horse," she murmured, relieved.

"Eh?" Rollo moved unsteadily, still more than a little

disguised from too much brandy and wine. "Got the right of it—Charlie's nag," he admitted, his voice slightly thick. "C'mon, Jess—got to see the bloody dolly mopper sometime, after all."

"Rollo!"

"Sorry—your bloody husband, then." As she hung back, he reached for her hand, tucking it into the crook of his elbow gallantly. "Don't be in a pelter, Jess," he said soothingly. "Fellow ain't such a dashed loose screw as to throw you down again—not with me and Sturbridge to stop him."

"Rollo, I—I cannot."

"Oh, for mercy!" Kitty snapped in disgust. "The man's half-dead, coz."

"But what if he recovers?"

"I certainly hope he does. Otherwise, you will be bringing me baskets to Newgate." She moved to lift the door handle. "Try to keep your voices down in case he sleeps."

At first, she thought the outer room was deserted, but then she saw Sturbridge asleep in a leaned-back chair, a half-guttered candle spluttering in a dish nearby. "Charles!" she hissed.

He lost his balance as he came awake guiltily. "What—? Oh, tis you, Kitty." Then, as his mind cleared, he frowned. "What the devil are you doing out at night? Mrs. Merriman will tan both our hides if we are discovered."

"I brought Rollo and Jess," she answered, as though that ought to explain everything. "How is Haverhill?"

"Worse, I think. Don't know how we'll do it without rousing the neighborhood, but he's got to have a doctor. Fever's come up, and he was more'n half out of his head when I came. Kept talking about dead fellows, as far as I could collect him. And when I tried to calm him down, he urged me not to tarry—said we had to charge or lose the day."

"Charge where?" Rollo asked curiously. "Did he say where?"

"No—just 'Charge!' "

"I'd best see to him first," Kitty declared. "Has he drunk anything?"

He nodded. "Brought some Madeira—mixed it with Mama's sleeping daught. Thought if I was to sleep with a havey-cavey stranger, I'd like to know he was out. But you got no business being here, not at night."

She ignored the uneasiness in his voice. "Then 'tis no wonder Haverhill is confused."

She slipped into the other room and waited for her eyes to adjust to the darkness. The baron's steady, rhythmic breathing reassured her somewhat as she approached the bed.

"My lord . . ." When he did not answer, she leaned over him and whispered more loudly, " 'Tis Kitty Gordon, sir."

"Unnnnhhhhh." He shifted slightly, but did not rouse. She touched his forehead and found it warmer than before. Hopefully, it was but that her hands were cold, but she feared the worst. She tried again. "My lord, 'tis I—Kitty Gordon!"

"Kitty Gordon," he mumbled thickly. "Go 'way. No case . . ." His voice ended in a sigh. He turned over, cradling his head on his arm.

"Is he awake?" Jessica whispered timidly, stepping inside the door.

"I think Charles has got him utterly foxed, if you want the truth of it," Kitty snapped irritably. "And I think him feverish. Here—feel of him and tell me what you think."

"Touch him? Oh, but I—"

"He's as out as if he had his cork drawn, Jess!"

"But—"

"Of all the cowardly, the—the *goosish* nonsense! Have you no gumption at all?" Kitty fumed. "No, I suppose you have not," she decided, sighing. "I forget."

"Kitty!" Nonetheless, Jessica edged closer to where Haverhill lay, moving for all the world as though if he should so much as breathe loudly, she would run. Very gingerly, she extended her hand, ready to snatch it back on the instant.

Her fingertips brushed over his forehead, barely touching it.

"He *does* seem a trifle hot," she agreed.

Just then, his eyes fluttered open, and he stared up at her. She jumped back, screeching, "Aiiiiiieeeeeeeeeee! Aiiiiiieeeeeeee!"

"What the devil—" he muttered.

Both Sturbridge and Rollo came running. "My dear Jessica, if he has so much as—"

"Stuff!" Kitty snapped.

"I say, Jess, but what the deuce? Scare a man out of a year of his life," Rollo remonstrated, his voice severe.

But Jessica was still staring, white-faced, at the baron. "I do not know who he is, Kitty, but this man is not Haverhill!"

"Of course he is. You have but forgotten after six years," Rollo assured her. "Bound to be."

"Well, he is not," Jessica maintained stoutly. "Do you think I could ever forget his face—or his fat fingers? Haverhill is *old*!" Emboldened by the presence of the others, she raised an accusing hand. "Just who are you, sir?" she demanded.

"Haverhill," Jack croaked.

"Says he is the baron, Jess," Rollo said, coming up behind her. "And he ought to know—Egad!" For a long moment, he could only stare at Jack. " 'Tis Red Jack Rayne!"

"Do not be ab—*who*?" Kitty stared also. "Are you saying he is *not* Haverhill?" she demanded.

"I tell you 'tis Red Jack!" Roland all but shouted.

"Are you quite certain?" Sturbridge asked, crowding his shoulder.

"Know him anywheres," the younger man insisted. "Went to London to see Prinny decorate him—stood as close as Kitty is to him right now, I tell you. Ain't Haverhill—'tis Colonel John Rayne, hero of—"

"It does not matter what he is hero of." Kitty cut him off abruptly. She stared down at the offending fellow. "You told me you were Baron Haverhill," she said accusingly.

By now, though still more than a little befuddled, Jack was awake. "Ears will never be the same," he muttered. His eyes met Kitty's. "Am."

"Am what?" Sturbridge demanded.

"Haverhill."

"Oh, no, you are not!" Jessica all but shouted at him.

"Henry's dead—last month. Inherited." Reflecting the glow of the candle the viscount carried, Jack's eyes were almost gold. "Sorry to disappoint you, Miss Gordon."

Kitty sank to the edge of the bed and sat there, feeling numb. "Red Jack Rayne—I have abducted Colonel Rayne," she said finally, as though she could make herself believe it. Swallowing as though it would help her grasp the enormity of what she had done, she repeated it. "Red Jack Rayne."

"Haverhill's *dead*?" Jessica demanded. "Are you quite certain, sir?"

"Heir."

"Been wanting to meet you, sir," Rollo told him sincerely. "Followed the reports since Cuidad Rodrigo, you know, and—"

"Not now," Sturbridge interrupted him. "Can you not see the man's in no case for civilities? Red Jack Rayne— lud! Got to get him to a doctor forthwith, Rollo, ere he is the late Jack Rayne."

"I am not wed! I am not wed!" Jessica repeated.

"Course you ain't wed, now!" Rollo retorted, stung by Sturbridge's tone to him. "Widow!"

"Black does not become me."

"It don't make no difference! If there was none to know of the wedding, then there's none to know if you mourn the fellow! Go to London now, if you want."

Instead of having the desired effect on his sister, Rollo's pronouncement seemed to overset her more. Casting a look at Lord Sturbridge, she burst into tears.

"Stifle it, Jess!" Kitty ordered curtly. "We've got to think of Haverhill now."

"Haverhill's dead, Kit!" the younger girl wailed. "Dead! There was no need!"

"*This* Haverhill, peagoose!"

"Kitty—Miss Gordon!" Sturbridge protested. "There is no need—dreadful shock, after all!"

"Take him home with us," Rollo decided. "Mama knows about the abduction, and when she finds 'tis Red Jack Rayne, she ain't going to cavil at it one bit."

"Do you think we ought to move him?" Kitty asked anxiously. "What if his wound should break open?" Recovering from her earlier shock, her common sense reasserted itself. "Perhaps we ought to summon the doctor here."

"And say what? That you have abducted the fellow and got him shot?" Rollo asked derisively. "Best let Mama tend to the matter. Are we agreed, Sturbridge?"

"Well, I—"

"Charles—Charles!"

The viscount reddened at the sound of his mother's voice in the outer room. Thrusting the candle into Roland's hand, he groped his way toward the door.

"Mama, what the devil are you doing here?" he wondered almost plaintively.

"I demand an explanation, Charles, and I will not be put off! 'Tis quite one thing to sow one's oats with the demimonde, quite another to dally with a neighbor! If Kitty Gordon is there, you'd both best come out!" As he stumbled into the outer room, she fixed him with the look of an avenging angel. "We shall take her home, Charles, though what the Merriman woman is to say, I am sure I do not know! Betrothed indeed! I'll not have an indecent female in the family, Charles Trevor—do you hear me?"

"Yes, and so does everyone else, Mama. I assure you—"

" 'Tis to be hoped that Isabella has the sense to send her back to America. No doubt there they will not refine so much on her lack of breeding."

Kitty rose hastily and slipped behind her beleaguered betrothed to support him. "Really, madam, but—" she began coldly.

"I knew it! When Pennyman saw you creep—and *creep* is all you can call it, Charles! When Pennyman saw you creep from the house, she recalled the nightshirt, and it did not take much imagination to think the worst. Charles, how could you?" Before he could answer, she turned wrathful eyes to Kitty. "And you! You hussy! If you dare to say you have been compromised by my son, we shall see about it! I'll tell the truth of the matter ere I'll see him legshackled to a—"

Rollo thrust himself through the doorway between Kitty and Sturbridge. "It ain't that way at all, Lady Sturbridge— it ain't! And none's to believe she's been compromised, 'cause me and Jess is with her!" Manfully, he faced the dowager. "Owe her an apology, you do."

"Roland Merriman!" she exclaimed. "Whatever—?"

"Lady Sturbridge, we can explain," Jessica promised, standing on tiptoe to peer over her brother's shoulder.

"Miss Merriman! 'Tis night! There can be no—"

"Came as soon as Sturbridge summoned us," Roland insisted, exercising his mind to invent a plausible tale. "Didn't we, Kit?" he asked, hoping she would help him.

"Well, yes, but—"

"Got Red Jack Rayne here. Fellow's hurt, if you want the truth of it, and Charles—"

"*The* Red Jack Rayne? I would that you told the truth, young man," Louise interrupted him. "If this is not an assignation, what is it?"

"Trying to tell you," he retorted. "Charles found Red Jack and brought him here. Sent to me 'cause . . ." At *point non plus* in his story, he looked again at Kitty for help.

"Because he knew Roland would be interested. That is, he *knew* Rollo could tell him if 'twas truly Red Jack."

"I have never heard such a Banbury tale in my life, Kitty Gordon," Charles's mother declared forcefully. "Red Jack

Rayne indeed! What would someone like that be doing here?''

"Beset by highwaymen," Rollo maintained stoutly.

"In Sussex?"

Ignoring the incredulity in her voice, he nodded. "Charles found him."

"And when we heard that 'twas Red Jack Rayne," Jessica murmured behind her brother, "Kitty and I had to see him."

"In the middle of the night, miss?" Turning to her son, the dowager demanded, "I'd have the story from you, I think."

"Not much to tell," he began evasively. " 'Tis as Rollo says."

"If you found a wounded man, why did you not bring him to Blackstone Hall? Why is he in an abandoned crofter's cottage?" she asked awfully.

"Can't bring just anyone home," Roland answered for him. "What if he was a flash-cove or something? Man don't bring home what he don't know, after all. Sent to me—knew I'd seen Red Jack in London." Then, reddening under her icy stare, he added hopefully, "You ain't going to tell m'mother, are you? Shouldn't have brought the girls with me. She'll read a regular peal over me, you know, for it."

Sensing that Roland had seized the advantage, Sturbridge addressed his mother. "You owe Kitty an apology, Mama."

His mother's eyes dropped. "Well, what was I to think? First the nightshirt, then you sneaked from the house—"

"Quite an understandable thing," Jessica admitted.

The dowager favored her with a look of gratitude. "Thank you, dear child. You at least seem able to know a mother's concern for her only son."

"I'm not in short coats, Mama," Sturbridge muttered.

"Kit's waiting to hear it," Rollo reminded her.

"It does not matter," Kitty said tiredly. "We've got to do something about Haverhill."

"Haverhill? I thought you said 'twas Red Jack Rayne," the dowager said suspiciously.

"Colonel Rayne is Baron Haverhill also, ma'am," Jessica volunteered.

"Oh." Realizing that they all still waited for her to acknowledge her mistake, Louise Trevor inhaled deeply and drew herself up to her full height. "Well, I own I had hoped I was wrong, Kitty dearest."

"Paltry, Mama."

"And as no harm is done, I would that you gave me a kiss of forgiveness, my love," she added. "You will hear no more on this head from me, I assure you."

"Just now, I should imagine my cousin would rather kiss a viper," Roland told her. "Don't have to do it if you don't want to, coz."

"I am sure Lady Sturbridge did not mean it," Jessica insisted. "Please, Kitty. Remember Pope—or was it Gray?"

"It was Pope." For the sake of peace, Kitty held out her hand. "I accept the apology, Lady Sturbridge."

Knowing she was beaten, the dowager managed to smile at the rival for her son's affection. "You dear girl. La, but I can scarce wait until you feel able to call me Mama also."

"It's settled then." Roland sighed his relief. "Now, all that remains is to get Colonel Rayne to Rose Farm. Hope you girls do not mind it, but I'll have to come back for you—two-seater, you know," he murmured apologetically. "The carriage is down, alas."

"To Rose Farm?" Lady Sturbridge's voice rose. "You'll do no such thing! If 'tis indeed Red Jack, he will be carried to Blackstone Hall immediately. Charles, you will see to it on the instant. And I shall send to Dr. Crawford this very night."

"I'd thought Dr. Ellis," her son admitted, "for he is closer."

"Ellis? A country bonesetter at best," she sniffed. "I

would not have it said for the world that we did not get the colonel the best care possible. No, 'twill be Crawford.''

"But he'd be more comfortable at Rose Farm!" Roland saw his opportunity to acquaint himself to Red Jack slipping away. "Got more people to tend him there."

"Nonsense. There are more servants at Blackstone Hall," the dowager declared. "He will of course come there."

"Servants! Wasn't speaking of servants, Lady Sturbridge —mean family. Mean to treat him like family."

"Yes, of course. Well, if he is truly ill, you would not wish to make him worse, would you? Tell you what, young man—look in on him at the Hall. I am sure he would welcome the company when he is better, but for now, I think he ought to be carried to the closest place."

"I think she's right, Rollo," Jessica agreed.

"Thank you, dear. When Roland comes to visit, you come also." Then perceiving that her son was again about to protest, she added with less enthusiasm, "And it goes without saying that I am always eager to see dear Kitty."

He was beaten and he knew it. Roland nodded. "Be there in the morning—in case he should wish to have someone who understands the military mind about." Then, seeing the skeptical expressions on those around him, he added, "Bring Kitty and Jess too."

It was not until much later, after the baron had been bundled into the Sturbridge carriage, that Kitty felt a great sense of loss. It was as though Lady Sturbridge had taken him from her. "Rollo, I hope you intend to visit often," she told him grimly as she and Jess squeezed into one seat of the two-seater together.

"Run tame in the house," he assured her. "The dragon'll have to throw me out. Daresay you'll want to go also—give me an excuse. Mama will not complain if you are wishful of seeing your betrothed."

And in the Sturbridge carriage, Louise held Red Jack's

hand solicitously. "La, but who would have thought it—Colonel Rayne at Blackstone Hall! I do hope you recover quickly, for I should like to hold a soiree in your honor—nothing large, mind you—just a gathering of friends. I suppose you were robbed of your medals," she murmured regretfully, "but 'twill not matter. Everyone has heard of Red Jack, after all."

"Mama, he is Haverhill now," Charles reminded her.

"Well, if I were to say that, no one would know who he was," she pointed out practically. "We will explain he is Haverhill when they come to call."

Jack lay there, his head supported by the carriage door, wishing for Kitty Gordon.

KITTY ROSE EARLY after a nearly sleepless night and made her way downstairs, where she discovered her aunt and Roland already at breakfast. From the doorway, she discerned that he was telling Isabella about Lady Sturbridge's peremptory possession of Colonel Rayne. To her relief, he failed to mention that Kitty and Jessica had been there also.

"Encroaching female," Mrs. Merriman murmured. "As if he ought not to be brought here. After all, 'tis Kitty who abducted him, and therefore we who are responsible for his well-being, I should think." She looked up, seeing her niece, and for once she did not appear vexed in the least. "La, love, but what a tale Rollo has brought home!"

"Really?" Kitty took her place across from her cousin and tried not to betray herself. "I am all ears, coz."

"Naughty girl! Only fancy—Jessica's Haverhill has passed on, poor man," Isabella answered for her son. She paused, waiting for the news to have the desired effect on Kitty.

To her credit, the young woman appeared dismayed. "Oh—surely not! I mean, he is not—"

"Not *this* Haverhill, my love. As far as is known yet this morning, he survives still." Favoring her niece with an excited smile, she announced triumphantly, "I own I could not credit it, but you have abducted Colonel Rayne! Haverhill is none other than Red Jack Rayne!"

"Haverhill, Aunt Bella?" Kitty asked, feigning shock. "Oh, but I don't think—"

" 'Tis he! Just think—he is in Sussex!" She stopped again,

peering closely at Kitty. "You appear a trifle hagged, dearest, did you not rest well?"

"I had the headache," Kitty lied.

"Again? I am afraid we shall have to consult Dr. Crawford about these megrims of yours. Lud, where was I? Oh, yes— Rollo stopped by the cottage on his way home from the village pub, and 'twas he who discovered Haverhill is not the Haverhill we thought."

"Red Jack Rayne," Rollo stated. "Hero of more battles than I can count."

"A truly dashing fellow, or so I have read," Isabella added. "I wish you had brought him directly here, though, for Louise Trevor has stolen the march on us and had him carried to Blackstone Hall. I must say, I think it rather odious of her to simply appropriate the colonel to herself," she complained. "As if we should not have taken full responsibility for regaining his health." Her eyes narrowed as Kitty buttered a piece of bread. "I must say that you do not appear overly surprised by this turn of events."

"Daresay she don't know who Jack Rayne is," Roland interposed smoothly, coming to Kitty's rescue. "In America during the Peninsular campaigns, after all."

"I collect he must be a soldier."

"Oh, my dear girl! Not just a soldier! Prinny decorated him with all London watching! Even Rollo left Oxford to see it."

"An officer, then."

"More than that—*much* more than that, my love! As I recall it, one of the papers called him a national treasure!"

"A national treasure? Surely not," Kitty managed faintly. "He is but one man, after all."

"Well, he ain't Wellington," Rollo conceded, "but he was with Old Douro through much of the war. Wounded more than once, too. Lud, coz, but I could not believe m'eyes when I saw him last night. To think that a little dab of a female like you brought him all the way from London at pistol point."

"Oh, dear—I hope he will not take us in dislike because of it," Isabella said nervously. "I had hopes that perhaps Jessica—"

"Dash it, Mama, but she was wed to his cousin!" Roland protested. "Cannot go throwing her at his head ere Haverhill is cold, you know."

"As if I would do such a thing, Roland Merriman! No, you mistake me. I merely wished that she make his acquaintance. Then, if after the proper time has passed, he should discover—"

"He ain't going to discover a passion for Jess, Mama. My sister, I know, but the girl's more than a trifle flighty—a widgeon, in fact. Be more likely to fix his interest with Kit here than Jess—and that ain't too likely neither."

"I should hope not," his mother sniffed. "Catherine is betrothed to Sturbridge, after all, and I am sure that the colonel is not so lost to propriety that he would make sheep's eyes at another man's affianced bride. Besides, I cannot think she is in his style at all." She turned to Kitty. " 'Tis useless to ask one man what another looks like, for they never seem to know. Is he as handsome as I have read?"

"Well, he is red-headed," Kitty muttered dryly, "so I must suppose 'tis why he is called Red Jack."

"But what does he *look* like?" her aunt persisted.

It was an impossible task to describe him without betraying the attraction she'd felt for him, so Kitty hedged again. "I didn't precisely notice," she said. " 'Twas rather dark, after all."

"Catherine Gordon, never in all my life have I ever known you to have so little opinion on anything," her aunt declared in disgust. "Can you recall nothing?"

"He has hazel eyes."

"Hazel eyes. Is he tall? Fat or thin? A mustache, perhaps?"

"Mama, officers cannot sport hair on their faces," Roland reminded her. "And he is quite tall, not at all fat, and I'm told all the ladies think him exceedingly handsome. There.

Leave the poor girl alone—this whole affair has been a dreadful shock to her, I should think." He rose from the table. "Now, if you will excuse me, I mean to ride over to Blackstone Hall to see how he fares this morning."

"Well, of all the unfeeling—"

Kitty looked up at him. "I should like to go with you, Rollo."

"You ain't ready," he protested.

"I can be at the door in a trice," she promised. "I have but to get my wrap and bonnet."

"But you have not eaten, and I cannot think he would wish to see you after all that has befallen," her aunt said.

"I am not hungry."

"And 'tis why you have the headache so often, I'll be bound. No, I don't think 'tis wise, my dear."

"Don't see why not, I suppose, but you'd best hurry, Kit. I ain't no hand to wait on a female." Roland met his mother's reproachful eyes. "Dash it, but daresay she wants to see Sturbridge, don't you know?"

At that moment, Jessica came into the dining room, her eyes still heavy from too little sleep. "Hullo, Mama. Rollo. Kit." Sinking down next to Kitty, she held her head. "Lud, but I cannot think," she added, groaning.

"Never say you have the headache also?" her mother asked. "I wonder if 'twas something we had for supper, do you think? But then Rollo and I do not seem to be suffering for it," she decided. "Perhaps you ought to go back to bed."

"Couldn't sleep," Jessica mumbled, not wanting to admit that she'd left word with her maid to waken her early. She reached for the teapot.

"You will not credit the news, my love," Isabella told her, "but Haverhill's dead."

"*Dead?* But he was—"

"Dash it, Jess! Watch what you are doing! You are pouring the demned tea on the cloth!" Roland remonstrated with her.

"Well, she can be forgiven. 'Tis the shock, no doubt." Isabella fixed her daughter with a sober gaze. "Alas, but 'tis true—the baron need trouble you no longer, Jessica.''

The girl blinked. "Oh, I knew—"

"Jess, Rollo has been telling Aunt Bella about how he went to see Haverhill last night," Kitty cut in quickly. "And only fancy, Haverhill is not our Haverhill, after all, but rather someone called Red Jack," she added significantly.

"Yes."

"Mighty calm about it, missy," Isabella observed, suddenly suspicious.

"Of course she ain't in raptures yet, Mama! Gel's got the headache! Take time for it to sink in."

To Kitty, it was obvious that Jess was still more than a little weasel-bit from the night's brandy. Taking the teapot from her, she poured a cup and carefully added a chunk of sugar. "You'll feel more the thing after you drink this down, dearest," she murmured solicitously. "Rollo and I mean to go to Blackstone Hall, else I'd put a cool cloth on your head for you."

"I want to go with you."

"Eh? Now, Jess, there ain't but two seats! Besides, you got no reason—and I ain't waiting for two females, I ain't!"

"Rollo!" Isabella turned to him. "You will, of course, take your sister."

"Cannot. Ain't got a carriage right now," he reminded her. "And I dashed well ain't going to drive up to see Red Jack with a female a-hanging off the back of a two-seater! Should look like the veriest cake." ·

But Kitty had little hope that before the day was out Jessica would have spilled the tale. "I'll sit on the groom's step, Rollo," she said tiredly. "And Jess will hurry, I promise you."

"No!"

"And after you have delivered them to Blackstone Hall, you will return for me," Isabella decided. "I am sure that dear Louise will need support in caring for Lord Haverhill."

"Mama, 'twill be like a damned invasion!"

"Nonsense. Besides, it cannot be thought odd in the least,

for there is Kitty's wedding to discuss, after all. And I should imagine that while Kitty is occupied with Sturbridge, and I am with Louise, you and Jessica will be more than useful in amusing the colonel.''

"Uh—I don't think he will wish to be amused, Aunt Bella. When Charles and I saw him yesterday, he was already fevered from the wound,'' Kitty pointed out reasonably. "I should imagine that he ought to rest.''

"Exactly so.''

"You also, Rollo.''

"Don't want to amuse him—want to ask him about Cuidad Rodrigo,'' he retorted defensively. "Ain't the same thing.''

But Isabella would not be moved. "Run up and make yourself presentable, my love,'' she told her daughter. "And wear your blue-figured muslin—the one we bought of Mrs. Hill this spring.'' She surveyed the girl critically. "I would that you were not so peaked this morning, but there's naught we can do about that, I suppose. Kitty will have to pinch your cheeks ere you go in.''

"Mama, I can see taking Kit because of Sturbridge,'' Rollo complained, "but Jess ain't got a reason in the world to go.''

"Stuff! Much you know about anything, Roland Merriman!'' his sister retorted. "And you will wait while I have Annie do my hair.''

As the two girls hurried upstairs, Isabella shook her head. "Poor child. She does not yet realize the significance of it all, does she?'' she said softly.

"The significance is that Red Jack is being invaded,'' Rollo muttered glumly. "And he ain't even up to mounting a defense.''

" 'Tis no such thing, Roland Merriman,'' his mother declared severely. "Though I own I have heard that men are particularly vulnerable to females when they ail.''

"Ain't a man I know as likes an ailing female, Mama.''

"No—no, you mistake my meaning! Sometimes, Rollo, I think you are a slow top,'' she complained. "But it does not signify, I suppose. 'Tis Red Jack who must see Jessica to advantage.''

"Told you—she ain't in his style."

"As to that, we shall see. But first we shall have to get past Louise, for I have not the least doubt that she means to guard him like a dragon at the gate. I should expect she will wish to appropriate him to her own consequence, you know. Being that she is daughter to an earl, she seems to feel that 'tis her right to have everything, which I think most unfair of her, for she has not that much to feed her pride. Indeed, if she had not snared Charles's father, her papa would have gone to debtor's prison.'' She looked up at him, shaking her head. "But 'tis spilled cream now, is it not? One could only wish that Kitty had brought him here first.''

LOUISE TREVOR PRESSED THE DAMP, scented handkerchief to her temples, while Mrs. Pennyman hovered nearby. Had it not been for the coup of having Red Jack Rayne in her house, she would have wished for a different night. As it was, Charles had kept her up long after the doctor had left, and the quarrel had not been a very civil one.

He had, he told her furiously, offered for Kitty Gordon, and he'd be hanged before he would allow her to insult his intended again. And if that meant that Louise must leave Blackstone Hall, then so be it. As for the unfortunate incident at the cottage, he was not an infant in need of his mother's protection, and "By God," he'd roared in most unseemly fashion, "if I wished to have an assignation with anyone, which I do not, 'tis none of your affair, madam! I am nine and twenty, after all!"

It had been an ill-calculated mistake, and she realized it now. Dabbing at her eyes with the same cloth, she looked about her unhappily. Leave Blackstone Hall? Never.

"My lady, Mr. Merriman is come with Miss Gordon and his sister," a footman ventured diffidently. "Kennet would know if you wish them turned away?"

"Of course, I wish them at Jericho!" her ladyship snapped, then she recalled herself. "No, no—must not say that precisely. He has brought Miss Gordon, you say?"

"And Miss Merriman."

"Lud!"

"You like Miss Merriman," Clara Pennyman reminded her timidly. "Said so to Lord Sturbridge but yesterday."

"What time is it, Edward?" the dowager asked tiredly.

"Just after ten o'clock, madam."

"They cannot have slept at all," she muttered under her breath. Rising, she dropped the cloth into the basin of perfumed water. "I should rather tame lions at a menagerie, but there is no help for this, I suppose. I would not have Charles discover that I have sent the wretched girl away."

Belowstairs, Kitty paced before the small fire that had been laid in the reception parlor, while Roland and Jessica sat at proper attention, waiting for Lady Sturbridge to come down. "Ain't ladylike to go to and fro like a bear on a chain," Roland chided her. "Sit down."

"Why did you not ask how he fares?"

"Ask Lady Sturbridge. It ain't the thing to gossip with the servants."

"I should scarce call it gossip to inquire if—"

"Kitty dearest!" Lady Sturbridge swept into the room, her hands outstretched. "You poor child! You look positively hagged this morning!" She turned accusing eyes on Roland. "Young man, you ought to take better care of our little Catherine." She caught Kitty's fingers in her cold ones, then bent to brush the barest kiss against the girl's cheek. "You need more rest, my love."

"Lady Sturbridge—"

"Such formality, child! If you cannot bring yourself to call me Mama, it must be Louise." Releasing her hands, she managed to keep her voice light as she added, "La, but I hope that you will not refine too much on last night, my dear, for I can quite see I was wrong. I ought to have known you are just what you should be, after all, for how else would Charles have come to offer for you? Come—cry peace between us, for I am sure we both love him, do we not?"

"Kitty is not one to nurse ill feelings, Lady Sturbridge," Jessica answered hastily for her cousin. Then, before Kitty could say anything untoward, she asked, "And how is Colonel Rayne? Lord Haverhill, that is?"

The dowager shot the younger girl a look of gratitude.

"Not well, I am afraid. Dr. Crawford could not come on such notice, so we had to make do with Ellis, you know, and I am not at all certain he knows his business."

"But he's better, ain't he?"

"Alas, young man, but he is not. Dr. Ellis is of the opinion that had he not been brought here he possibly would not have survived. At first 'twas feared that there was still a fragment in him, but then after probing, he discovered 'twas not so. The poor, poor man."

"He opened the wound?" Kitty uttered incredulously.

"Yes. Charles protested also, but what could we do? I mean, *I* am certainly not a physician." She dropped into a chair. "We were up much of the night."

"But what did Ellis say?" Kitty persisted.

"That if nothing else dreadful happens, he ought to mend. The greatest fear seems to be that the wound will putrify."

"Red Jack's been through worse," Roland maintained stoutly. "Cannot have come through the war to die in bed here."

"No, of course not. Though one could wish it will not take him so long to recover. I had hopes he would be better in time that we could have a small party to introduce him into the neighborhood ere everyone went to London," she murmured regretfully. "But Dr. Ellis is of the opinion that he will not be up much before the fortnight, and then when I asked about having a soiree of sorts, he allowed as how the colonel should most definitely not have any excitement."

"Shouldn't think so," Roland agreed. "Too weak to dance."

"Yes, and by the time he is up, we shall be thin of company here," Lady Sturbridge complained. "But I daresay he cannot help that, after all." She looked up at Kitty, who still stood. "Tell me, love, do you think perhaps I ought to send a notice to the papers that he is here? I mean, there must be those who will worry about him," she added, realizing how she sounded. "And I would wish that Mrs. Peavley and Mrs. Shoreham should know."

"Why?" Kitty asked bluntly. "Do they know him?"

"Of course they do not, dearest," the dowager admitted, the edge in her voice unmistakable. "But I have not forgotten how Emily Peavley carried on about the fact that Byron attended Cynthia's come-out—as though he ought to be held up as desirable, which I am sure I do not think he is. Lud, but you would have thought 'twas Prinny. And everyone has heard of Colonel John Rayne, after all."

"Well, I cannot but think 'twill appear self-serving," Kitty pointed out reasonably.

"I assure you 'tis no such thing!" Affronted by the girl's candor, Louise sought to disabuse her of the notion. "Surely you do not think that I would seek to—to—"

"Of course she does not," Jessica murmured soothingly. "And I for one see nothing wrong with apprising people that Red Jack is here. Indeed, but as you said, there must be those who are worried about him."

"Thank you, dear."

Lord Sturbridge stepped into the room. "Kitty! And Miss Merriman! Hullo, Rollo."

"They are come to see how Lord Haverhill does, Charles," his mother explained. "And 'tis scarce a proper greeting for your betrothed."

"Sorry." He bent to plant a chaste kiss on Kitty's cheek. "Forgot. He's been asking for you, by the by."

"Haverhill's been asking for Kitty?" the dowager asked incredulously. "But he does not know her."

"Uh—actually, he saw her last night. Asked if I thought the pretty female might be persuaded to call," he improvised quickly.

"Then you mistook him. I am quite certain he must have meant Miss Merriman."

"Uh—no, I believe he said Miss Gordon."

"Oh, I should like to see him again—to inquire how he feels," Kitty admitted quickly.

The dowager's mouth drew into a thin, flat line. "I cannot think—well, after all he has been through—"

"Eh? Just the thing for him!" Roland insisted. "I'll go up with her, in fact. Been wantin' to talk to him, you know—great admirer."

"Rollo, I do not think that—"

"Dash it, Kit! You don't know a dragoon from a grenadier! Me and Red Jack got things to talk about, don't you know?"

"Actually, Rollo, you have forgotten Mama," Jessica reminded him. "I am sure that if Colonel Rayne—Lord Haverhill—is to be recovering for weeks, there will be more than enough time for you to speak with him."

"Your mama?" Lady Sturbridge asked.

"Our carriage is down just now, so Rollo is to fetch Mama in the two-seater. She is wishful of helping you through this," the girl responded, straight-faced.

"Well, I cannot think of anything she could do that I cannot," the dowager protested peevishly. "Really—"

"Take you up to see him," Charles told Kitty. "Miss Merriman?"

"Oh, no. I shall just wait with Lady Sturbridge, I think. It cannot be very good for him to have everyone hovering him while he mends."

"But I thought you wished to see him," her brother protested. "Told me so, in fact."

Casting a quick look at the viscount, Jessica blushed rosily. "Oh—no, you mistook me. I am sure I said I wished to visit Lady Sturbridge."

Resigned to the prospect of seeing her house at sixes and sevens, the dowager said nothing further until Roland, Kitty, and Charles had left the room. Then, sighing deeply, she murmured, "I have loved this house so much, Miss Merriman. I cannot think I shall like the dower house half so well, you know. It will be so confining with Mrs. Pennyman there."

"Oh—no! Dear Lady Sturbridge, you must not think of it!" Jessica said warmly. "I am sure that Kitty will not expect such a thing. Indeed, but I would not—I should ask you to stay, and so she shall also. Why, 'twould not be Blackstone Hall without you!''

For a moment, the older woman stared into the girl's face, expecting guile. But Jessica Merriman's eyes mirrored her sincerity.

"You dear, dear child," was all Louise could manage to say. Reaching out to clasp Jessica's hand, she squeezed her fingers. "You are all that a mother could wish for," she added finally.

Upstairs, Kitty approached the poster bed anxiously. The baron lay propped among a bank of pillows, his eyes closed. He appeared pale and drained of blood against the white of the sheets and nightshirt. As she leaned over him, his hazel eyes opened.

"You wretch," he murmured.

"I am so sorry," she whispered contritely.

"I cannot believe you gave up the field so easily."

"What?"

"Ought to have taken me home with you." He twisted to see what Charles did, but the viscount had already left the room. "As it was, the woman held my hand all the way here, prating about giving me a damned party."

"Oh, dear. Yes, well, you have to understand Lady Sturbridge, you see," she began, trying to suppress a giggle. "You are a social catch."

"I've got a hole in my shoulder," he retorted.

"But that is an inconvenience merely. And she will wait until you are better, even if it means that we shall be thin of company then," she explained, her mouth twitching. "But it would be better socially if you could recover post haste, you understand. That way, perhaps not everyone will have already gone to London."

"Egad."

"But you do have something for which to be thankful," she added impishly. "There are no daughters in the house. Otherwise, you would not get out of here without being legshackled, I assure you."

"My dear Miss Gordon, even in my weakened state, I am not so easily taken."

"As it is," she went on blithely, "now that the other Lord Haverhill has departed this earth, Aunt Bella means to throw Jess at your head." She pulled up a chair and leaned toward him. "It must be awful to have every matchmaking mama in the country casting out lures to you, I expect."

"Awful."

"But I daresay you are getting used to the notion," she added impishly. "Or do you get tired of being toad-eaten?"

"Dashed tired of it already." A faint smile played at his mouth. "But you seem to be rather impervious to my supposed charm."

She regarded him for a moment, then answered evasively, "Well, there is Sturbridge, after all, is there not? And I must say, I have not seen you at your best." A trace of mischief lurking within, her blue eyes regarded him for a long moment. "Under other circumstances, I should expect rather more heroism from Red Jack Rayne. If Rollo is to be believed, you won at least five battles by yourself."

"Doing it too brown, Miss Gordon! And from the outset, you have held the advantage on me."

"I own it must be difficult for a man of your stature to be abducted at all, and by—"

"Very lowering, thank you," he admitted ruefully. "There is something about a pistol that makes for a rather poor introduction." His hazel eyes betrayed a hint of amusement. "Tell me, did you never wonder how I came to go with you?"

" 'Twas the pistol."

" 'Twas curiosity, Miss Gordon." His hand crept to the bandage that bulged at his shoulder. " 'Twas a mistake. 'Pon reflection, I ought to have disarmed you and made you tell me the tale then and there. As it was, my curiosity very nearly killed me."

He struggled to pull himself up against the pillows, and fell back. She moved to assist him, lifting him by his good arm, bracing her knee against the side of the bed for leverage. He was heavy, far heavier than she remembered even, and the thought crossed her mind that he was not helping her at all. In fact, he seemed to be pulling the other way, and she was in grave danger of sprawling over him. She let him fall and straightened up in exasperation.

"If you are in such bad case, my lord," she told him severely, "you ought not to be bothered with company. I shall come again when you are feeling more the thing."

"Sit down, Miss Gordon."

"Really, sir, but—"

"Up in the boughs, eh? I shouldn't stay there, were I you." Grinning, he nodded. "Aye. You'd best consider what I mean to tell the magistrate."

"The magistrate? But—"

"The magistrate," he repeated definitely. "There is bound to be an inquiry of some sort, my dear—or did you think a man could get shot without comment in England? 'Tis not America, after all." As she sank back into the chair, he met her eyes reproachfully. "Besides, 'tis a trifle difficult to explain how I came to be lying at the side of the road, my shoulder already bandaged. There will be those who will wonder at that, you know, for not too many highwaymen stop to tend to their victims." Seeing that the color had drained from her face, he relented. "Not that I mean to tell anyone precisely what happened, I assure you. I should look the veriest fool, don't you think?"

"No," she answered low. " 'Tis I who must appear the fool, for 'twas my mistake."

"I suppose I can forgive you for that," he allowed magnanimously, "but if you think to abandon me to that encroaching female, you are mistaken. The price of my silence, Miss Gordon, is *your* company. You at least amuse me."

"I cannot just run tame here, sir," she protested weakly. "Lady Sturbridge dislikes me."

"Being an inventive, resourceful female, you will no doubt

discover a way.'' He favored her with what he hoped was his most beguiling smile. "Offer to assist her, for I can assure you she is no hand in the sickroom at all. She very nearly cast up her accounts while the quack dug again for the ball. Indeed, but if she had not been avoiding Sturbridge, I think she would have preferred to be nearly anywhere else. Devil of a row they had afterward, anyway.''

"She would sooner discover a viper underfoot than me, sir,'' Kitty declared. "And Aunt Bella has such plans for Jess, you see, that she will not approve either.''

"The screaming widgeon? Tell her she wastes her hopes on that head.''

"Well, you *were* a shock to the poor girl, you must admit, for she quite expected to see your cousin,'' she pointed out judiciously. "As for Aunt Bella, I must take leave to tell you that once she gets a notion in her head, 'tis nigh to impossible to disabuse her of it. I ought to know—there *is* Sturbridge, after all,'' she recalled dryly.

"Ah, yes—the mistake.''

Thinking he was funning with her, she stiffened visibly. "The mistake was you, sir. Charles was the cost.''

"The practical Miss Gordon,'' he murmured. "I collect 'tis not a love match, then.''

"You are to collect nothing, my lord. Indeed, but 'tis improper of you to pry.''

"Still, I cannot think you will suit.''

Later, she was to chide herself for a fool, but there was something quite disconcerting in the baron's gaze. And she was not so green as to be taken in by an obviously accomplished flirt. "Charles and I shall suit very well, for there is a great deal of affection between us,'' she insisted.

He sighed. "Well, if 'tis your wish to rule the roost, I suppose you could do worse. Myself, I should prefer some passion in the arrangement, but then I am not a female.''

She opened her mouth, then snapped it shut. "My affairs are none of your concern,'' she managed finally through clenched teeth.

"No. No, they are not," he admitted, disappointing her. "You must pardon the meanderings of a fevered fool."

Without thinking, she reached to touch his head. "I do not believe you are as warm this morning as you were last night. Perhaps the doctor's attention . . . Well, I could not forgive myself if you were to take a turn for the worse."

"Kitty, dearest, you must not tire the colonel, you know," Lady Sturbridge chided, coming into the room. "Lud, but you need to be abed yourself." Turning to Jack, she added a trifle too brightly, "We have to have *such* a care for her health, you know, else she will not be up to the rigors of a wedding next year. Small females simply do not have robust constitutions."

"Really, but I am quite well, and—"

"So like her, my lord. She fears to admit to weakness, not realizing that we shall love her just as she is." Dismissing Kitty, she told her, "Do wear your bonnet when you go out, my love, for I could swear I see a spot coming on your nose, and Charles abhors freckles."

Making a face that the dowager couldn't see, Kitty turned to address the baron again. "I shall come again to see how you fare, my lord. In the meantime, I shall leave you in Lady Sturbridge's care," she added sweetly.

"You will find Charles in the garden with Miss Merriman, my dear. I had him show her the crocuses," Louise told her. "Such a sweet, lovely girl. Your aunt must be so proud of her."

Behind her ladyship, Red Jack gave Kitty a look of long suffering, which she wisely chose to ignore. "Well, my lord, I must apologize," she heard Charles's mother say as she reached the hallway, "but there was simply no way to keep her away with any civility at all. And I would not for the world slight Charles's betrothed, you know, but if you shall not wish her to visit, I am sure you have but to mention the matter to Sturbridge."

"She seems like an amiable girl," Jack observed noncommittally, disappointing Kitty again.

Amiable? Was that all he could think to say? Telling herself
it was most impolite to eavesdrop, Kitty forced herself to
go on down the stairs.

"Girl? I should scarce call her that," Louise protested.
"Indeed, but I could have wished she were younger." She
sighed expressively and looked away. "Alas, but 'tis not for
me to choose whom he weds . . ." Her voice trailed off,
letting him know that Kitty would not have been on any list
of her making. "She is so free-mannered, you see. I suppose
that comes from being bred in America. How she will
manage as Charles's viscountess, I am sure I do not know.
Indeed, but I cringe to think what Sally Jersey will say of
her—'Sturbridge's little savage,' no doubt."

"I find her manners refreshing."

The dowager looked at him sharply. "Oh. Yes, well, 'tis
none of my affair, in any event. But I own I could wish she
were a trifle taller for the children's sake."

" 'Twould be a pity if she were. There is something about
a small female that bears protecting," he countered with a
straight face.

"I suppose." Louise sighed again. "If only she were
not likely to turn brown—the Indian influence, you
know."

"I think Miss Gordon is one of the loveliest females I have
ever seen. You son is most fortunate, Lady Sturbridge. In
fact, I envy him."

"You do? But then you are a man, and—" She stopped
in midsentence, digesting the possible import of his words,
and a slow, almost devious smile warmed her countenance.
"Of course you are right, my lord! A most unexceptional
girl! Lud, but how I do go on. You must think I do not like
Kitty, which is most certainly not the case. Indeed, but I shall
enjoy her company while you recover, for I have hopes she
means to come every day, especially since you have assured
me you do not dislike her."

"Not at all."

"Such an amusing, clever girl really. Charles tells me she is a Mistress Sharp at whist. Do you play the game, sir?"

"I am a fair hand at it myself," he admitted.

"Then you simply must play cards with her, my lord—la, and I have been worrying how to amuse you while you are here. I have but to look to dear Kitty for help with the task. And considering all that has befallen you, I am sure that Charles will understand . . ."

"I should be pleased to see her," he murmured, amused by the dowager's rather abrupt and certainly transparent change of heart.

"And see her you shall," she promised almost enthusiastically. "Yes, indeed. And I shall insist that she bring Miss Merriman with her, of course. La, but why did I not think of that?"

"I have never favored a three-handed game."

"What? Oh, I should not dream of that," she assured him. "Goodness, how I do go on, don't I? Well, we must see that you get your rest now. Later, I shall have Charles's man shave you and make you more presentable—make you feel more the thing, you know."

"Thank you. And I'd have someone write to Haverhill House to apprise my solicitor as to what has happened. Poor fellow must think I have fallen off the earth."

"Of course. But there is no need to send any servants to attend you, for we are well-staffed here, my lord, and quite capable of the task."

As she left, he could hear her talking, presumably to herself, congratulating herself on a godsend. He lay back, staring at the ornate ceiling above him, wondering if he ought to save Kitty Gordon from the dragon. And the more he thought on it, the more heroic the mission became. But he was at a disadvantage lying abed—or was he? It was difficult to show to one's best when one could not do the things one did well, after all, he conceded. But for all her unconventional manners, he'd wager that Kitty Gordon was as tender-hearted as the rest of her sex. That, coupled with the guilt she felt, ought to aid him in his campaign. He certainly had hopes of it, anyway.

"LUD, LOUISE, but I came as soon as Rollo apprised me," Isabella murmured, brushing a kiss against Lady Sturbridge's cheek. "You must be beside yourself with worry over Lord Haverhill. La—Red Jack Rayne!"

"In truth, but I am honored to have him here, dear Bella," the dowager said, drawing away.

"The poor man! Is there any notion who did this dreadful thing?"

"No, but I—"

"No, I suppose not," Isabella answered herself quickly. "I own I am surprised to discover they carried him here, you know, for he is distantly related to us. One would think—"

"Distantly related to you? I am sure I have never heard of the connection," Louise sniffed.

"You forget that the late Lord Haverhill visited us some six years past. Indeed, but I could not help wondering if perhaps 'twas to Rose Farm that the colonel was coming."

"If he was, he has not mentioned it," the dowager answered dryly. "What is the relationship, by the by?"

" 'Twas by marriage—some years back. But it does not signify now," Isabella added hastily. "More to the point, my dear Louise, is what I can do to aid you, for I know this arrival has caught you unwares, and—"

"It was a shock, I own, but we shall manage."

"Well, if you find yourself overset, you have but to call on me, for with the younger girls gone to boarding school, there is more than enough room to accommodate the colonel at Rose Farm.''

The dowager's eyebrows lifted. ''Are you suggesting that you have more room than I? Or that you are more capable than I of attending to a guest?'' she demanded awfully.

''Lud, no! You mistake me, my dear Louise. But as he is a relation of ours, however distantly, I thought I should offer.''

''Nonsense.''

''Well, when he is up and about, I should hope he means to visit Rose Farm.''

'' 'Twill be an age before he goes anywhere—I had it of Dr. Ellis myself.''

''Ellis? Louise, you ought to have had Crawford. I for one would not refine on anything Dr. Ellis said. My late husband, dear Mr. Merriman, was of the opinion that Ellis is more than a trifle crack-brained.''

The dowager, who held much the same opinion, nonetheless felt it incumbent upon herself to defend him. ''I am sure that there are many more significant people who hold him in esteem,'' she retorted stiffly.

''Still, I would that you called in Crawford. Indeed, if you would have me pay for the consult—''

''Of all the—the *brass*, Isabella Merriman! When I have need—'' She stopped short at the sight of her son, with Kitty on one arm and Jessica on the other, coming in from the garden. Clamping her mouth shut, she managed to hold her tongue. One brangle with Charles was more than enough.

''Oh, I collect you have company, Mama,'' he observed mildly. ''Mrs. Merriman.''

''What did you think of the crocuses? Are they not lovely despite all the rain?'' Louise asked Jessica.

''Lovely, madam.''

''Charles, I would that you discovered what Pennyman is doing, and if 'tis more needlework, tell her I have need of her this instant.'' Her temper in check, she turned again to Mrs. Merriman. ''You and Pennyman simply must view them before you go. The poor dear ruins her eyes with her infernal stitching, so the air will do her good.''

"Finally got the clunch of a groom to understand I want the horses walked,'' Roland explained to his mother as he joined them. ''Your servant, Lady Sturbridge,'' he murmured, bowing over Louise's hand.

"Such pretty manners your children have, Isabella dear. The Merriman manners, I daresay.''

Unaware his mother had just been delivered a set down, Roland beamed. ''Try to be a credit to m'family. Well, now that everyone's here, I think I shall look in on Red Jack— Haverhill, I mean.''

"The poor man is terribly overtaxed, I fear,'' Louise murmured. ''I don't think he ought to be disturbed again today.''

"What?'' Roland fairly howled. Appealing to Charles, he said plaintively, ''I made two trips over, and it don't seem right—I mean, I'm the only one as *wants* to see him, I'll be bound. Besides, I ain't ready to make two trips back just yet.''

"Roland!''

"Sorry, Mama—but I ain't. Couldn't speak with him last night for the commotion, and now—''

"What commotion?''

Unwilling to remind anyone of her part in the previous night's fiasco, the dowager relented quickly. ''Kitty dearest, perhaps you could take your cousin up, after all,'' she suggested. ''I know that you will not let him tire the colonel overmuch, will you?'' As they left, she turned to Isabella, astounding Charles by adding, ''I shall so enjoy having Kitty here—such a lovely girl—and such refreshing manners. You simply must allow her to come over more often, particularly now that I have need of her.''

"Well, I—''

"As Charles's betrothed, her presence will not be remarked, I am sure, and I expect the colonel will find *youthful* company more to his liking, don't you think?'' Louise continued pointedly. ''Indeed, but if you would wish to send Miss Merriman also, I daresay that between them they will be able to keep him tolerably amused as he mends.''

Ignoring the barb, Isabella forced herself to smile. After all, she'd managed to insinuate her daughter into the house at least. ''Well, I see no harm to it—no harm at all. Jessica has many accomplishments,'' she said proudly. ''I am sure the colonel will appreciate her company.''

''Yes. Ah—there you are, Pennyman—I was about to send Charles up for you,'' Louise said brightly, drawing the elderly woman into their midst. ''Well, now that you are here, perhaps you will wish to take Mrs. Merriman for a turn about the gardens—and I would you showed her the greenhouse also, for Joseph has started some of the loveliest plants.''

''Oh, I should like to see them also,'' Jessica admitted.

''Not you, dear—I will have Charles show them to you tomorrow. For now, I think you ought to fetch your brother back before he tires the colonel. Perhaps you and Rollo and Charles could take the carriage into the village to apprise the vicar that Haverhill is here. I am sure he will wish to remember the colonel in Sunday's prayers, after all.''

''But should not Kitty be the one to go?'' Jessica asked. Even as she said it, she could have bitten her tongue for her foolishness. ''But I suppose—''

''Dear me, no! I have need of Kitty here today, for now that your mama is here, we should be putting our heads together over this wedding, don't you think?'' the dowager answered slyly. ''I mean, there is so much to do, after all, and if they have hopes of a winter wedding, we shall have to rush as it is.''

Charles frowned. ''Mama, if Mrs. Merriman is in the garden, I cannot think there will be much planning done.''

''Foolish me! I did not mean she was to stay there all day, Charles. Did I say that? I meant that perhaps we could all share a cold nuncheon when you are come back from the village. And whilst you are gone, *after* she has seen my lovely flowers, Isabella and I shall have a cose about the wedding.

I am positively full of ideas, I assure you, Madame Cecile shall do Kitty's trousseau, for I own I have some influence there—though 'tis doubtful her services can be had before autumn . . . well, there *is* time, anyway, so that will not signify."

"Really, Louise, but we are capable of tending to the matter ourselves," Isabella said stiffly.

"Of course you are! Did I imply you are not?" the dowager asked soothingly. " 'Twas not my intent, I assure you. Indeed, but I merely meant to offer my assistance."

Unmollified, yet not wishing to throw a spoke in the wheel of what could only be considered an advantageous marriage for Kitty, Isabella addressed Mrs. Pennyman. "Indeed, but a turn about the garden would be most welcome," she managed. "Then we shall come to terms over the wedding at nuncheon," she added to Louise.

Jessica climbed the stairs, feeling quite guilty but nonetheless grateful for the chance to accompany Sturbridge even if it meant the vexatious company of her younger brother. And if she had to allow her mother to think she was throwing her cap over the windmill for Haverhill, she would do it. She stopped outside the bedchamber and listened. Roland's voice carried through the partially opened door.

"Things might have been different, don't you think, if Prince Jerome had held his division back rather than attacking the Prussians and the British Guards first? I mean, they were so badly cut up by the artillery, they lost fifteen hundred Frogs in the first forty minutes, don't you know?"

"No."

"No? How can you say so? The losses was awful, as I read 'em."

"Very true, but they were not deterred by that. The telling point was that Wellington did not commit any more troops than were needed to hold the positions until Bülow and the rest of the Prussian army moved."

"I know, but—"

" 'Twas a stroke of brilliance on Wellington's part rather than an error by the French.''

"But I read where the Frogs' morale was low after it," Rollo protested.

"Not until they realized we were being reinforced by both Blücher and Bülow—only then did Boney know he'd made his battle plans on the wrong information," the colonel answered. "Napoleon's mistake was in continuing the battle at that juncture. What Jerome and Reille did, while foolish, was not the great blunder of Waterloo.''

"But Napoleon's twelve-pounders nearly won the day," Roland reminded him. "Read of that also.''

"It was a bloody awful sight," Red Jack conceded, "and even the Peninsular veterans were surprised by the ferocity of the French artillery. There were twenty-four cannon, each with more than a mile range. 'Twas the mud that saved us there, for many of the shells burst and lay where they fell. Had the ground been dry, they would have ricochetted and taken a greater toll. In the end, 'twas mostly the Belgians who fell to the cannonfire.''

"I would that I had been there," the younger man said wistfully. "I would that I had seen the glory of it all.''

"Glory?" Jack snorted derisively. "There was no glory there—nor anywhere else I fought. 'Twas smoke and fire and the screams of wounded and dying men and animals. 'Twas hell on earth, and nothing less.''

"But we won," Roland reminded him proudly.

"We won, and for that we ought to be thankful. But never say what we did was glorious, for 'twas not. I can still see in my nightmares the charge of Uxbridge's cavalry—and of the Union Brigade. The flower of our cavalry saved the middle of the line, all right, but in their pursuit of your glory they were destroyed. Will Ponsonby fell at their head needlessly.''

"But—"

"Speak no more of war to me, for I'd forget it all," Jack said, his voice low. "I saw my friends fall, I carried the dying back to our line too many times to count, and I saw the folly of those who thought glory worth dying for.''

"Read of it—of every battle—''.

"Oh, Rollo, cut line!'' Kitty snapped, exasperated by her cousin's unwillingness to let the matter drop. "The man is too ill to be bothered with this.''

"Dash it, Kit, but I been waiting years—years! I read every word that was written about him. I—''

Jack shook his head wearily. "Words on paper can never convey the horror. If the numbers in dispatches had faces, the public would rise up and demand an end to every war.''

To Roland, it was as though his hero had admitted to heresy and he could not accept it. "But you yourself was wounded—aye, and decorated by the Crown for it.''

" 'Tis ludicrous to be honored for living when so many died.''

"You are too modest merely. We all read of how you—''.

"I said I had no wish to speak of it,'' Jack cut in curtly, then relented as the younger man's face fell. "Maybe another day 'twill not pain me so much, but just now I'd not remember what I saw.''

"Rollo—'' Kitty's voice warned her cousin to have done.

"La, Rollo, but you are sent for,'' Jessica said, opening the door wider. "You and Charles and I are to go into the village, while Mama and Kitty discuss wedding plans with Lady Sturbridge.''

"I just got here!'' Roland cried. "Me and Red Jack—''

"Lord Haverhill is overtired, Rollo,'' Kitty announced, rising. "Indeed, but he looks more than a trifle out of sorts just now.''

"Dash it, Kit!''

"Oh, come on, Rollo,'' Jessica urged him. "Let the poor man mend. I daresay there will be more than enough time to regale him with what you know of the military ere he goes back to London.''

"Females! They got no notion of a man's interests! It ain't right for a man to be plagued with a houseful of 'em!'' Roland

declared forcefully. Then, looking down, he could see that
his idol's eyes were closed. "Daresay you *are* overtired, ain't
you?"

"Yes."

"Sorry for it," the young man mumbled. "Didn't
mean—"

"You can come back," the baron murmured. "Another
time."

"You mean it? I say, deuced good of you, sir! Be back
tomorrow and every day after—and if you don't want to talk
about battles, we'll think of something else," Roland
promised. "You hear that, Kit? He wants me to come back!"

"I heard."

She hung back until the other two had left. "I am sorry,
my lord. 'Tis just that Rollo has always wanted to be a
soldier, and you are a particular hero to him."

"I know." He reached a hand to her. "I'd have you sit
again, for I'd not face the demons alone."

It was the second time she'd heard him speak of demons.
Sinking back into the chair, she leaned closer, for he spoke
at little more than a whisper. "You are far too tired, my
lord," she said softly as she clasped his hand.

"I've been in worse case."

"You feel guilt that others died and you did not, I suppose,
but you must not look on it like that, you know. If you did
not fall, there was a reason for it."

"Is this to be a sermon, Miss Gordon? For if it is, I can
do without it."

"No, not a sermon precisely. But I do believe that if you
were spared, 'twas because the Almighty was not quite done
with you yet."

"He's been rather close-lipped with His plans," he
muttered. "Damned if I can discover anything." A harsh,
almost derisive laugh shook his shoulders. " 'Tis more like
the devil's jest, don't you think? Red Jack Rayne, a baron—
'tis funny." He coughed, then winced, paling. "Don't feel
like a baron. Feel like a deuced infant."

"Well, you will be better on the morrow, and more so the day after that," she said bracingly. "And if you like, I will read to you when I come again."

"What?"

"Whatever you like. Perhaps you would hear a novel— or a play, do you think?"

"Shakespeare's sonnets—or whist. Regular Jack Handy at whist."

She looked down to where his fingers curved over hers, and the first thought that came to mind was how strong they appeared despite his being wounded. The second thought was that she had no business touching him at all. Reluctantly, she pulled her hand away.

"Yes, well, if you are up to whist, then whist it will be." She rose again. "Do try to sleep, sir."

"You will come back tomorrow?"

"I'll come every day until you are better."

" 'Twill be weeks, Miss Gordon—weeks," he promised.

FOR TWO WEEKS, it seemed that Red Jack regained his strength even more rapidly than expected, despite the ever increasing numbers of the curious who came to call. Indeed, as word of his presence at Blackstone Hall spread, there were those who traveled a full day's carriage ride to pay respects to a revered hero. And within the neighborhood, there were those who postponed leaving for London in order to present marriageable daughters to him in hopes that one might somehow gain favorable attention.

But it was Kitty, Rollo, and Jessica that he saw every day, the latter only when no excuse to be with Lord Sturbridge could be found. The hours she spent with Jack were interminable to both of them, for she was so self-conscious in his presence that much of her conversation was monosyllabic and punctuated with blushes that bespoke simplicity rather than artifice. He discovered he preferred her sycophantic brother's determined adulation to her inane civility.

And it was Kitty he awaited eagerly every morning, Kitty who played whist when he felt like it, who read to him, who did not plague him with infernal questions about the war he'd rather forget. Unlike the others, she would listen to him speak of other things, and she supplied conversation that did not center around him. She was, he discovered, a female of her own opinions, and she was not above defending them to him, quite a novelty to one who was used to women who pandered to his supposedly superior male intellect. In short, she was refreshing, she was intelligent, she was lovely. From their certainly unusual introduction, through her frantic attempts to save his life, to her current devotion to his regaining his health, she had been a daring, unconventional girl, far more unfettered by convention than the usual English miss.

He was, he realized, in a fair way to being head over heels for her, and for the first time in his life, he was uncertain of his campaign. As he saw it, analyzing the situation at length, there were two rubs in his way—she was Sturbridge's betrothed, and she yearned to return to America. In the first instant, he'd not serve Charles an ill turn, not after accepting the hospitality of his house; and in the second, if she were freed of her engagement to the viscount, there was a far greater certainty that she'd book passage across the Atlantic than that she'd accept Baron Haverhill's suit. It was a devil of a coil.

He realized he'd been mulling the matter for possibly a quarter of an hour on this particular occasion, while Jessica Merriman sat placidly across from him in the morning room, keeping her own thoughts, whatever they were, as usual. How was it that the girl had so little conversation in his presence when she could talk at length to her brother and Sturbridge? he wondered irritably. To draw his mind from her cousin, he determined to speak with her.

"You seem in another world, Miss Merriman," he chided.

"Ah—no, no, I don't think so." She blinked a couple of times before looking up at him, and there was the inevitable blush. "Where would I be?"

" 'Tis for you to tell," he teased.

Her color deepened. "It does not signify, sir."

He gave up pursuit of that vein, turning instead to a subject closer to his heart. "I have not seen your cousin or your brother this morning."

"No." She met his eyes again, then looked away. "Mama has sent Rollo to town to see about our carriage wheel, and Kitty is gone with Charles—with Lord Sturbridge, that is— and his mama to visit the vicar's wife, who complains of a weakness in her legs."

It was perhaps the most words she'd put together for him

since he'd met her. "Then 'tis just you and I today?"

"Oh no! At least I hope 'tis not," she admitted artlessly. Then, realizing what she'd said, she blushed again. "Oh, dear—I am not supposed to say such things, am I? Besides, there is Mrs. Pennyman for propriety."

"No, but I suspect 'tis the truth," he answered a trifle dryly. "Just why do you come every day, Miss Merriman?"

Her color went from rosy to a deep red, and she looked studiously at her slippers. "I don't know," she mumbled finally, much in the manner of a chastened child.

"Your mama makes you," he hazarded.

"Well, she is gratified that I am in your company, sir," she admitted. "But I should come anyway." She looked up almost defiantly, then dropped her eyes again. Her hands nervously pleated the skirt of her figured muslin over her knees. "I am not wed to Haverhill now, after all," she added low.

It was difficult to follow her. He fought an urge to throttle whatever she hid out of her. "No, you are not. But what is that to me, my dear? I cannot say that you are casting out lures to me, so there must be another reason."

"Lady Sturbridge likes me," she declared naively.

"Because she is throwing you at Charles's head, I think," he muttered. "She does not appear to like your cousin in the least."

"Because Kitty is different from what she expects!"

The sudden flare of passion opened a new vista for him. "Ah, yes—she is an American."

"Well, I can quite see why she would not," she defended Louise Trevor. "After all, Kitty does not know how to go on at all. I mean, look at what she has done!"

"What has she done?" he asked.

"She abducted you, my lord. And she is forever going about without her abigail, saying she does not need one for she is four and twenty—as though that is to the purpose when she is unwed." She turned a fine, straight profile to the window and stared for a time. "She has not the least notion how to go on," she repeated slowly, "and she does not seem to care."

"And she is betrothed to Charles," he added gently.

Startled, she looked into his hazel eyes. "Well, of course Lady Sturbridge does not like that. She would prefer he wed someone who would be a credit to him."

"I was not speaking of Lady Sturbridge just now," he said quietly. "'Twas of you."

The green and gold flecks in his beautiful eyes seemed to hold her. "I—I—well, I wish him well, of course," she managed lamely.

"I was of the opinion the courtship between them was of longstanding."

"No—uh, yes."

"Miss Merriman, plain speaking will serve us best, I think. I collect that you fancy Charles Trevor yourself."

"Oh, dear—does it show so much?" she asked miserably. "Yes."

Her hands twisted the fabric of her skirt more tightly until he reached over to disengage them. "Well," she began, exhaling heavily, "he was used to come to see me, you see, but 'twas impossible because of Haverhill. No one knew of it, for we were wed in the North at Papa's insistence, but still I was not free."

"I know about that, Miss Merriman."

"Yes, of course you do. But Mama would have it that 'twas Kitty he came to see, that he was attempting to fix his interest with her."

"And it served you to let her think it."

"Yes."

"And to free you, Kitty Gordon abducted me."

"And 'twas folly on her part, sir! Oh, I know she meant well," she conceded, "but she cast us in a worse pickle than before!" Tears welled in her eyes. "Do you not see? When 'twas discovered that she'd spent the night with you at the Hawk and Hog, Charles had to offer for her!"

For a moment, he was lost, and the only thing he could

think to say was, " 'Twas the Pig, Miss Merriman."

She blinked again, releasing a trickle of tears down each cheek. "What is that to anything?" she wailed. "Because we thought you were *my* husband, there was no help for it—it had to b-be Charles! And 'tis all my fault!"

"Your fault?" Her reasoning was beyond him. "How is that your fault?"

"S-she did it for me, don't you see? So I had him offer f-for her!" Her throat constricted visibly, then she nodded. "And I did not know Haverhill was dead!"

"I see." He reached into the jacket he'd borrowed from Sturbridge and drew out a handkerchief. "No need to be in a pelter over it, Miss Merriman," he murmured soothingly. "He can cry off."

She looked up through wet tears. "Charles Trevor is a gentleman, sir!" she declared forcefully before dissolving into tears again. "He c-cannot! Oh, I am the most miserable of females!"

"Then she will have to do it. She does not seem to have a deep passion for him, does she?" he found himself asking almost casually.

"But she cannot! For if she did, then there would be no excuse—that is, well, I do not think she would."

"Miss Merriman, you have an ally—possibly two," he amended, considering Lady Sturbridge. Leaning over, he took the handkerchief from her hand and dabbed at her face. "Buck up, for I—"

"La, but what a sight! Can it be that there are two sets of lovers at Blackstone Hall?" Mrs. Pennyman tittered, coming into the room. "Dear Louise will be so pleased, I vow! To think that Red Jack Rayne discovered his lady here!"

"Mrs. Pennyman, 'tis no such—"

"Oh, there they are now! La, when I tell Louise my news, won't she be surprised!" She reached to squeeze Jessica's hand. "Such a handsome fellow for you, my dear!"

"Miss Pennyman, I assure you that you are mistaken," Jack insisted.

But she had already turned to greet her employer, who stood in the foyer with Kitty and Charles. "Only fancy, Louise!" she gushed loudly, "Lord Haverhill has offered for Miss Merriman!"

"What? Oh, no! 'Tis no such thing!" Jessica protested.

"Well, it had certainly better be, for I discovered them in a most compromising situation, I can assure you," Mrs. Pennyman declared.

"What the devil have you done to Jess—to Miss Merriman?" Charles demanded, advancing into the room.

"I was drying her tears," Jack muttered through clenched teeth.

"You fiend!" The viscount turned to Jessica. "What did he do that you were crying? Afore God, I'll see he pays for it!"

There was such protectiveness, such intensity in his face, and some imp within her wanted to prompt his jealousy. "Oh, Charles!" she cried, bursting into tears anew. "He—he—asked—"

"Devil a bit!" Jack protested. "If you think—"

"Stifle it!" Sturbridge snarled. "Another word from you, and I'd like nothing so much as to give you a hole in the other shoulder, Haverhill! And it don't matter if you *are* Red Jack Rayne—don't care if you was Wellington himself!"

White-faced, Kitty stared at Jack. "I don't believe it—not for one minute do I believe it. Jess—"

"Surely you would not take his side against mine?" the younger girl asked incredulously. "Kitty Gordon, I am your cousin!"

Dismayed, Lady Sturbridge looked from one to the other of them, trying to digest what must have happened. "Pennyman," she demanded, "what did you see?"

"The baron had his arms around Miss Merriman. 'Twas

obvious that I interrupted what can only be termed an assignation.''

"Both arms?" Jack asked. "I cannot raise but one."

"In the morning room?" Kitty fought an urge to laugh and lost. Dissolving into giggles, she shook her head. "I cannot think 'tis the place for it. I should look to somewhere more private, in fact.''

Charles favored his betrothed with a wrathful look. "Shows you what an innocent you are—it don't make any difference where a man is.'' Turning to Red Jack, he declared stiffly, "You will, of course, do the right thing, sir. I shall see you send the notice of the betrothal off to the papers myself.''

"Oh, Charles—*no!*''

"Dash it, but he ain't getting away with it, Miss Merriman! Not while there is breath in my body, anyway. Now if he don't want to do what is right, I'll meet him over it."

"I don't think that will be necessary, Charles," his mother said quickly. "I am sure Haverhill will do all that is proper, won't you, sir?''

"No," Jack answered baldly. "I have no interest in wedding Miss Merriman, I assure you.''

"Of all the dastardly—'' The viscount looked to Jessica. "Miss Merriman, did he behave in an untoward manner to you?''

"This is ridiculous," Kitty snapped. "Jess, tell him the truth.''

But to Jessica, doing that would be the same as admitting she'd lied to Charles, and she could not bear to lose his regard. Not daring to look at Red Jack, she nodded. "Yes," she answered almost inaudibly.

"That settles it. The notice will go off forthwith," Charles decided. "No female will ever be compromised in my house.''

"I say, but what's the commotion?" Roland Merriman walked in unannounced. "Couldn't raise anyone, for they was all at the keyhole. "Uh—?" He stopped, aware that something was amiss.

"La, Mr. Merriman, but Colonel Reade has offered for your sister!" Mrs. Pennyman told him excitedly. "Two weddings this year!"

It took a moment for the young man to digest the information, then his face broke into a wide grin. "You don't say!" Walking to pump Jack's hand enthusiastically, he exclaimed, "If this don't beat the Dutch! My sister and Red Jack Rayne! Good to welcome you into the family, sir!"

"Merriman, I assure you that I never—"

He did not finish the words before Charles hit him a glancing blow to the shoulder. For a moment, he staggered as the pain shot through him, then he managed to recover. "Deuced clever of you to hit the bad side," he muttered.

"Dolly mopper!" the viscount flung at him. Then, perceiving what he'd done, he added defensively, "Meant to get the other one."

"*Will* everyone be calm?" Kitty shouted.

For once, the dowager gave her son's betrothed an approving smile. "Just so. Must let the tempers cool ere we can sort this out, don't you think, Kitty dear?"

"Sort what out," Roland demanded suspiciously. "Is he marrying my sister or not?"

"He is," Sturbridge insisted.

"Jess?"

"Oh, Rollo!"

"Don't come the watering pot to me, Jess! Dash it, but I cannot deal with female sensibilities!" He turned to Lady Sturbridge. "Do you know what's going on?"

Her gaze moved around the room, taking in each participant in turn. "Yes," she said finally, "I think I do. It appears that Lord Haverhill has led Miss Merriman to believe he meant to offer for her, and Charles means to hold him to it."

"You don't say!"

" 'Twas poor-spirited of you, Jess." Kitty's eyes accused her cousin of utter perfidy. " 'Tis two Haverhills now you have ensnared with your foolishness."

"Kitty! 'Twas no such thing," the younger girl insisted. "You were not here."

"Er—may I speak privately with Miss Merriman?" Jack asked suddenly.

"Won't have you oversetting her," Sturbridge maintained stoutly. "Don't think it necessary."

"Charles, I see no harm," his mother countered. "I mean, he cannot do very much with all of us in earshot, after all."

"I—uh, I'd very much rather not," Jessica whispered, coloring.

"Nonsense!" Roland declared. "Utter rubbish! If he's going to marry you, it don't make no sense for you to act like a peagoose around him." He turned to address Jack. "Take her out into the garden," he advised. "Ain't raining yet today."

"Charles—"

"Jess Merriman, I am disappointed in you," Kitty declared with feeling. "You ought to be ashamed of yourself."

"Girl's overset," Sturbridge began, then held his tongue.

"Miss Merriman?" Jack asked softly.

Jessica had gotten herself into a sorry plight, and she knew it. Yet if she disavowed everything, Charles would certainly lower his opinion of her. Aware that everyone watched her expectantly, she nodded.

"After you, Miss Merriman."

"If he offers you any violence, I shall be there on the instant," the viscount promised. "And he shall pay for it," he added menacingly to Jack.

Red Jack did not say anything to her until they reached the garden gate. Unlatching it, he waited for her to pass beneath his good arm. She looked up hesitantly, seeing not a handsome auburn-haired gentleman but rather a stern fellow who reminded her much in this instant of her late father when he was vexed. She ducked beneath, and walked quickly up one of the neat walkways.

"Have you not thought that I shall made a devil of a husband, Miss Merriman, if you persist in holding me to this nonsense?" he asked without preamble.

"Well, I—" She considered batting her eyelashes for effect, but the cold fury she saw in his hazel eyes stopped her.

He moved closer, and before she could run, he reached out to clasp her chin in strong fingers, forcing her to meet his gaze. "You see, I am not like my cousin Henry—not at all. When I wed, I expect to produce children."

"Really, my lord, but this is most improper. I—"

"Is it?" he asked silkily. "I shall not be satisfied for what passes for marriage among the rest of the *ton*, I assure you. Wed with me and I am all you will get, Miss Merriman. There will be no dalliance with Sturbridge or any other fool, and you'd best believe it. Play me false, and I'll see your lover dead—do you understand that?"

She shuddered visibly, and tried to shake her head, but his fingers were like a vise. "Please," she gasped.

He laughed derisively, then bent his head to hers. At first she was too shocked to stop him, but then she began to struggle to no avail. He kissed her ruthlessly before releasing her. As she stumbled away, he asked, "Is this what you want? A man you cannot lead with your wiles?"

"No. No, of course not . . ." She felt her lips gingerly as if to see if they were still there. "I'm sorry, my lord," she mumbled contritely. "I should not have done it, but I did not want Charles to think . . . well, you heard what that woman said . . . and I could not . . ." Her voice faded as her humiliation rose.

"She is a tittery old fool."

She swallowed hard, her mortification making it difficult. "I—I shall tell them—and—and I shall never see Charles again," she managed miserably, hanging her head. "I shall lose his regard, you know. And Lady Sturbridge will send me home to Mama in disgrace for being fast."

"No more Cheltenham tragedies, Miss Merriman, if you please." But even as he spoke, the harshness was gone from his voice. "Devil of a coil, isn't it?" he asked tiredly. "But I am afraid you will have to admit to the error, for I am not the sort of man to marry in some mistaken gesture of nobility."

"But there will be such a row when Rollo tells Mama. And she will not let Kitty and me ever come here again—I know it." She sucked back a sob and lifted her chin. "I suppose I must," she decided, sighing heavily.

He walked away, combing his hair with his hand as though he could somehow clear a cluttered mind. "You want Charles Trevor very much, don't you?"

"Yes," she whispered.

"Then why the devil the subterfuge, Miss Merriman?" he demanded, exasperated.

"Because he is betrothed to Kitty! Because he has too much honor to cry off! Oh, I am the most miserable of females!"

"Why can you not just tell him the truth?"

"Because it won't fadge!" Tears coursed down her cheeks freely. "You do not understand! After this, I have lost him. If I say I lied—that I misled him—that 'twas not the way Pennyman saw it, he will despise me."

"If you are betrothed to me, he'd have to be a pretty havey-cavey fellow to hang after you," he pointed out reasonably.

"If he thought I was going to wed you, he might become jealous enough to cry off!"

"But you just said—"

"I don't care what I just said!"

"Jealousy is a powerful thing, Miss Merriman. And sometimes we are not prepared for what it unleashes."

But he spoke to the air, for she'd turned and run back toward the house. For a long moment, he stared after her, considering what he ought to do. And somehow the thought that Kitty Gordon might not come to see him again was almost beyond bearing. Duplicity was not something he liked at all, and yet . . . well, perhaps it would be justified much as a ruse in a campaign. He would do it. Holding his shoulder with one hand and his thigh with the other, he tried to hurry after Jessica Merriman.

"Charles—" She stood in the doorway, her face white, her body trembling. "Charles, I have to tell you—"

Red Jack caught up to her and placed his hands on her shoulders. "Wish me happy, Charles," he said. "Miss Merriman and I have an understanding."

"My congratulations, sir," Sturbridge said stiffly.

"I say, 'tis jolly great, ain't it?" Roland chortled. "My sister and Red Jack!"

The dowager managed a tight smile that told everyone she was quite disappointed in both Jessica and Lord Haverhill, for they'd thrown a spoke in her wheel also. "Well, I hope you know what you are about, of course," was all she could bring herself to say.

"La, but we shall have two weddings in the same season!" Mrs. Pennyman exclaimed. "How diverting!" Then, as her employer's smile grew even colder, she added lamely, "Well, perhaps not two . . ."

Turning in hopes of catching sight of Kitty Gordon, Jack saw her leave. "Your pardon," he murmured, moving for the door. "Be back in a trice."

Hobbling as fast as his bad leg would take him, he caught her in the drive. "Going somewhere, Miss Gordon?"

"Home," she answered shortly.

"May I ask why?"

She spun around to face him angrily. "You were a fool to be so taken in, my lord—a bloody fool."

"And a gentleman," he reminded her.

"I am sick unto death of manners that make people do what they ought not!" she snapped. "As far as I am concerned, England is a nation of fools! Men duel over nothing, commit themselves to the ridiculous, and call it honor!"

"Miss Gordon—"

"No. I am going back to America—to South Carolina, to be precise."

He fell into step beside her, limping heavily to favor his aching leg. "Not by walking, I hope."

"No. I shall merely walk to Rose Farm, then I shall take the stage to Plymouth. I'll go if I have to sell my mother's jewelry for passage."

"Miss Gordon, I wish you would not."

"I have no patience with fools, my lord."

She walked faster, making it more difficult for him to keep up. Two weeks of bed rest, coupled with his old wound, made his leg weaker than usual. "Cannot walk so fast," he muttered under his breath. "Got to stop."

"Good day, my lord."

"Wait—cannot—" Beads of perspiration formed on his forehead as he struggled after her. "Miss Gordon—"

She was angry, as angry as she could ever remember being, and yet there was that within her that wanted him to say it had been a mistake. She slowed down, then looked up at him. He was pale beneath his red hair, and obviously in distress. For an awful moment, she feared he meant to faint.

"Lud! Why did you come after me?" she demanded furiously. "Here—lean on me. Of all the cork-brained things to do, this is the most idiotish—" Words failed her. "How the *deuce* am I to walk off if you fall?" she demanded finally.

"Got to get back—to lie down—"

"Of course you do, you clunch!" She stood there for a moment, torn by indecision. And then she remembered how he'd fallen for Jessica's foolishness, and she was angered all over again. "You!" she called out to one of Blackstone Hall's stableboys. "Yes—you! Come take Lord Haverhill back to the house ere he swoons!"

When the boy arrived to aid her, she fairly shoved Jack onto him. "Good day, my lord. I wash my hands of you."

"Owe you—a week's pay—for whist," he gasped, bending over to hold his leg.

"Play Jessica—you'll win it back," she retorted brutally.

There was no help for it—he had to let her go. For a few

moments, he stood there, leaning on the stableboy, watching her walk down the lane. Then, with the boy's help, he limped slowly back. Roland was coming down the portico steps after him as he reached the end of the drive.

"What the deuce—? Where's Kit?"

"Walking home."

" 'Tis two miles!"

"I know." Jack leaned over and half-fell onto a step. "Useless," he muttered. "Couldn't stop her."

"You ain't useless," Roland insisted, stooping to help him stand. "You are Red Jack Rayne, and that's more than any of the rest of us can claim to be." He threw Jack's good arm over his shoulder and hoisted him. "Don't know why Kitty didn't come back with you—it ain't like her to let anything hurt, you know. Farm's full of animals she's brought home—too tender-hearted by half."

"I hope so—I certainly hope so."

"Eh?"

"Just help me to bed. And fetch Miss Merriman—got to talk to her."

"WHAT DO YOU MEAN he's suffered a setback? He was getting on well enough when I last saw him." Kitty stopped, recalling how he'd looked nigh to fainting when she left. "Well," she owned, sighing, "perhaps not well, precisely, but certainly not at death's door." She eyed Jessica irritably. "Though I cannot say that he probably does not wish for a way out of this ridiculous betrothal you have foisted on him."

"I didn't foist it on him, Kit! 'Twas that totty-headed Pennyman!"

"You went along with her!" Kitty said accusingly. "And don't fib to me, for it won't fadge, Jessica Merriman! 'Tis to Catherine Gordon you would tell such a farradiddle, and I know better!"

"Kitty! But I didn't!"

"Are you telling me that Red Jack Rayne—that Rollo's hero of dashed near everything—tried to seduce you?"

"No, but that woman *twisted* it, Kitty." As was her wont whenever something went awry, Jessica burst into tears. "You don't understand!"

"Oh, stuff! Either he did or he didn't, Jess—and if he didn't, then you have trapped an innocent man into marriage."

"You make it sound as though marrying me is like going to prison," Jessica muttered, sniffling. "Charles—"

"And you can have Charles! Though how you are to wed two of them, I am sure I don't know!"

"I don't want Red Jack, Kitty! He—he *scares* me! He does! When he k-kissed me, I thought I should die!"

For an awful moment, Kitty did not want to believe her ears. "He kissed you—Red Jack Rayne kissed you?" she asked hollowly. "When?"

"In the garden when we went outside—and he—he told me if I wed him, he'd expect me to have his children! And he'd kill my lovers! Kitty, I cannot wed him—I cannot!" Jess finished tragically. "We should not suit at all!"

"Then why the deuce did he say you had an understanding?" Kitty demanded angrily.

"I don't know. I was coming back to tell Charles that it wasn't so—that Red Jack had done nothing beyond listen to me speak of him. And then there he was, saying we had this understanding, Kit—but I swear we did not."

"But he kissed you."

"It was the most unloverlike kiss in my life, Kit—I hated it. It—it was *brutal*—like he wanted me to run away—to have a disgust of him."

"No doubt," her cousin observed dryly. "If you watered the plants for him as much as you have for me, he probably wished you at Jericho." She eyed Jess curiously. "Just how many times have you been kissed, coz? I thought in England 'twas considered fast."

"Not often," Jessica retorted indignantly. "Before this Haverhill, there was but the time with the other Haverhill— and Charles, of course."

"Oh—of course," Kitty repeated sarcastically.

"Kitty Gordon, *will* you listen to me?" Jess demanded, recalling Red Jack's instructions to her. "Colonel Rayne is in bad case—he may be dying even."

"I doubt that."

"His fever came up, and we feared his wound had broken open, and—"

"After two weeks?" Kitty asked, lifting one brow. "I don't think so, Jess."

"After you left, Lady Sturbridge sent to Dr. Ellis. You can ask Rollo—'twas he who went for him."

"He ought not to have been out walking."

"Well, I have never seen you so—so mean-spirited, Kitty Gordon, never in my life!"

"Maybe I've never been quite so vexed," her cousin replied acidly. "And with reason."

"Lud, is there nothing I can say to you?"

"Good-bye." Kitty saw the younger girl's eyes widen. "I am going home, Jess."

It was that moment that Isabella Merriman chose to convey her pleasure with her eldest daughter. "There you are, my love! You naughty puss! Why did you leave it to Rollo to tell me the good news?"

"Uh—"

"La, Kitty will be a viscountess and you a baroness! I vow the two of you have cast me into transports! And we need never worry that the other Haverhill will out, for this one already knows of it—'tis the very thing I have prayed for."

"Mama—"

"Do you think Louise would approve joining the weddings? 'Twould save on the expense, and—"

"Mama, there is a problem." Jess waited for her mother's attention, then she nodded. "I am afraid Haverhill has suffered a dreadful setback."

"Surely not—why I had it of Rollo but the other day that the doctor was more than pleased with his progress, my love."

"That was before he ran after Kitty."

"Ran after Kitty?" Isabella asked faintly. "Whatever for?"

"That doesn't matter, Mama," Jess answered tiredly. "I guess he must have injured his wounds. And he is fevered."

"Fevered! From running?"

"I daresay he was not well before, but now he is worse."

Isabella sank onto Kitty's bed and reached for the latest book of fashion plates to fan herself. "I have never heard of such a thing. Well, I daresay he will recover, won't he?''

"I expect so, but the doctor despairs of the fever." Out of the corner of her eye, Jessica watched Kitty. "He believed Red Jack's wound is putrifying underneath—that the scab covers an infection.''

"Oh, dear. I have heard of such things, of course, but I never suspected—I mean, I thought he was recovering.''

"As did we all."

"Kitty ready yet?" Roland called through the door.

"Oh, Rollo, I cannot persuade her!''

"Eh? Why not?" he asked, coming in.

"Roland Merriman, what would you have done had I been *en deshabille*?" Kitty demanded angrily. "You cannot just barge in here.''

His eyes traveled over her neat pink muslin gown. "But you ain't. Dash it, Kit—I knowed you wasn't! Always dressed this time of day, ain't you?''

" 'Tis Bedlam," she muttered with feeling. "Utter Bedlam.''

"You ain't going? Red Jack was asking for you, Kit.''

"No.''

"But he was.''

"No, I am not going.''

"Dash it, the man may be dying!''

"Just after he offered for Jessica?" Isabella wailed. "He cannot!''

"Got a fever hotter than a kitchen stove.''

"Since when?" Kitty asked suspiciously.

"Since we carried him upstairs. I went back up to see him, and he was a-burning up, I tell you—a burning! Never seen nothing like it, I swear!''

"Rollo, is this your idea of a whisker?''

"Kitty, I'm telling you Red Jack's in bad case—bad case! Out of his head with it, and asking for you.''

"Are you quite certain 'twas not Jess?" she asked slyly. "His betrothed?''

"Saw her already. Asked for you also.''

Isabella, who'd been trying to follow everything, put down the magazine. "But why would he wish to see Catherine?"

"Quarreled with her. A dying man wants to set things to right."

"Of all the nonsense—"

"That way, even if he don't die, he's got his house in order," he continued. "Now, Kit—d'you go or not?"

"Rollo, I think this is perhaps the biggest gammon you have ever pulled, and I am not about to be taken in by it. You can tell Red Jack Rayne that I hope he rots."

"Kitty!" Isabella gasped.

"Tell you what—go see him," Roland coaxed, "and if it's a hum, you can punch him in the shoulder."

"But I still don't see why it has to be Catherine," Isabella murmured. "If he is betrothed to Jessica, it seems—well . . ."

"Told you," her son answered impatiently. "Wants to make amends while he can."

"Aunt Bella, he was fine this morning. In fact, I collect he was about to kiss Jess. Does that sound like a dying man to you?"

"No—no, of course not." Turning a reproachful eye on her daughter, Isabella wondered, "Was that before or after you were become engaged, my love?"

"After, Mama. But that is nothing to the purpose now, after all. Kitty, I am telling you the man is as sick as a—a—"

"A dog," Roland supplied. "Shot the cat twice after we got him to bed."

"Well, Catherine, if it will make the baron feel better, perhaps you ought to go," Isabella suggested tentatively. "I mean, what will Charles and his mother think if you do not?"

"But I have no wish to!"

"Nonsense. One does one's duty, after all. Your dear papa was used to put duty before all else, my love. Indeed, but if it had not been for duty, I daresay he would have preferred to stay in England."

"I pray you will leave Papa out of this. There is no relevancy, I assure you."

"Never knew you was a quitter, Kit," Roland told her. "Always thought you was up to anything, you know."

Goaded, Kitty snapped, "Cut line, Rollo! When I abducted Haverhill, you did not think so much of me."

"Did when I discovered 'twas Red Jack."

"Please, Kitty," Jessica pleaded. "For me."

"For you? That's rich, it is, Jessica Merriman!"

"I think we should all go," Isabella decided. "I mean, if Jessica's betrothed is in dire situation, perhaps the family ought to be there."

"Kitty, I swear he is terribly ill," Jess insisted. "I swear it. And if he is not, you can have my new white muslin with the blue sash—'twill become your eyes."

"If he is not, I will not need it in prison," Kitty muttered. "Do they hang females in this country?"

"Well, I am not precisely sure—oh, I collect you are funning, aren't you, Kit?"

"No, Rollo, I am not."

Isabella rose from the bed. " 'Tis settled then. Thankfully, the carriage wheel is fixed, so we will not have to make two trips this time." She surveyed each girl critically. "Jessica, my dearest, you really ought to put a little rouge on the harsefoot. And Kitty, my love, I think the sprigged muslin becomes you better. Indeed, but the one you are wearing looks like a rag."

" 'Cause she walked home in it."

The older woman blinked as she digested the notion. "Oh. Well, I suppose that explains it, of course. Not at all the thing to do, my love," she scolded mildly. "What if you had been seen? The neighbors would think it exceedingly odd of you."

"They think me odd already," Kitty retorted, unrepentant.

"Nonsense. Come on—Rollo will order 'round the carriage."

Much against her better judgment, Kitty found herself on

the way to Blackstone Hall in the repaired coach. As Isabella chattered about two weddings, her niece stared out into the newly green countryside. It was foolish to go back, to face Red Jack again. He was, she told herself severely, an accomplished flirt, no more and no less. And if he had not offered for Jess, then he ought not to have said he had, she recalled, seething. But then it was all of a piece, for had not Sturbridge come up to scratch for all the wrong reasons also?

"If you pulled your face any longer, Kitty Gordon, your chin would rest on the floor," Roland teased her.

"And if you do not leave her alone, she just might plant you a facer," his sister told him.

"Females do not use cant, Jessica."

"Kit does."

"Catherine, coming from America, is different."

Ignoring them, Kitty studiously kept her eyes on the window. Yes, she was different, and she was glad of it, she told herself mutinously. She believed in saying what she meant, for one thing.

Lady Sturbridge met them on the portico herself, not bothering to wait for the butler to admit them. "Thank heavens you are come!"

It was the first time that Kitty considered the possibility that the baron was indeed ill, for Charles's mama would certainly not be party to any prank. Her heart rising in her throat, she dared to ask, "Lord Haverhill has taken worse?"

"Worse?" Louise cried tragically. "My dear, he is out of his head! And poor Dr. Ellis can think of no reason for it!"

"But he was getting well—he was!"

"Ellis has called in Crawford for a consult, and they are both with him now," Charles explained, coming out behind her. "Deuced odd thing, it was, too, for we'd just gotten him to bed. Queasy, you know. Ought not to have been out and about so soon, and certainly not trying to run on that leg of his." Ignoring the fact that Kitty flushed guiltily, he continued, "Thing was, after he spoke with Jessica, she came down and told me he was feverish. Thought it was from the exertion, don't you know? Short of it was that I went up and found him too hot to touch.''

"Oh, my.''

"Sent for Ellis on the instant—Rollo went. Doctor came back and said he was hanged if he knew what had happened. Was on the mend yesterday, after all.'' His eyes met Kitty's briefly. "Deuced odd,'' he repeated.

"Oh, good heavens—what you must think me, Isabella dear,'' the dowager tittered nervously. "Do come inside, and I'll ring for tea—or would you prefer ratafia?''

"Brandy for me,'' Rollo insisted.

The two physicians were coming down the stairs together as Kitty followed Charles inside. Seeing him, Dr. Ellis cleared his throat. "Don't know what to make of it, my lord, and neither does Crawford.''

"Surely you must have some idea,'' Kitty protested weakly.

"Eh?'' He looked at her from beneath bushy brows. "Young woman, if I knew, I'd say,'' he retorted testily. Turning to his colleague, he shook his head. "Odd business, don't you think?''

"Odd. The only possibility I see is that the fellow has an infection beneath where 'tis healed—that perhaps a piece of the ball is still there.''

"Probed for it myself,'' Dr. Ellis reminded him. "Told you so, in fact.''

"But would an infection come on so suddenly?'' Kitty asked.

"No.'' Crawford appeared to consider the matter further, then added, "Not unless he's been sicker than was thought from the beginning. Red Jack Rayne, ain't he? Always heard as how he cannot be brought down, and perhaps that's got something to do with it. Took a ball that ought to have cost his leg, but didn't.''

"Not to mention the other balls that were dug out of him,'' Ellis reminded him.

"Thing is, he ain't used to being down from things like

this. Overdid it, I daresay. Latent infection has got him from it.''

Kitty's heart sank. ''Can I see him?''

''Shouldn't think it advisable,'' Crawford answered.

''Dash it, but he's asked for her,'' Rollo told him.

''Well—'' The two physicians exchanged glances, then Dr. Ellis decided. ''If you do not tax his strength, I suppose—''

''Thank you, sir.''

As she hurried up the stairs, she heard Lady Sturbridge offer the doctors brandy while they determined a course of treatment for the baron. Kitty found the bedchamber door slightly ajar, but even before she opened it fully, she was surprised by the heat coming from the room. It reminded her of the bakehouse at Rose Farm on bread day.

''Colonel Rayne?'' she whispered, entering the stifling warmth. When he did not answer, she approached the bed, saying more loudly, ''Lord Haverhill?''

He was swathed in blankets despite the intense heat, and his face was red beneath his auburn hair. To her relief, his forehead was wet with perspiration. His eyes fluttered open, and for a moment, it seemed that he had difficulty focusing them.

''Good of you to come,'' he said in croaks.

''What happened?'' she asked, moving to the side of the bed.

''Sick.''

She felt as though she were in an oven herself. The heat from the blazing fire overwhelmed her. ''Would you that I opened the window, my lord? Surely you cannot breathe in here.''

''Cold,'' he muttered.

''Cold? But you cannot be!''

''Cold,'' he repeated.

''Do you hurt anywhere?''

He slipped one hand from beneath the covers, reaching out to her. His fingers were hot where they touched hers.

Placing her hand over his shoulder, he nodded. "Like the devil."

"When did this happen?"

"After you left me. Tried to walk back on my own—leg wouldn't hold me."

Telling herself that she could endure the heat if he could, she sank onto the chair beside the bed and leaned over him. "It came on rather suddenly, did it not?"

He nodded. "Ridiculous, isn't it?"

"I feel awful, my lord—awful," she admitted painfully. "But I cannot see how—"

"Stay with me."

"What?"

"Stay with me."

"Jess—"

"No. Didn't offer for her." His eyes closed as though he were too weak to keep them open.

There were a lot of things she wanted to ask, but she realized he was in no condition to answer her, so she forbore saying anything more. Instead, she sat there, her hand held against his breast by his. When she could stand it no longer, she reached with her free one to pick up a discarded newspaper to use for a fan. After a while, she wondered if he slept or was unconscious, if perhaps she ought to fetch his doctors.

"Woooeeee, Kit! Damned if it ain't an inferno in here," Roland complained, joining her. His eyes dropped to where her hand rested beneath Red Jack's, and his eyebrow shot up.

"Uh—he was showing me where he hurt," Kitty muttered, retrieving her fingers gingerly.

"Hot," Jack croaked.

"Should think so," Roland agreed with feeling. "Damned hot—er, *deuced* hot."

Bathed in sweat herself, Kitty breathed relief. "Open the windows for air, Rollo."

She had not needed to ask, for her cousin already busied

himself with throwing open the sashes. Cool spring air blew in, fluttering the canopy above the bed. For a long moment, she sucked in the fresh air, filling her lungs with it. She felt like a dying man saved. As Roland pulled up a chair beside her, she picked up a cloth and poured water from the pitcher over it, catching the excess in the basin. Leaning over Jack, she wiped the sweat from his brow and smoothed the unruly auburn hair back from his forehead. His eyes opened, showing his gratitude. And once again, she was struck by the unusual beauty of them.

"My thanks," he whispered.

The task done, she turned the cloth to herself, mopping her own streaming face, cooling it. And then she proceeded to wipe her neck and arms.

"What do you think?" Roland asked anxiously at her elbow.

"If he needed this much heat to warm himself, he must be exceedingly ill," Kitty admitted.

"Told you he was." Her cousin's forehead creased in a frown. "Wish I had more confidence in the demned physicians, though—cannot agree on what to do with him. Crawford wants to reopen the wound and probe, while Ellis wants to bleed him."

"Bleed him? Rollo, he lost far too much blood when it happened." She looked down at Jack, who lay quiet again. "Rollo, we cannot allow it."

"Now, Kit, I ain't a doctor! Cannot tell 'em what to do."

"Well, I will," she declared forcefully. "Bleed him indeed!"

"Got to get the poison out somehow."

"Well, there must be another way."

"Cold," Red Jack muttered. "Deuced cold."

"Cold?" Rollo fairly howled. "Just got to where I could breathe!"

"Got to have the fire."

Kitty exchanged glances with her cousin. "I suppose you

will have to shut the windows, Rollo, but how he stands it, I am sure I do not know.''

"Sick man," Rollo said succinctly.

"No doubt."

As the younger man went about closing up the room, Kitty started to rise, promising Red Jack, "I shall return later, sir."

"No. Stay with me . . . please." His hand closed over hers again. "Please."

"Best stay, Kit," Roland advised. "Call me later, and I'll sit with him." He eyed the fire that still roared in the hearth dubiously. "Tell you what—send for me when he's hot, will you?"

"Wretch," Kitty muttered after him, sitting down again.

It was, she reflected grimly, going to be an exceedingly miserable evening. Then, looking down on the baron's pale countenance, she realized it would be nothing to what he must be suffering. And guilt for what had happened to him washed over her. If he could stand it, so could she. The important thing would be to get him well again. Without thinking, she tenderly brushed his wet locks back from his face.

IT WAS MISERABLE in the sickroom, for Red Jack insisted on either having the room at stifling temperatures or too cold for comfort. And, despite the offers of help from Rollo, Charles, Jessica, and numerous servants, Kitty could not bring herself to leave him for more than a few hours rest. Every time she rose, he clasped her hand and begged her to stay.

And any protests about the unseemliness of her presence in a man's bedchamber were overridden by the fact that he was considered far too ill to compromise anyone. Throughout the ordeal, Kitty maintained an almost stoic tolerance, telling herself that the paramount thing was making him well. If he died, she could never forgive herself—never. And so she fed him spoonfuls of sustaining broth and held him to drink, praying all the while that he would recover fully.

Finally, in the middle of the second morning, she deemed he was resting peacefully enough for her to partake of breakfast downstairs with the others, for Louise had invited Kitty's family to join in the vigil below. Emerging from the sickroom, Kitty exercised cramped legs, and tried to tell herself that she was not too tired to think.

"Egad, my dear, but you look hagged!" Charles exclaimed as she joined them.

"Peaked," Rollo agreed. "And it ain't a wonder."

"Well," Isabella complained to the viscount, "what an unloverlike thing to say to your betrothed."

"Yes, what we should do without poor Kitty, I am sure

I do not know," the dowager murmured. "Tea, dear?" she asked solicitously.

"The physicker is here, by the by," Roland told her.

"Well, he will not be cupped."

"Now, Kit—it ain't your business."

"I am afraid I must agree with dear Kitty," Louise stated mildly, pouring a cup of tea for the younger woman. "It seems to me there must be another way, after all."

"Got to lower the poison in his body, Mama," Charles reminded her. "Got to do it somehow." He cut off a piece of sugar from the loaf and added it to his betrothed's tea. "Do you think he is any better?"

"I don't know," Kitty answered tiredly.

"Well, dear, for what 'tis worth, I think you a positive saint," his mother announced. "For a small female, your strength is nothing less than boggling. I am sure that I could never have managed without you."

"Really, but—"

"Such devotion to a stranger."

"Kit's got substance—do it for anyone, wouldn't you?" Roland asked.

"Of course she would," Louise answered for her. "One can only admire her for it."

Unused to such encomiums from Charles's mother, Kitty bent her head in embarrassment and began to butter her bread. No, she would not do it for anyone, she had to admit. In fact, she was not at all sure she could even bring herself to endure such heat and cold for her own family. But Red Jack Rayne had become a far different matter.

"I have asked Dr. Crawford to join us momentarily that he may discuss treatment," Louise added.

"At the breakfast table, Mama?" Charles protested. "I don't think—"

"Don't see why not," Roland countered. "Got strong stomachs—except Jess, that is."

"Rollo, I cannot help it."

"Seems to me you cannot help much of anything, Jess," her brother gibed. "Leaving it to Kit to tend your betrothed—it ain't right."

"What an awful thing to say, Roland Merriman!" Jess threw down her napkin and stalked from the room.

"Your pardon, Louise," Isabella said, rising.

"No—no. I'll go after her," Charles decided hastily.

The dowager watched her son leave with a small, secretive smile. "I do not refine too much on it, Bella, for I am sure she is overset." Turning to Kitty, she asked slyly, "Do *you* want her to take care of Haverhill?"

"No."

"Somehow I did not think so."

While Kitty still pondered the dowager's meaning, Dr. Crawford arrived. After partaking heartily of coddled eggs, sausages, and bread and jam, he turned his attention to the matter at hand. "Two ways to go," he announced, wiping his mouth with his napkin. "Can cup him or purge him. Ellis and I are agreed—got to get rid of the poison. The short of it is, he ain't getting better, and Ellis is loath to open the wound again. Says he *knows* he got it all."

"Oh, but he's so weak!" Kitty protested. "I don't see how he will stand for either procedure."

"Got to do it, Miss Gordon," Crawford maintained stoutly. "Got to."

"I cannot understand why he is forever too hot or too cold," Roland said.

"Strangest case I have ever had," the doctor agreed. "Defies everything I know. Got to be a poison from the lead in the ball."

"Well, I am against it."

"Dash it, Kit, but he ain't getting any better! Got to do something! Don't know precisely what, but something."

"Just so, young man."

"Well, I am more familiar with cupping, of course," Isabella murmured. "Having been bled myself when I contracted a fever some years ago, I am proof of the efficacy of that. I recovered within a fortnight.''

"When was that, Bella? I for one do not recall it," the dowager challenged her.

"Well, 'twas when the youngest girl had the measles, and we were in quarantine, Louise dear.''

"Still, one would think I would have heard, after all.''

Kitty slipped from the room as her aunt prepared to regale both Sturbridge's mama and the physician with an account of her miraculous recovery. It was ridiculous to think that further weakening a truly sick man would improve his condition, she was certain, and yet if she did not stop them, they would agree to either purge or bleed Red Jack.

She stopped outside the sickroom door and considered what she could do to stop them. Perhaps Crawford would consider some of the Egyptian bark for the fever, but she doubted it. He did not appear to be a physician overgiven to innovation.

Out of the corner of her eye, she caught movement from within the bedchamber, and at first she supposed it must be Charles's valet come to shave and wash the baron. And then she detected the distinct limp. Slipping just to the edge of the door, she watched in dawning fury as Red Jack Rayne leaned his face into the heat of the fire for a long moment. And then he warmed his hands also. Sweat poured from his face. Very carefully, he wiped it away, then hobbled back to bed. She waited until he was again between the covers. Thinking he was alone, he took a few quick fans with one of the papers she'd carried up to read to him.

As she stepped inside the door, he dropped the paper behind the bed and gestured weakly to her. "Feeling better, my lord?" she asked solicitously.

"No. Fever's up again, I think," he said.

She walked over to him and touched his almost fiery forehead. "You *are* a trifle hot," she admitted.

"A trifle?" He looked up reproachfully. "Burning up. Got to cool off.''

"Oh, dear. Perhaps if you were given a cool bath . . ."

"Too weak," he gasped.

"Yes. Yes, I suppose you are." She picked up the wet cloth she'd been using to wipe his fevered face and wet it again. This time, she did not wring it out. "Perhaps I can help," she murmured soothingly.

"So good to me . . . so good . . ."

"Here, hold this to your head while I fetch the doctor," she said, dropping the dripping cloth onto his forehead.

"Don't need him."

"Nonsense."

He reached out to her, but she eluded his grasp this time. "I shall be back directly," she promised him.

Outside, she shook with the intensity of her anger. She'd been bamboozled royally, and she knew it. Ill, he was? With each step, she reviewed the care she had given him, the heat and cold she'd endured for his sake, and the hours she had spent holding his sweaty hand. Seething, she determined to get revenge on him.

"Is he any better, Kitty dear?" the dowager asked, looking up. "I vow you look as though you are utterly overset."

"No, he is not one whit better, Lady Sturbridge," Kitty managed. "And I am not overset in the least." Turning to the doctor, who was finishing his coffee, she said, "I have reconsidered, sir, and in view of his deteriorating condition, I find I must conclude that a remedy should be undertaken."

"Ought to be cupped," he agreed, nodding.

"Actually, I was more inclined to think of a purge."

"A purge? Deuced hard on a man," Rollo protested. "A little blood would be easier, I'd think."

"But a purge is so much more thorough, Rollo, and Red Jack is so filled with poison that I have all but given up hope."

"Still . . ."

She looked to Dr. Crawford. "Would you not agree, sir, that a purge cleanses all the systems?"

"Most certainly. Got to balance the humors, after all."

"His humors are definitely in need of balancing," Kitty muttered. "Most definitely."

"Could cup him just a trifle—a few ounces at most, I suppose. And a little senna or some salts ought to take care of the other," the doctor mused.

"But he lost so much blood to begin with," Lady Sturbridge complained. "And he is so weak."

"You ain't seen weak until you have seen a purge," Roland told her with feeling. "I remember when I was sick with the ague, and Mama—"

"That will be enough, Rollo," his mother declared flatly. "You are here, and that is the important thing."

"Dear lady," Crawford murmured to the dowager, "I shall, of course, bow to your good sense. 'Twill be the senna, followed by the salts."

"Both of them?" Isabella asked doubtfully.

"Both of them, Aunt Bella. I quite agree."

"He ain't going to like it," Roland predicted direly. "And I cannot say as I'd blame him."

"Rollo, sometimes one must endure for the sake of one's health," Kitty answered him. " 'Tis for the best, I am sure."

"Give you the powders to make them up." Crawford rose from the table, bowing to the ladies. "Be back directly," he promised, following Kitty out.

He found his bag and opened it to reveal a number of evil-appearing instruments as well as an assortment of containers filled with salves, ointments, powders, and liquids. Rummaging through them, he drew out two jars, and after opening and smelling them, handed them to her. "One spoon of the powder in half a glass of water, followed by two spoons of the salts in another half glass—ought to be quite thorough, I should say."

"Thank you, sir."

"Can you get them down him, do you think?" He appeared to consider her. "Little for a grown female. Perhaps I ought to do it."

"I shall manage," Kitty promised him grimly. "And you ought to enjoy another cup of coffee."

"Drink it for its virtues, Miss Gordon—good for the spleen. Yes, well . . ." He cleared his throat. "If you have any difficulty, you have but to ask for help, don't you?"

"Exactly."

Armed with the two jars, she made her way back upstairs to find her patient pressing the wet cloth to his head. As the cloth slipped to one side, one hazel eye gazed at her almost warily. "Thought you'd abandoned me."

"Gracious, no, my lord—why would you think that?"

"Acting deuced odd."

"If I am out of reason cross, 'tis because I am beside myself with worry over you." She poured water from the pitcher into his glass, then carefully measured out two spoons of the powder into it. "Hopefully, this will make you feel more the thing."

"What is it?"

"I am not entirely certain—'tis for the fever, I think."

"Fever's better," he said feebly. "Feel."

" 'Tis just because the cloth was cool." She stirred the mixture and leaned over him. "Can you sit, do you think?"

"Hold me."

"Gladly." Sitting beside him, she slipped an arm behind him and lifted his head. "Drink this, if you please," she ordered crisply.

"Strong for a small woman," he observed, postponing the moment.

"Yes." Not to be deterred, she held it to his lips. "All of it."

He gulped noisily, draining the glass. "Ugh! Not much to recommend it." He shuddered as the taste overwhelmed him. "Water."

"Bitter?" she asked solicitously. "Well, we are almost done, in any event, and then you will be better." Turning back to the table, she opened the other jar and measured a liberal amount of the salts into the glass, then added more water. "Perhaps this will be more to your taste."

"What is it?" He eyed the mixture suspiciously. "I don't think I ought to take two kinds of medicine at the same time."

"Nonsense." Again, she lifted him, cradling him almost tenderly. "We are almost done."

"Easy for you to say," he grumbled. Thcn, sighing as though he were badly goaded, he swallowed it. "Aaaaaarrrrrgghhhhhh! Awful!" For a moment, it looked as though he might shoot the cat, then he lay back in her arms. She moved aside, letting him fall, and stood over him.

"Hopefully, we have discovered a cure for fire-sickness," she said sweetly. "Good day, my lord."

"Wait! What the devil?"

"I don't think you will wish me here when the medicine takes effect. You see, you have been roundly purged."

"Purged?" For an awful moment, he looked as though he might come out of the bed. "Egad."

"Just so." She'd meant to leave and let him discover his predicament for himself, but there was that perversity within her that wished him to know she *knew*. "How could you, my lord? How *could* you? I worried about you—I prayed over you! You—you fakir! You bamboozled me!" Drawing herself up to her full five feet, she turned on her heel. "I shall not, of course, tell the others, for 'twill only make my gullibility even more apparent."

"Miss Gordon—Kitty—"

"Hero of everything, indeed! Did you spend the war in the sick tents?" she asked sarcastically as she reached the door.

"Kitty, I merely wished—"

"I don't care." She wrenched the door open fully. "Good day, my lord."

"I did not wish you to wed Sturbridge." Throwing the covers off, he lunged from the bed, trying to reach her before she left him. " 'Twould be a mistake."

"There was never any question of that. And my mistake, sir, is you," she told him coldly, stepping into the hall.

"Kitty!"

"Good-bye, my lord."

He considered going after her and trying to explain, but he had little hope that she could be brought to listen to him. Instead, he would only make a bigger cake of himself than he already had. He sank back to sit on the side of the bed, his head in his hands, feeling as though he'd gotten his just desserts.

It had been a foolish ploy, and one unworthy of him, and he knew it. But he'd not been able to show to advantage, to court her as he ought. And there had been the presence of Sturbridge to contend with. But it didn't matter—he'd played the game abominably, and lost. It was his first losing campaign, he realized bitterly.

"Hallo, sir," Rollo spoke from the doorway. "Is aught amiss? Kit came down as mad as fire, and said if I wouldn't take her home, she'd walk again."

"You'd best take her."

"Are you all right?" the boy asked anxiously. "Look more than a trifle queasy to me."

The two mixtures churned in Jack's stomach, reminding him of what she'd done to him. "No, I am going to be thoroughly, completely sick."

"It ain't too bad, Red Jack—had it done once to me. Ain't what a man'd like, of course, but bound to get rid of any poison anywheres in your body. Tell you what—take Kit home and come back to sit with you," Roland promised him.

"Been hoisted on my own petard," Jack muttered. "The Bard was wrong—hell hath no fury like a woman bamboozled."

"What? Oh, collect you mean Kit. She'll come around, I daresay."

"No. Underestimated the whole thing—bungled it." He looked up miserably. "No way to explain."

"Females is queer creatures. I know—been living with a

bunch of 'em since I was in short coats, and I can tell you there ain't no telling what they'll let go by. No telling what they won't, neither," he added judiciously. "Just got to give her time, that's all."

"No. Got to get well and go home."

"Red Jack Rayne give up the field?" Roland's voice rose incredulously. "Never! If you'd have thought like that in the war, we'd have never beaten Boney!"

"My dear Rollo," Jack countered tiredly, "I had help with that."

"GAWD, but he was sick, Kit!"

"Was he now?" Kitty asked mildly. "All I can say is that he is well served for it."

"Crawford said you must have misunderstood the directions and gave him too much of the stuff."

"Possibly," she agreed almost noncommitally.

"Feeling like the devil over everything."

"I expect he was turned inside out."

"Dash it, Kit, but that ain't what I meant! Never saw a man as was so cast down—and that's the truth of it."

"Rollo, I don't care if he was cast into the pits of hell."

"Kitty!"

"Stuff, Jess!"

Kitty rose angrily and stomped from the room, leaving her cousins to stare after her. "Uh—I'd best see to her," Jessica mumbled guiltily. " 'Tis my fault, after all."

"Your fault? How the devil can it be your fault?" Roland demanded.

"Actually, it was both our faults, Rollo. You told him she was tender-hearted, and I allowed as how if he were helpless, she'd fall in his arms." As her brother looked at her in dawning horror, she snapped, "Well, how was I to know she'd discover him out?"

"You mean he was bamming her?"

"Of course he was, sapskull! We put our heads together to keep Charles at bay!"

"I say, I don't—"

"Oh, Rollo, use *your* head for something besides playing soldier!"

"If you are meaning I am a slowtop, I ain't. Just cannot follow this roundaboutation you are giving me, that's all."

"Very well. I don't want to marry Lord Haverhill—yes, your Red Jack Rayne, Rollo—and he does not wish to wed me." As he stared incredulously at her, she sighed. " 'Twas always Charles."

"You mean Sturbridge wasn't head over heels for Kitty?"

"Of course not! 'Twas for me—but there was the other Haverhill, as you will recall."

He digested the story for a moment. "Then it seems to me, Jess Merriman, as you got to set a few things straight. The clunch in this family ain't me—'tis you."

"Rollo—"

"And if you start blowing the blubber, I'll tell Mama—this is your brother, Jess, and I'm proof to your tears," he declared forcefully. "Save 'em for those as isn't."

Her chin set mulishly. "I wasn't going to cry."

"See as you don't. Now, the whole, if you please, and don't be giving me no Cheltenham tragedy."

She gulped, then nodded. "Well, I pushed Charles to take Kitty in the first place, because I was not free. And then when I was, Charles was too much the gentleman to cry off, so I thought—"

"So you thought if you was engaged to Red Jack, you'd get Charles? Jess, it don't make no sense!"

"I don't want Red Jack Rayne, Rollo! I don't care if he defeated Boney all by himself! I should hate being married to him—I should hate it!"

"They why the devil did you do it?"

" 'Twas Old Pennyman—she's too blind to know what she saw!"

"Dash it, Jess, but you don't have to yell—I got ears on both sides of my head," he complained. "Why didn't you just say she was mistaken?"

"Because Charles acted like he cared! Oh, Rollo!" she cried, flinging herself against his shoulder and bursting into tears.

"Now, damn it, I ain't Sturbridge or Haverhill," he muttered, disengaging her hands from his lapels. "And I ain't got enough coats to ruin one of 'em." Nonetheless, he patted her shoulder awkwardly. "Come on, Jess—it ain't that bad—it cannot be."

"Mama will make me wed the colonel, and Charles will marry Kitty—I know it!" she wailed.

"Cannot make you marry anybody you don't want," he murmured soothingly. "But it ain't right, what you did to Red Jack. Put him in a deuced bad spot, you know."

"Him? Rollo Merriman, all you care about is your stupid war hero! What about me?"

"If it was me, I'd go to Charles."

"Obviously, you are not a female, Rollo."

"No, and damned glad of it, thank you. Why is it that females can never say what they mean to a man? Here you make Sturbridge offer for Kitty in some sort of mistaken notion, then you ain't got sense enough to tell him you have changed your mind."

"Charles is a man of honor. I was hoping that Kitty would display a *tendre* for Haverhill and cry off."

"Well, she didn't. Hates him now, in fact."

"Rollo, you *are* a slowtop. Her hat's been over the windmill ever since she saw him. And I quite understand it, for next to Charles, I do not believe I have ever seen a handsomer man," she admitted.

"A female don't purge a man if she wants his attention, Jess. Got to be deuced mad to do it. Uh-oh. Mama," he uttered in warning.

"I vow I have never been so overset in my life," Isabella Merriman declared, dropping to the cushioned settee. "What can that vexatious girl have been thinking of? If Charles does not think her positively rude, I am sure I will not know why. And Louise. After Kitty left so precipitously, *she* was like a tabby over spilt cream. Said I ought not to refine too much on the girl's lack of manners, for she is American—as though that explains the girl's queer starts!''

"Well, daresay it does," Rollo said soothingly.

" 'Twill be all over the neighborhood how she nearly killed Haverhill. I shall not be able to hold my head up before the world, I shan't.''

"It ain't that bad, Mama. She just overphysicked him, that's all. Be kinda funny if it weren't Red Jack, you know.''

His mother cast a baleful eye over him. "Sometimes, Rollo, I think you are a changeling.''

"Well, if you think we are ruined for it, I say we go away for a while—London or Bath," he suggested. "Don't mind going, I suppose, for it don't look like Red Jack is going to want my company now, anyways.''

"Rollo, 'tis the Season—there will not be a decent address to be had in all of the city," Jessica reminded him.

"Not to mention that we have no connections there," his mother added. "I should rather stay home than be a nobody.''

"Got Cousin Margaret, don't we? Tartar, I own, but she ain't bad *ton*.''

"I have not even written to her in years.''

"Write now. Tell her we got business—need to talk to Papa's man of affairs anyway, so's we know how bad this thing with the Funds is. Tell her we ain't there for the Season precisely, so she don't need to put herself out.''

"Rollo, nobody goes to London during the Season with the intention of not going to anything," his sister protested.

"Stay a couple of weeks, take in the opera, Vauxhall, the Mint, and come home," he responded reasonably. "Nobody here has to know why we went.''

"Oh, Rollo.''

"I don't know," Isabella said slowly. "I am so mortified . . . mortified, Rollo.''

"And it ain't like Kitty and Jess were going to the Marriage Mart, anyway, for they are betrothed, ain't they?''

"No." Jessica's chin came up as her eyes met her

mother's. "Mama, I am sorry for it, but Lord Haverhill and I are agreed we should not suit."

For a long moment, Isabella stared at her eldest daughter through narrowed eyes, then she sighed. "Well, after what Catherine did to him, I cannot think he would wish to ally himself with this family anyway."

"No."

"Do you think Catherine would go?" she asked suddenly. "I mean, she has not seen London at all, and she has a liking for museums and things."

"And libraries," Jessica recalled. "She reads almost every night."

"Too many demned romances, if you was to ask me," Roland muttered. "But don't know why she wouldn't. Wants to go back to America, you know, and she cannot go if she ain't got the money. Tell her we mean to inquire about the Funds."

"We most certainly do. But 'tis the first I have ever heard of her returning to America, Rollo. Females say things they do not mean when they are in disgrace."

"I've got no clothes for London!"

"Get 'em made, Jess."

"Where? All the modistes will be too busy!"

"Hire a seamstress then. Daresay Cousin Margaret will know of someone."

"I could not go about in old clothes while I waited," the girl wailed. "I could not."

"Fiddle," her mother said. "Fiddle. It is not as though we shall be invited to any *ton* parties—unless someone notes that Catherine is betrothed to Sturbridge, and then I cannot think—"

"Don't think she wants Sturbridge, Mama."

Mrs. Merriman fixed her only son with a look reserved for imbeciles. "Nonsense. Sturbridge is a catch. Jessica, run tell Catherine that we are going to London for a few weeks," she decided impulsively. "And if she cavils at it, tell her that I am determined. Hopefully, by the time we are returned,

Lord Haverhill will have departed and Charles will have forgotten the embarrassment she has caused."

"We shall look like the veriest country dowds," the girl complained.

"The guards at the Mint ain't going to know it," Roland retorted. "Go on."

Jessica found her cousin lying upon her bed, staring at the ceiling. "La, Kitty, but Mama has discovered the best diversion! We shall be going to London!" Without waiting for the older girl to react to the momentous news, Jessica sat down beside her. "Only fancy—we shall have new gowns, and we shall see so many things! Rollo is promised to take us to the Mint and to Vauxhall and—"

"We are in disgrace then," Kitty observed tonelessly. Rolling over to face Jessica, she sighed. "I don't belong here, you know."

"What fustian."

"Was she very angry with me?"

"Not angry—vexed, perhaps," Jessica conceded. "And then Rollo proposed that we go to either London or Bath so that we need not see the baron again. Mama agrees 'tis the veriest thing, Kit."

"I am too old for the Marriage Mart," Kit said tiredly. "If Aunt Bella thinks—"

"You are forgetting Charles."

"No, I am crying off. 'Tis up to you to bring him up to scratch, Jess. I am wearied of the business."

"You are hagged, 'tis all. I daresay 'twill look better in the morning," her cousin murmured soothingly. "And then we shall think what we shall pack—for the museums and libraries, of course," she added judiciously.

"Hagged? You have no notion, Jess," Kitty murmured. "I was frozen and cooked in alternation, while Red Jack Rayne was laughing up his sleeve at me. I shall never forgive him for it." She exhaled heavily as though she could expel the awful memory. "But I don't think London is the answer for me."

"Mama and Roland are going to discover what happened with the Funds, Kit. There is a rumor they are turned around a bit." Jessica slid off the bed and stood. "You'll feel more the thing in the morning—I know it. What you need is sleep."

After she left, Kitty continued to stare at the ceiling. She was in such disgrace that her family had to flee. Everything about Red Jack had been a mistake from the very beginning, and she was heartily sorry for most of it. For a brief moment, she closed her eyes, but then she saw his face again. And it seemed his hazel eyes mocked her from beneath that unruly auburn hair. Her heart aching in her breast, she forced herself to rise and undress for bed.

ISABELLA'S COUSIN MARGARET, Lady Millhaven, welcomed them on short notice, and after the customary kiss between the two widows, turned to survey Jessica and Kitty critically. It was, Kitty was to fume later, as though they were horses at auction.

"So this is Jessica," she murmured, walking around the younger girl first. "A pity she had no Season, for she most surely would have taken. Such carriage, such a trim figure. Why is it that she wasn't brought to town?"

"Er—measles," Isabella invented hastily. "And then poor Mr. Merriman passed on, and there was mourning, of course."

"How old is she?"

"Twenty-two."

"Hmmmmmm. Nearly impossible, I should suppose." Turning her attention to Kitty, she observed, "And this is the American cousin, is it not?"

"Yes. But really, Meg, we are not come for the Season— not at all."

The other woman waved an imperious hand to silence Isabella and continued to study the girl before her. "One could wish you were taller, my dear, for short women are not in fashion this year."

"I refuse to go on the rack," Kitty managed through gritted teeth.

"So droll." Lady Millhaven cocked her head to one side for a moment. "But the face is good, the complexion excellent, and I like the hair. How old is this one?"

"Twenty-four."

"Twenty-four! Oh, my! Well, I have heard 'tis done differently in America, but here I am afraid—"

"I am resigned to leading apes in hell, Lady Millhaven."

"Dash it, but she ain't *that* long in the tooth!" Rollo protested, taking offense at the woman's attitude. "Dashed taking little thing, if you was to ask me!"

She turned a frigid face to him. "And this must be Roland. Yes, the name suits him. Young man," she addressed him coldly, "you will hold your tongue until I am done."

As he fell into mollified silence, she continued to consider Kitty. "A widower perhaps—or an older gentleman. There is Mr. Threll or Lord Pemberton, I suppose."

"Pemberton?" Roland howled. "Fellow's fifty if he's a day!"

"And she is not in the first blush of youth," Lady Millhaven retorted.

Isabella, who was also beginning to take umbrage at her cousin's perceived criticism of her niece, felt it incumbent upon her to set her straight. "We are quite proud of Catherine, for she is promised to Lord Sturbridge. He would think it a pity if she were to grow."

"Charles Trevor?" Lady Millhaven asked with renewed interest. "You don't say!"

"Well—" Kitty opened her mouth to deny it, then shut it. For Isabella's sake, she would try to hold her usually ungovernable tongue.

"Well, if he does not mind that she is so short, I am sure I must not," Margaret decided. Abruptly, she returned to Isabella. "I attempted to gain an appointment with Madame Cecile, but to no avail, I am afraid. However, there is another emigré, a Madame Francine, who does creditable work, and she is agreed to take a look at them. She will not, of course, do them herself, but she has an assistant who has hopes of gaining custom."

"Meg, I thought I made myself quite clear in my letter,"

Isabella protested. "We are come to see Mr. Merriman's man of affairs."

"And the Mint," Rollo added in support of his mother.

"No one comes to see the Mint this time of year, young man. There is no point in being in London now if one is not to be seen."

"Meg, I have not the money for a Season," Isabella told her bluntly.

"Oh, a Season is out of the question, Bella dear, for they are far too old to be presented now. But that does not mean that I shall not contrive to have a small party or two of introduction, after all. And we shall, of course, be seen about a bit."

"I say, but we ain't staying overlong," Roland insisted.

"How old is he, by the by?" she asked Isabella, ignoring him.

"Roland is twenty."

"Quite old enough to provide escort for unmarried females. One could wish for broader shoulders, but perhaps a good tailor can remedy that. Does he drive?"

"To an inch," Jessica declared proudly. "And there is nothing wrong with Rollo's shoulders. The Misses Peavley admire him excessively."

"They do? Egad." Then, as Lady Millhaven's intent sank in, he knew he'd been had. "I say, but I ain't going to parties and routs! Maybe the opera once, or to see a play—the girls can have their choice of that—but I ain't about to do the pretty for 'em. Told 'em as I'd take in a few of the sights, but that's all."

"Nonsense. You cannot wish your sister to remain unwed, young man. There is nothing worse than a maiden aunt in your household, which is what you will have one day."

"Really, Margaret, but I cannot think—"

"A few gowns merely. A few drives in the Park. A party here and there. See and be seen, Bella—'tis how it is done."

Lady Millhaven fixed her cousin with a sober gaze. "I should be remiss to do less."

"But we shall not stay above two weeks," Isabella protested weakly. "There is not time."

"Nonsense. Jessica's future demands the time. And if she returns to Rose Farm without an offer, she has at least gained some town bronze with which to dazzle the country gentlemen."

"Please, Mama—I should like it, I think," Jessica coaxed.

"Jess, if you think I—"

"Stuff, Rollo!"

"Then 'tis settled." Lady Millhaven looked to where Kitty stood silently studying a painting. "Is she always so quiet?"

Roland snorted. "Them that knows her don't think so."

Later, as the two girls got into bed, Kitty allowed that she was not about to be paraded around for anyone's gratification. But Jess snuggled beneath the covers happily. "Just think, Kit!" she crowed. "I shall go home with new gowns, and Charles cannot help but note it." Then, turning over to face her cousin, she added anxiously, "You did post the note to him, did you not?"

"Yes, I have cried off," Kitty said wearily. "You can have him. I just could not let the woman think I was too short to get anyone."

"You aren't that short, Kit. The French would say merely that you are petite."

"Which translates into little, Jess. I cannot help it, you know. I was used to pray to grow, but it did not happen."

"I don't think Haverhill minded it one bit."

"I never want to hear that man's name again, Jess," her cousin declared emphatically. "Never. And if 'tis discovered that I have the price of passage, I shall go home and forget I ever met him."

"I sent my note also," Jessica murmured, adjusting the covers beneath her chin. "So we shall both have to wait."

"For what?"

"Something to happen. Do you still pray, Kitty?"

"Often. Why?"

"Just wondered. G'night."

THE FIRST FOUR WEEKS were spent in an endless round of shopping, fittings, and sightseeing, the latter at Roland's aggrieved insistence. It was, he reminded Jessica, the real reason he'd come. And if he was going to have to spend his days driving Lady Millhaven's equippage in Hyde Park and his evenings somewhere besides White's, then afore God, they were going to see what he wished to see also.

And all the while, Kitty fretted about the state of her money that had been invested in the Funds. One day, on the pretext of having a headache, she had stayed behind and, with the conspiracy of one of the housemaids, hired a hackney to take her to discover the price of coachfare to Plymouth and the cost of passage to Charleston. It was, she had discovered, rather an exorbitant amount, given her resources. And she resented the expense of her new clothes, for they would have more than covered the journey. That was different, Isabella told her, for the money for them was a loan from Margaret.

Roland came upon her as she descended the stairs in a smart new blue twill driving dress. "Jess ain't down yet?" he demanded querulously. "Told her if I was expected to parade around the Park, I'd not wait, and if she thinks I mean to cool my heels awaiting her, she can think again."

His sister leaned over the balustrade above him. "I am coming, but I cannot get my bonnet just right."

He looked up. "Egad—don't you look as fine as fivepence! Both of you, in fact. Credit to me."

"Oh, Rollo, do you think so?" Jess asked, skipping down the stairs excitedly. "I cannot wait to get to the Park."

"Don't know why—a dashed bore, if you was to ask me," he muttered, offering her his arm.

"But I have been waiting until I had just the right hat." She adjusted the ribbon to one side of her chin. "Well?"

"Hat's a hat," he declared, then relented. "But that is a regular confection, ain't it, Kit?"

"Definitely."

He cocked his head to study her also. "Look fashionable yourself, Kit—favor the military look, don't you? Like that, I do," he said. "Like the Hussar shako, especially atop that yaller hair."

"Thank you. I was afraid it was overmuch."

"Gives you height."

It was an exceedingly pleasant day for a drive, and Lady Millhaven's phaeton, pulled by a pair of well-matched, glossy bays, was smart indeed. Roland pulled into the line of conveyances already making the drive, and flicked the fine carriage whip over his cattle expertly.

"So this is what the fashionable world does for amusement?" Kitty asked, settling back against the leather seat.

"See and be seen," Jess agreed. "Cousin Margaret says 'tis everything."

"I feel like I am in a dashed parade."

A gentleman on horseback pulled alongside. "Servant, Merriman. Your sisters?"

"Hallo, Revenham. Jess—Baron Revenham. M'sister Jessica. Kit—Baron Revenham. M'cousin Catherine, but we call her Kitty."

"Charming." The baron tipped his hat rakishly, then rode on.

And so it went for a good half hour until Jessica clutched Kitty's arm. "Kit, I vow 'tis Charles!"

"Don't be absurd. He—" For an awful moment, she thought her heart had stopped, but her cousin did not note it.

"And Lord Haverhill!"

The two men rode side by side, their former animosity apparently gone. Kitty blinked, unable to tear her eyes from the resplendent uniform, its brass buttons gleaming in the late afternoon sun. Swallowing the lump that rose, she watched him approach. Her hands clenched her handkerchief in her lap.

"Miss Merriman! Miss Gordon! Rollo," Sturbridge called out, grinning. "Pleasant surprise, ain't it, Jack?"

"Lord Sturbridge," Jessica murmured demurely. "So nice to see you here. And Lord Haverhill also."

"Nothing to keep us at Blackstone Hall, after all. Sorry you missed the party Mama had for the colonel, but I daresay you prefer being here, don't you? Bang-up affair, actually." He looked over to Roland. "Miss Amelia and Miss Cynthia Peavley were asking after you, old chap."

"Charles—Lord Sturbridge, that is," Jessica amended hastily. "Er—did you get Kitty's letter?"

"Actually, 'tis why I am come to London," he admitted, his grin broadening further. "Mean to call on you tomorrow, in fact."

"You do?"

"With Mama's blessing."

She colored rosily and looked down. "We should be happy to receive you, sir."

Jack watched Kitty, saying nothing until she thought she could not stand it. "Well, I see you are recovered," she said rather lamely.

"Yes." His mouth twitched slightly at the corners. "I am beginning to regain the weight I lost."

"How—how very good for you, sir. And your shoulder?"

"A twinge now and then, nothing more."

"I am glad of it. And your leg?"

"As it does not rain, 'tis better also." His hazel eyes seemed to warm to gold. "As it keeps me from dancing, not all is lost."

Jessica, still blushing happily at the import of Sturbridge's words, turned to Red Jack. "Er—did you receive my note also, my lord?"

"Yes, and I shall cherish it always," he promised.

For a moment, her brow creased, for she'd said naught but that they would not suit. "Yes, well," she said, sighing, " 'twas for the best, I think."

"Damme if it ain't Red Jack!" someone shouted, hailing him.

Heads within hearing distance turned, and soon a number of vehicles were jockeying for position as their occupants waved frantically to attract his attention. To Kitty's chagrin, an exceedingly elegant female actually leaned out and beckoned him. He flashed her a smile, then turned again to Kitty.

"You look well, you know."

"Thank you."

"The hat becomes you."

"Thank you."

"Jack, dear, are you coming to my musicale?" another woman called out as she drove past.

"Damn!" Roland muttered under his breath. "Place is all clogged up. Got to move. Servant, Sturbridge. Haverhill."

"Wait—do you bring Miss Merriman to Lady Childredge's little affair this evening?" Charles asked. "I hear there is to be dancing."

"Uh, I don't—"

"Yes. Yes, he does," Jessica answered for her brother.

"Then I have hopes of seeing you there." Lord Sturbridge tipped his hat and backed away to let them pass.

Red Jack Rayne saluted Kitty as though she were an officer, then smiled as the carriage pulled away. She lifted her hand to wave, then dropped it. She'd be hanged if she let him think she was like the rest of the females who fawned over him.

"Oh, Kitty, did you hear? I vow I am transported!"

"No, I did not hear," Kitty muttered.

"He said he had his mother's blessing, Kit!"

"For what?"

"Oh, what a clunch you are today, Kitty!" Jessica complained. "He's going to offer for me!"

"How wonderful," her cousin observed without enthusiasm.

"And did you see Red Jack? Lud, what a figure of a man!"

"Thought they was going to wreck us trying to get to him," Roland commented. "He's a lion here. Did you note that, Kit?"

"He seems to be every female's 'dear,' " she retorted. "A lion indeed."

"Oh, but he is! When Mama told Cousin Margaret that we were acquainted with him, Margaret would not believe her at first. She told Mama that with the Season open now, every hostess is vying for him," Jessica confided artlessly.

"I hope they bag him."

"Bag him? Dash it, Kit, but he ain't an animal!"

"I wouldn't know," Kitty maintained woodenly.

Somehow, she managed to endure another half hour of endless circling of the Park, and from time to time, try as she would to ignore the colonel, she could not help seeing the press of those who stopped to hail him.

"La, Margaret, but you are in such looks," Lady Childredge murmured in greeting. "And these are the Misses Merriman?"

"One of them. The short one is Miss Gordon."

"Gordon?" For a moment, the woman's interest was piqued.

"A different family," Lady Millhaven said.

"Oh. So kind of you to come, dear—both of you. And you also, young man."

Roland leaned closer to his sister and whispered, "If he ain't here within the hour, I ain't staying."

"Merriman." A tall, slender young man bore down upon them, with a thin, freckled girl in tow. "Wanted you to meet m'sister Gussie—Augusta, actually."

"Miss Dunham," Roland murmured politely.

Her brother half covered his mouth and said in a low aside, "For God's sake, get on her card, will you?"

Mortified, the girl turned a deep red. Kitty reached out to her quickly. "I am Catherine Gordon, but my friends call me Kitty. And may I present my cousin Jessica?"

"Miss Gordon," the girl mumbled.

"Rollo, why do you not fetch us some punch? And one for Miss Dunham also."

Behind her, she could hear a stir, but she paid no attention. Impulsively taking the thin girl's hand, she led her to a chair along the wall. "Do sit with us, will you? I vow I know almost no one here," she told her.

"Not quite true, Miss Gordon."

She spun around at the sound of Red Jack Rayne's voice, and for a moment she was speechless. Recovering, she managed to hold out her hand. "Good evening, sir."

In full view of everyone, he bent over it and kissed her fingers. "Pleasure to see you—as always."

"There you are, Lord Haverhill!" Lady Childredge rushed up to him, gushing, "There are so many come to see you, sir! I have promised Lady Epperson that I would present you."

"Hold a chair for me, will you?" he said to Kitty as his hostess bore him away. "Be back."

Miss Dunham stared, goggling. " 'Twas Red Jack," she choked out finally.

"Yes," Kitty agreed simply, sinking into the chair beside her.

Roland returned, awkwardly carrying three glasses of fruit punch. "Did you see Red Jack?" he asked, handing one to Kitty.

"He was right here. Kissed Miss Gordon's hand even," the girl told him excitedly. "I saw it with my own eyes."

He looked to where Haverhill stood, surrounded by those who waited for the chance to speak to him. "Told you he was a lion!" he crowed triumphantly. "Told you!"

"One would have thought he was Wellington," Kitty muttered sourly.

"Eh? No, Wellington don't like to come out—cannot stand the fawning."

"Well, your Red Jack seems to delight in it."

"Don't like it above half. Had it from Charles that he don't go about much either."

"Really? One would never know it."

"You know something? You are out of reason cross tonight, Kit. It ain't like you at all."

"I have the headache," she lied.

"Again? Get too many of 'em. Daresay ought to have Mama take you to a physicker while we are here. Get you a powder or something." He looked down guiltily. "Guess I ought not to have said that, huh?"

"No."

"Charles says he don't hold no grudge, you know."

"How very charitable of him."

"Oh, look—he's coming back!" Miss Dunham whispered excitedly. "He is. Wait until I tell Mama I have seen Red Jack Rayne in person."

"Lud."

"Buck up," Rollo urged, then he disappeared, leaving only her and Miss Dunham to face Red Jack. She looked around quickly for Jessica, then realized that Sturbridge was in attendance also. They sat alone near a potted fern, and the look on Jess's face gave Kitty a stab of envy.

"Devilish crush," the colonel commented, taking the seat beside her. A twinge of pain crossed his face as he adjusted his leg. "Cannot dance, so might as well sit it out with you."

"May I present Miss Dunham?" she asked politely.

He leaned past her, giving her a whiff of the Hungary water he wore, to take the girl's hand. "Miss Dunham," he acknowledged gravely. "A pleasure."

"B-Baron Haverhill," the girl stammered. "Oh."

He looked down to where her empty card dangled from her wrist, and he nodded sympathetically. "I should sign on, but I would embarrass you, I am sure."

As the girl's blush deepened, some imp prompted Kitty

to say, "I don't know—perhaps one of the more staid ones . . ."

"Nothing you could do could embarrass me, sir," the girl blurted out.

Kitty did not fail to note the faint lift in his brow or the quirk at the corner of his mouth. Nonetheless, he nodded. "The first quadrille then, but I take leave to warn you that we may be laughed at," he promised gallantly.

Later, it seemed as all eyes watched him lead Miss Dunham out, and as the sets formed, none seemed to note that he moved stiffly. The light from the glittering chandeliers reflected off the buttons and braid of his dress uniform, and his dark red hair gleamed. Even Kitty was moved by the sight of him as he attempted to negotiate the steps.

"Heard he nearly lost that leg," a man said beside her.

"Held the surgeon and his saw off at gunpoint," his companion replied. "Wouldn't take the laudanum nor sleep for fear they would take it."

"Half a regiment's alive today because of him."

"Aye—I heard that after he was shot, he crawled to put a cannon out."

"Ask Wilmington—he was there. Said he saw him do it."

"Wonder he's alive."

"Wasn't the first time neither. Carried a man two miles when he was wounded himself. Poor soul died, but 'twasn't because Red Jack did not try."

"Wouldn't be an England, if there was not men like him."

Kitty sat and listened to them, feeling very much the fool. This was the man she'd abducted, the man she'd caused to be shot, and the man she'd purged so unmercifully. And he was not above speaking to her still. As she watched him, it came home to her that Roland's youthful adulation was shared by too many to count.

As the music died, he and Miss Dunham were surrounded, then a young buck took the girl back onto the floor again. Roland, who'd been watching also, walked over to where Kitty sat. "Made the chit fashionable as surely as he was

Brummell,'' he said. "Deuced good of him to do it, as she
is a plain girl.''

"Yes. Yes, it was.''

It seemed an age before he came back, and then he bore
the harried look of one hounded. "I'd hoped to speak with
you, Miss Gordon, but I see not how,'' he muttered in
exasperation. He sat down and drew out his handkerchief
to wipe his brow. "I despise crushes.''

"It was exceedingly kind of you to lead Miss Dunham
out,'' she said softly.

His eyebrows lifted. "Doing it too brown, Miss Gordon.
As you will recall, I was prodded into it.''

"Still, you could have resisted.''

"What—the Ice Maiden thaws? Can it be that I am finally
to be forgiven?''

"I suppose there is something to be forgiven on either side,
and your attempt at revenge was justified,'' she conceded.

"Revenge had nothing to do with it, I assure you.''

Her eyes widened at the warmth in his voice, and she dared
to meet his gaze. He was smiling in a manner that almost
curled her toes. It was as though they were the only people
in the room.

"I am heartily sorry for overdosing you,'' she said finally.
"Truly sorry. And for everything else.''

"Well, the price was worth—''

"Red Jack! Red Jack Rayne! And damme if it ain't—Mrs.
Smith!''

For an awful moment, she stared up into Colonel
Barswell's thunderstruck face, wishing that somehow she
could sink from view. "Uh, there must be some—''

"Hullo, James.'' Jack's hand took possession of Kitty's
in her lap. "May I present Miss Catherine Gordon, my
betrothed?''

The room spun around her, and there was a sudden air
of unreality about her. His warm fingers clasped her suddenly
cold ones tightly. Above her, Colonel Barswell's face swam.

"I say, but—" He looked from Kitty to Jack suspiciously. "It was you!" he announced suddenly. "John Smith indeed!"

" 'Tis a long tale, but I can explain," Jack insisted. "Come over to my house and we'll split a bottle of Madeira over it. Suffice it to say that I had reason."

"Don't see what—lying to a magistrate—"

"Over the Madeira, James." He rose stiffly. "Got to see Miss Gordon home first, then meet you there. Haverhill House in Arlington Street." He tugged at Kitty's hand. "Let us find Miss Merriman and Rollo."

"Damme if I know what to make of it," Barswell muttered. Turning to the first person he saw, he asked, "Did you know Red Jack was engaged to the little chit?"

Neither Rollo nor Jessica seemed to be anywhere to be found. Dragging Kitty through the crowd, Jack criss-crossed the room until he saw Sturbridge. "Got to discover Merriman, Charles," he muttered in a low undervoice. "In the basket—magistrate's recognized Miss Gordon."

"What? Uh—"

"Lord Haverhill! Lord Haverhill!" Lady Childredge waved her handkerchief frantically to gain his attention, then glided through the group that pressed against them. "I have just heard the most diverting tale, I vow! 'Twas told to me that you and Miss Gordon are become engaged!"

As Kitty stiffened in mortification, he slid an arm around her shoulders. "Puffing it off to the papers in the morning, in fact," he announced.

"Then you are?" she asked incredulously. Her eyes took in Kitty as though she could see no good reason for this travesty. "La, but you have broken half the hearts in London, Miss Gordon," she said finally. "To think an American has stolen the march to his heart."

"Going to have a summer wedding," he added, squeezing Kitty. "Aren't we, my love?"

"Uh—"

"Charles, I leave it to you to speak of the matter with Rollo and Lady Millhaven. Your servant, Lady Childredge. Got to run—Kitty has the headache."

"Burn some camphor and feathers!" Lady Childredge called after her, waving her handkerchief again.

It was not until he had bundled her into his carriage that it came home to her what he had done. He leaned across the seat to chide her. "You do not look precisely overjoyed, Miss Gordon."

"Tell me, my lord, do you make it a habit to become betrothed to every female in distress?" she asked archly.

"First time ever."

"What about Jess?"

"You never listened. If you had, you would have heard me say we had an understanding. I never used the word betrothed. She'd already told me about Sturbridge, you see."

The moonlight seemed to reflect off his eyes and his dark red hair. But his face was sober and very, very close, so close in fact that she could feel his breath on her face. And the smell of Hungary water mingled with the lilac scent she used.

"Never," he repeated softly.

She closed her eyes. "You cannot wish to marry me," she said weakly just before she felt his lips against hers.

It was a kiss she would always remember, she was certain. His arms closed around her, cradling her, and his mouth was gentle at first, then more insistent. She was overwhelmed by it all—the scent, the warmth of his body and his breath, the strength of his arms about her. In the beginning, it seemed as though her own arms were superfluous appendages, then she slid them around his waist and returned his embrace. It was a heady, dizzying experience.

When at last he released her, he whispered, "I am getting used to the notion, believe me."

"But why?"

"I have never forgotten how you pulled up your skirt and

lay atop your wadded petticoat to keep me from bleeding to death,'' he answered fondly.

Grateful for the darkness, she turned her flaming face away. ''You were supposed to be unconscious.''

''I would not have missed that for the world.''

NOT SINCE SHE'D COME HOME from Blackstone Hall the last time had Kitty spent such a sleepless night. And it had not been helped by the fact that even Lady Millhaven was beside herself over Kitty's conquest of Red Jack Rayne. Then, to make matters worse, Jessica had come home and spent the better part of two hours regaling her with every detail of Lord Sturbridge's proposal, which he'd finally made in the Childredge garden. It was, Kitty reflected tiredly, an insignificant development when compared to the near ignominy of the Barswell incident.

The Barswell incident. 'Twas all she could call it, and she felt the veriest fool for allowing it to happen. She ought not to have gone to the Childredge party or to any other party, for that matter. See and be seen indeed! Well, she'd been seen by the wrong person, that was a certainty.

And now Red Jack Rayne, hero of everything, had gallantly offered for her, and it was in a fair way to being all over London, she supposed. That Colonel Barswell had trapped him into it was utterly lowering.

What had Jack answered when she said he could not wish to wed her? That he was getting used to the notion. And why had he offered? Because despite everything she'd done to him, he remembered that she'd possibly saved his life.

Well, she would not do it. If she ever did get a husband, she'd like to think that he had not been trapped into the marriage, after all, that he'd offered because he loved her. And Red Jack had never said one word about the tender passion. She had only that one kiss, and as much as that meant to her, she was not such a fool that she did not know men viewed such things differently. He'd probably kissed a dozen females before her—in fact, in view of the expertise he'd demonstrated, she was sure of it.

No, it was the ridiculous English notion of honor that had made him do it, the same thing that had made Charles offer earlier. Well, she was not English and therefore not governed by such silly constraints. Not that it was all that much easier for a female in America, she had to admit fairly. And what she'd done would not have been condoned in Charleston any more than at Blackstone Hall. But, she consoled herself, they would not know of it there.

Rising early, she rummaged through her writing case for pen and ink, then sat down to compose a letter to Red Jack.

"My dear Lord Haverhill," she began, "I very much regret all that has befallen you since first we met." She stopped. Well, perhaps not quite *all*. And the greeting sounded so terribly formal. She crumpled the paper and reached for another sheet. "My dear Haverhill," she scratched across the paper, "Though I am cognizant of the signal honor you do me, I simply cannot . . ." She stopped. That sounded even worse. A second ball of paper joined the first.

It had been so easy writing to Charles, but then she'd never wanted to wed him in the first place. Red Jack, she realized suddenly, was quite another matter. Even as she sat there, nibbling at the feather end of her pen, she could not forget the feel of his arms about her, the smell of his Hungary water, or the way he'd kissed her. A sense of intense longing flooded over her.

Forcing such traitorous thoughts from her mind, she resolutely tried again, writing,

Dear Lord Haverhill,
  I cannot thank you sufficiently for what you are prepared to do for me, but I simply cannot accept the protection of your name without the necessary regard to sustain a marriage.

She sat back and regarded the lines critically. They sounded foolish, but she did in fact mean them. Sighing, she continued,

> While I understand such things are viewed differently in England, I do not feel I could ever accept an arrangement where either of us was free to dally should the marriage prove to be an unhappy one.

Now she was indeed sounding like an utter ninnyhammer. Nonetheless, she had to go on.

> You see, I fear I am possessed of a romantical nature, and I should expect affection within the marital bond. I fear your sense of honor and duty alone would not be enough to sustain me through what you must come to think an onerous burden. The mistake was mine, not yours, after all.

She shuddered reading it. How pompous she must sound. She concluded with "I shall always remember you with great fondness, and remain your servant, Catherine Gordon."

Well, after he read this, he would be in whoops, but at least she would not be there to see it. She'd forgotten to beg his forgiveness for the abduction, she recalled, and she considered appending that, then discarded the notion. She never liked to get those letters where the writer insisted on adding all manner of things past the ending.

While she waited for the ink to dry, she dipped her quill into the inkpot again and composed a short note to Isabella, Jessica, and Roland, asking them to dispatch the letter to the baron. At the end of it, she promised to write more fully when she reached Charleston, then signed herself their affectionate niece and cousin.

Her task done, she sealed both missives, and filled her portmanteau with only the most necessary things. Hopefully, once they got over the shock of what she'd done, they'd dispatch her trunk after her, thinking it a good riddance. As she packed, she had to own that she must have vexed them terribly during her year and two months with them, for she'd certainly caused them more than a lifetime of embarrassment. Even now, she could remember the look on everyone's face when she'd stood in the foyer at Rose Farm in her bloody gown to announce that she'd abducted Lord Haverhill. And her Aunt Bella's expression of longsuffering when it had become obvious that she'd deliberately overdosed him with the physick.

She crept down the backstairs, stopping every step or so for the creaking boards. But as she was almost to the servant's entrance, she felt a hand on her shoulder.

"Kitty, what are you doing up this early?" she heard Jess ask. "And with your portmanteau!"

"I might ask the same of you," Kitty muttered tersely, turning around. "And I would that you kept your voice down, for I am leaving."

"I could not sleep for thinking of Charles," the other girl admitted. "Leaving? Kitty Gordon, you are running away!"

"Yes," Kitty admitted baldly.

"But *why*? Kit, you ought to be in alt! I mean, Red Jack has offered for you, and well—'twill be the talk of London, I vow. Indeed, there was not a female at the Childredges' party who did not envy you excessively, and—"

" 'Tis precisely why I am going, Jess!" she snapped. "He can do better than an American miss who is forever making mistakes and doing foolish things."

"Fustian. You may be able to tell Cousin Margaret such a farradiddle, but I know you better." Jessica peered into her face, then crowed, "You are in love with Red Jack!"

"Too much to make him wed me," Kitty acknowledged simply. "Now, will you stand aside?"

"You cannot wander the streets of London alone, Kit— this is not a country lane by Rose Farm, you know."

"I am not wandering precisely. I have sent a footman to hire a hackney," Kitty retorted. "I am not a complete fool,

Jess.'' Leaning over the portmanteau, she embraced her cousin quickly. "I shall write you from Charleston to let you know how I go on."

"Charleston! 'Tis America, Kit!" Jessica cried. "You cannot—oh, you cannot!"

"I have Mama's jewels, and I shall attempt to pawn them in Plymouth. Really, I shall be all right, I promise you."

"Rollo! Rollo!"

"No, Jess, I beg of you!" Kitty grabbed the heavy bag and started for the door.

"Mama! Rollo! Will somebody help me?" Jessica screamed loudly. "Mama, Kitty is running away!"

"Eh? What—?" Roland's rumpled head appeared in the stairway overhead. "What the devil, Jess! We ain't deaf!"

The younger girl pointed dramatically to the door through which Kitty had just left. "You've got to stop her!"

"Stop who? For God's sake, Jess, but you are raising the house," he hissed loudly, coming down.

"You don't understand! Kitty is running away to America! She just left, Rollo!"

"America? Deuced long swim, Jess. Besides, she ain't such a peagoose!" He stopped. "Oh, lud."

"By the time you get to the curb, Roland Merriman, she'll be halfway to the posting house!"

He pushed past her, running barefoot out the door. At the curb, he found his cousin stepping into the hackney. Catching her arm, he pulled her backward. She stumbled and tripped over the cracked leather bag, landing in a heap at his feet.

"Sorry," he muttered, helping her up. "What the deuce was you doing, Kit?" he demanded, looking down at the portmanteau.

"I am going home, Rollo."

"Home? Rose Farm is your home, Kit—you ain't got no home over there. No relations at all. Come on—got to get you inside before you are a spectacle. Come on," he coaxed.

"But I don't belong here!" Uncharacteristically, she burst into tears. "Rollo, I've got to go!"

"Dash it, Kit! Bad enough having Jess water the plants all the time! Come on—talk about it." He tugged gently at her arm. "You got Red Jack to think of."

"It is because of him that I am leaving!" she cried.

"What? Now, that don't make sense! Come on," he urged again. "Don't want to have to pick you up—look dashed silly if I was to do that."

"No." She sniffed back tears, wishing very much for a handkerchief. "My mind is set, Rollo. I will not be wed to satisfy a man's misplaced sense of honor."

"I owe I ain't quite awake, Kit, but I cannot make sense of you!"

"Kitty! Whatever . . . ?"

To her horror, her aunt, still tying her wrapper over her nightgown, was hurrying toward them. Kitty made a frantic attempt to pull away, but her cousin held her arm tightly. Exhaling sharply, she turned back to meet Isabella's reproachful eyes.

"Catherine Gordon, I demand to know the meaning of this. Well?"

"She's running away, Mama," Jess said behind her.

"Running away!" Isabella turned again to Kitty. "But why?"

"She's in love with Red Jack," Jess explained.

"She don't want to marry him," Rollo added.

"I have never heard such a Banbury tale in my life," Isabella declared, sinking to sit on the portmanteau. She looked up at her niece. "You were quite right, dear—we are in Bedlam."

"Good heavens, Bella!" Lady Millhaven hissed, hurrying toward them. She stopped when she realized what her cousin sat on. "We shall be a laughingstock," she complained. "The neighbors—"

"Hang the neighbors! 'Tis Kit who worries me," Roland retorted.

"Will someone tell me what is going on?" Lady Millhaven demanded awfully, looking from one to the other. "Well?"

Jessica nodded. "I could not sleep, so—"

"Dash it, Jess! She don't care that you wasn't asleep!" Roland expostulated.

"Well, I would not have caught her if I had been. In any event, I saw Kitty carrying her bag to the servant's entrance, you see, and I thought it exceedingly odd."

"Exceedingly odd!" her brother snorted.

She shot him a withering look, then went on calmly, "So I asked her where she was going, and she said she was leaving."

"Leaving!" Lady Millhaven uttered in disbelief. "Well, she cannot—not after last night's triumph."

"Kitty, you cannot run away from Lord Haverhill," Isabella said, trying to keep her voice calm. "If it becomes known you have cried off twice, you will be considered a heartless jilt."

"Aunt Bella, he only offered for me because I was recognized by the magistrate."

"The magistrate?" For a moment, Cousin Margaret looked as though she might faint. "The magistrate?"

"He recognized me from the night at the Hawk and Pig."

"I do not believe I wish to hear this," her ladyship declared definitely. "I know I do not."

"So you see I cannot do it," Kitty said simply.

"She loves him," Jessica repeated. "She does not wish to be wed for the wrong reason."

"Young lady, if he offers, it does not matter what the reason!" Lady Millhaven snapped. "She cannot let Haverhill slip through her fingers—she cannot. Full half of the females in London would give anything for just such a proposal."

"She don't want to marry him," Roland repeated. "And if she don't—" He stopped, aware that his mother, his sister, and Lady Millhaven were all regarding him indignantly. "Well, this is England, after all, and we don't force our females into wedding where they don't want to," he finished defiantly. He looked down at Kitty, and moved to place a

comforting hand on her shoulder. "Now, I am the man in
this family, and I say if she don't want him, she don't have
to take him."

"Rollo!" his mother gasped.

"But she loves him!" Jess insisted. "She admitted it."

"Daresay she must have her reasons. Thing is, we ain't
going about this in a havey-cavey manner, Kit. If you was
not to wanting to marry Red Jack, you got to tell him."

"I wrote him a letter—it's in my bedchamber."

"All right. Ain't the way I'd choose to do it, but then I'm
a man."

"Rollo—"

"No. If she wants to go, I am taking her as far as Plymouth
myself. It ain't proper for a female to travel alone in these
times, so I don't mind doing it."

Kitty's chin quivered dangerously, then she burst into tears
again. "Oh, Rollo!"

"Got to quit that, though. Now, if 'tis settled, I say we
pay off the hackney and go back inside. I'll be hanged if I
travel ere I've had my breakfast."

Lady Millhaven shook her head. "Young man, I think—"

"It ain't nothing to the point. What matters is what Kit
thinks. And I won't have her badgered over it." He squeezed
Kitty's shoulder. "Leave right after we eat," he promised.
To Jess, he added, "Run get Red Jack's letter, so's it can
be sent 'round to him."

"No!" Kitty cried. "That is, I should wish it to be
delivered after we are gone."

"All right."

"Roland Merriman, you are a complete fool," Isabella
declared. "Kitty dear," she said soothingly, "you are merely
overset. I am sure that Lord Haverhill holds you in the highest
regard, and—"

"Mama, you forget she physicked him," Roland cut in
impatiently. "A man don't forget that sort of thing. Might
make for an unhappy marriage."

"I think I shall wash my hands of the lot of you," Lady Millhaven muttered. "Magistrates. Inns. Physicks. I vow I have never heard the like."

"Now, I'd have you cry peace with Kit ere we leave."

"Rollo—"

"No, Mama, m'mind's settled."

"But I shall miss you, Kitty!" Jessica wailed, throwing her arms around her cousin. "I wanted you there when I wedded Charles!"

"Nonsense. You shall be q-quite h-happy without me," Kitty insisted, hugging her tightly.

"I ain't listening to two of you. Stifle it, Jess," Roland ordered. "Now, while breakfast is being cooked, I shall write Red Jack also. Only fitting as I am head of this family, after all." He looked at Kitty. "Best pack what you can—that ain't going to suffice all the way to Charleston, you know."

She stood on tiptoe to embrace him. "Oh, Rollo, if I'd had a brother, I would have wished for you."

"Proud of you, Kit—know why you did everything. Well, run on now—we got things to do."

SHE SAT IN THE small private parlor Roland had bespoken at the inn, waiting for her cousin to return from purchasing her passage across the Atlantic with her mother's brooch. Two days hence, she would be bound for Charleston and the home she'd left behind. She ought to be happy over that, for she'd been homesick much of the time she'd been in England. But as her departure approached, she discovered she was not.

Roland had been right, of course. She really had nothing to return home to anymore. Her papa was gone, the house she'd grown up in sold, and the business she loved belonged to others. She was not even certain that her papa's partners would welcome her back.

It did not matter, she told herself forcefully. If all else failed, she would teach, for her knowledge of sums was exceedingly good. And she was accounted to write a fine hand also. But the thought of years of facing reluctant pupils was nonetheless daunting.

She stared into the empty fireplace, wondering if Red Jack had felt relief upon receipt of her letter. Surely he had, for she'd been nothing but trouble to him from the moment she'd leveled the pistol on him.

"You were perhaps thinking of going on your wedding trip without me?" he drawled almost lazily behind her.

"What—?" She spun around to face him guiltily, her heart rising in her throat. "Oh."

He seemed to fill the room, looming over her. He wore the full dress uniform of a dragoon, its gold braid gleaming

221

in the sun that filtered through the window. Only his hat was missing, for his dark red head was bared, its unruly locks brushed into the semblance of a Brutus. Despite his words, he watched her, his mouth quirked into a halfsmile, his beautiful hazel eyes betraying amusement.

"Uh—did you not get my letter?" she asked lamely. "I— uh—I wrote to you."

"The one referring to the necessary regard to sustain a marriage?"

"Yes."

He reached behind him to close the door, then advanced on her. Her palms were suddenly damp where she pressed them against the skirt of her twilled cotton traveling dress. She took a step backward, and nearly tripped over the raised hearth. Her heart beat wildly, reverberating even in her head.

"The one where you disparage dalliance outside marriage?"

"Yes."

"The one where you call yourself romantical? The one where you express hopes of affection within the marital bond?"

"Uh—" She looked around her nervously. "Rollo—"

"Rollo is on his way back to Rose Farm, I believe. Yes, I am sure of that, in fact. He means to join Jess and your Aunt Bella there."

"But—he's booking my passage! He—"

He held out her mother's sapphire brooch, its jewels winking in the palm of his hand. "I don't think so." Almost impersonally, he leaned to pin it above her breast. And then he leveled the pistol.

"And now, my romantical Miss Gordon—"

She stared into the barrel in disbelief. "You cannot—that is, why—?"

"The reason ought to be obvious, but as it isn't, I take leave to inform you that this time, 'tis Red Jack who abducts you."

"What?"

"An elopement, Miss Gordon."

"You cannot be serious!"

"Never more serious in my life."

"But—"

"We tarry overlong. You will go out before me, and get into the red and black lacquered carriage, just outside the door."

"You cannot—"

"And I can do considerably better than hit a cider jar at twenty paces," he added, straight-faced. "So do not be thinking of sounding a warning, Miss Gordon, for I shall be directly behind you."

It was as though her own words had come back to haunt her. "Where are we going?"

"A great distance."

She tried to keep her voice light as she stepped in front of him. "Am I to collect you do not mean to compromise me, sir?"

"Not at all. I intend to do so thoroughly."

He was behind her so close that she could feel his breath above her head, and again she smelled the faint, pleasant scent of Hungary water. An odd, exhilarating thrill went through her. His hand closed on her arm, guiding her before him into the yard.

"Jem!"

"Morning, Miss Gordon."

"Er—I thought to employ a driver with experience in such things," Red Jack murmured.

"But how—?"

"While I was recovering at Blackstone Hall from our last encounter there, he returned to beg Charles for money," he explained, reaching around her to open the carriage door. "Somehow I felt responsible for his lack of a job."

"This is ridiculous," she muttered as he pushed her up into the coach. "You cannot wish to marry me."

He swung up behind her, but instead of taking the seat opposite, he settled against the squabs beside her. "That, my love, is a lie." Shifting his pistol to his left hand, he reached into his coat and drew out a folded paper. "Behold a Special License. By the time we reach Rose Farm, I should expect Rollo and Jessica and your aunt to be awaiting us."

"But I am not the sort of female you should wish to marry!"

Laying aside the license, he reached to untie her bonnet. "No?" he asked conversationally. "And just what sort of a female should I choose, do you think?"

"But you can have an Incomparable—a-a Toast!"

"I think I have one." He leaned closer. "I favor small women, you know. Romantical ones, too."

"Not someone who is forever making mistakes! You were a mistake! You ought to have someone who thinks about what she does, and—"

"A deuced bore, I should think." His fingertips traced a line lightly from the tip of her chin to her ear, sending a shiver of delight through her. "But go on."

"You are the dashing Red Jack Rayne," she protested feebly. "Every woman in London—"

The bonnet dropped to the floor in front of her, and his face was so close that she could not focus on it. His breath brushed softly against her face.

"There's only one I'd have," he whispered against her lips. "There's only one I'd love."

Her protest died in a thorough, lingering kiss that left her utterly, completely breathless. She clung to him, savoring the feel of his lips on hers, the warmth of him, the strength of him. It was, she decided happily, what she was made for.

Slowly, she became aware of the gun that lay between them, and she sat up in alarm. "Your pistol—"

For answer, he dropped it on top of her bonnet. "It isn't loaded," he murmured, reaching for her again. "I do hope that one of these days, you will cease referring to me as a mistake, my love," he added as she snuggled against him. "It might confuse the children."